My little sister Peri, *stolen*. My brother Koi and my father, *gone*.

Suddenly the truth comes back to me. I remember exactly where I am. *What* I am.

I am a prisoner of the Initiative, with a connection to the Murder Complex in my brain. I came here to destroy the Motherboard, shut the system down for good.

I am the only one who can end The Murder Complex. If I die, the system dies along with me.

That is the only way.

THE
DEATH
CODE

A MURDER COMPLEX NOVEL

LINDSAY CUMMINGS

GREENWILLOW BOOKS

An Imprint of HarperCollinsPublishers

The Death Code: A Murder Complex Novel

Copyright © 2015 by Lindsay Cummings

First published in hardcover by Greenwillow Books in 2015; first Greenwillow paperback edition, 2016

The text of this book is set in 11-point Adobe Garamond.

Book design by Paul Zakris

Library of Congress Cataloging-in-Publication Data is available.

16 17 18 19 20 CG/RRDH 10 9 8 7 6 5 4 3 2 1

ISBN 978-0-06-222004-2 (pbk.)

First Edition

GREENWILLOW BOOKS

To my dad, Don Cummings, who taught me how to be fearless.

And to my #booknerdigans, for all your love and support.

PART ONE
THE SHALLOWS

CHAPTER I

ZEPHYR

It's going to be a dark night.

Weeks ago, the darkest nights were the worst. Bodies dropped like flies around the Shallows, and blood dried in rivers all over the streets. The Dark Time meant dread. It meant the Murder Complex and its Patients came out to play.

That hasn't changed. If anything, the deaths have gotten worse.

But something good will happen tonight.

It's a new moon, and black clouds are gathering over the tops of the crumbling buildings. The thunder and lightning and the Dark Time combined make for the perfect distraction, the perfect storm.

And that means Lark Woodson will come out of hiding.

I've been tracking her for weeks, but every time I'm about to find her, she disappears. Like the wind.

Not tonight. Tonight, I'm going to catch her.

As I run, I see Meadow's face in my head. Her gray eyes, determined and cold as steel. Her dagger in her hand, slicing Patients and Leeches as she fights her way through the Leech Headquarters from the inside out.

It's been three weeks. She *has* to be alive. I'd know it if she were dead, wouldn't I?

Maybe not. Maybe she *is* dead. Like Talan.

Oh, god, Talan. My best friend. Dead, because of me. I try to shove the guilt away, but it's too strong.

"Damn it!" I growl and sprint harder, faster, down the streets of the Shallows. The gun sheathed at my thigh bobs with every step. I skid around the corner of an alleyway and stop. Fade into the mass of people heading for safety before the Dark Time takes over.

The Leeches are out in packs, searching, but they won't find me easily.

I pull a baseball cap low over my eyes. My arms are covered in temporary tattoos, drawn on just this morning.

Hiding in plain sight is exactly what the Leeches *wouldn't* expect me to do.

The crowd moves along, and I walk with them. I keep my head on a swivel, searching. Always searching, for the woman who created me. Turned me into a monster.

Five minutes, and the Night Siren will go off.

There's a crackle in my left ear, the only good ear I have left, where a stolen Leech earpiece sits. *Take the alley directly across the street. And hurry up. My little sister runs faster than you.*

It's Rhone, the guy from the Resistance who was so interested in sending Meadow into the Leech Headquarters in the first place. Now she's gone, stuck inside. And I can't reach her.

Zero, move! Now.

I do what he says, shove my way through way too many people. Running is still hard since losing my ear, and my balance isn't quite right. But I can't stop now. I wobble on my feet before I leap over the train tracks, then dive into the alley to my left. The setting sun disappears, and suddenly it's dark.

And quiet. Too quiet, almost like it's the Silent Hour.

I stop and look around.

There's a Leech lying all bent and broken up against

the brick building to my right. His rifle lies on the concrete at his side, and there are empty bullet casings all over the place. But no other body, which means if Lark was here . . . she's gone. I take a step closer to him. Fresh blood drips from a slit in his throat, a perfect line of red, like a smile. The Leech chokes, lifts a hand for help that he's not going to get.

"She was just here," I say into my wrist mic. "Slit throat, like all the others."

We'll get her next time, Zero, Rhone says, and I want to believe him, but he's been saying the same thing for weeks. 21 days, and 7 hours, to be exact. *I'm on my way.*

I sigh and run a hand through my hair. I have to find Lark. When I do, I'll take her to the Leeches, knock down their front door, and hand her over in exchange for Meadow. I've thought about killing Lark instead. But in the chaos that will come afterward, I might not get to my moonlit girl.

Trading Lark for Meadow is best. We'll be together again, and we'll find some way, *any* way, to leave the Shallows behind. Find where the Leeches have taken her family, set them free.

I promised her I'd rescue them.

But I won't leave without her. I refuse.

The Leech groans, one last time. He takes a rattling breath and dies.

"You deserved it," I say to his body. I lean down to grab his rifle, and that's when I see it.

A bloody footprint, just a few feet away from him.

And then another, and another, heading out of the alley, toward the exit that leads to the beach. The footprints are small, but not small enough to be a child's. They could be Lark's.

I lift my wrist to my mouth. "Rhone, I think she's hurt. She couldn't have gone far from—"

The Night Siren goes off.

It starts as a whoop, dipping low, and then goes so high it's like a piercing scream. I cover my ears and drop to my knees. My whole body shakes, all the way to my fingers and toes. I hear a voice in my head. Lark's voice, welcoming me to the Murder Complex.

And suddenly I want to *kill*, *destroy*, give in to the pull of the system in my mind. I feel myself slipping away, feel my heart turning cold and solid as stone, see a victim in my head, their Catalogue Number, 65098, in bright red numbers.

But I think of Meadow. I think of one word, with four letters, and it's stupid as hell but I don't care.

Because love is what saves me and sets me free. It's still working, for now, but each night it's becoming harder. If I don't save Meadow soon, I'm afraid of what I'll become.

I shake the Murder Complex from my mind and sprint into the darkness.

CHAPTER 2

MEADOW

Something is different tonight.

On normal evenings, when the sun begins to set into the sea, the waves are calm and quiet. They whisper and crawl and collapse onshore, as steady as a heartbeat.

Tonight, the sea is angry.

The waves crash harder than ever against the rocks. Sea spray erupts into the sky, stinging my skin. Out in the water, the shipwrecked boats rock and groan like they are begging for mercy.

"Meadow?"

I blink and look down. My little sister Peri sits beside me on the sand, her silver curls dancing in the wind.

"Yes?" I ask. My voice sounds hollow. Empty.

"How much longer?" Peri asks me. She grabs my hand, entwines her fingers in mine. They are so cold that I flinch. "I want to go home."

"I know you do," I say, as I look back out at the sea. "Me, too."

There is a storm on the horizon, a promise that chaos is soon to come. We should go home, back to our houseboat where my father and my brother Koi wait. But something tugs at my mind, begs me to stay. The gray clouds rumble just beyond the Perimeter. The Pulse blinks in time with the lightning, and the hair rises on my arms. I shiver.

"Just wait," I say. "A few more minutes."

Peri shifts beside me. "What are we waiting for?"

"I . . . I can't remember," I whisper. My breath comes out in a puff of fog. Something that has never happened before in the Shallows. It is whisked away by the wind, carried into the bleeding sky.

The colors of the sunset are the same, reds and oranges and pinks, like the citrus my mother used to love. But still, I sense it.

Something is different tonight.

Seagulls dip and dive, screeching a warning. But a warning for what?

"I'm cold," Peri says. She leans against me, and her body is like ice.

A voice tugs at the back of my mind, whispering my name over and over. *Meadow, Meadow. Wake up. Pay attention, Meadow.* The voice sounds like my father's.

Peri starts to sing. Her voice is soft and lovely, and for a moment I close my eyes and let it roll over me like the wind.

Somewhere in the distance, the Night Siren goes off. It is a wail that belongs to those who mourn the dead. A warning that soon, something will come.

But *what*? I can't place it, and everything feels off.

Peri stands up, suddenly, whirls around to look at the beach behind us. Sand sprays my face. "Is that what we've been waiting for?" she asks.

I can hear a sound, like shuffling feet moving across the top of the sand. But I don't want to turn. Something begs me not to.

"Meadow!" Peri tugs at my hand. "Meadow, look!"

I take a deep breath and turn, slowly, and in my head I hear my father's voice again. *Wake. Up.*

And that's when I see them. A wave of Patients stumbling toward us in the sand.

"Run," I hear myself say. "Peri. Run!"

But when I turn to look at her, my little sister is gone.

In her place sits a puddle of fresh blood.

CHAPTER 3

ZEPHYR

I sprint into the trees at the edge of the alley.

"Lark," I say. My voice is strong and steady. "I know you're in here."

Movement in the overgrowth catches my eye. I stand up just as Lark appears in the tall grass. She stumbles toward the beach like a wounded animal. At the sight of her, I lose what's left of my sanity.

I fire the gun in her direction. And *curse it all*, I miss.

So I run, sprinting across the jungle floor, the wind blowing into the hole in the side of my head where my ear should be.

"Stop!" I scream, voice ragged. Lark trips, and I close the distance between us. I dive, fingertips grazing her ankles. I land on top of her and she cries out, her eyes reflecting the craziness that's inside of her.

"You left us to die!" I spit. "You left your *daughter* to die!" I whirl her around so we're facing each other. For one second, seeing her is like a punch to the gut.

She looks *so much* like Meadow.

"They can't touch my daughter, Patient Zero," Lark says, smiling with blackened teeth. "She'll live."

I punch her in the face, and she groans, then bursts into laughter. "Go ahead and kill me," she says. "Kill me and drag my body back to the Initiative. Do you think they'll hand Meadow over then?" She laughs, and her breath is so bad I want to puke. "You're a murderer, and you always will be. I made you perfectly in that way."

"Then this will be easy," I say. I turn the gun, level it at her forehead, right over her Catalogue Number. I'm ready to do it. Ready to kill willingly, and I'm not afraid. As soon as her heart stops, the fail-safe she put into the Murder Complex will activate. The Patients will turn their attacks onto the Leeches, and the Shallows will erupt into chaos.

Should I do it? Do I kill Lark, and use the chaos to help

me rescue Meadow . . . or do I carry Lark in, alive, and use her in exchange for setting her daughter free?

"You're a fool," Lark spits up at me.

I'm about to squeeze the trigger when she looks right into my eyes and whispers something, a string of words and numbers and things that don't make any sense. But she seems to know exactly what she's doing, and she smiles as she finishes speaking.

That's when the pain comes. I see a bright white light in my head, and suddenly, Lark's voice whispers from deep inside of me.

Welcome back to the Murder Complex, Patient Zero.

Initiate Termination.

Lark squirms under my body. I roll away from her, clutching my skull. I've already fought the system tonight. I can't do it again, not twice, not when I'm exhausted, not when my stomach is empty and I haven't slept in days. I need Meadow near me, close by, to fight it.

We've been separated for way too long.

Before the system takes over, I see Lark stand up and stagger away, a trail of blood in her wake.

"Stop . . ." I groan. "We have to . . . Meadow . . ."

But it's too late. The pain intensifies, and my sight goes.

Somehow, the Murder Complex has me in its grip.

I have enough strength to lift my wrist to my mouth. "The beach," I gasp to Rhone.

Then darkness pulls me under as the system takes control.

CHAPTER 4
MEADOW

I wake up screaming for my father.

Someone has dumped a bucket of ice-cold water over my head, and it feels like knives against my skin.

"Where is your mother?" a man's voice asks. I try to get my bearings, figure out where I am, but my head is heavy. My mind is a million miles away.

"Where is Lark Woodson?"

I don't answer. More water. Cold, so cold that I fear I will never be warm again.

I cough, gasping for air. I try to wipe the water away from my face, but my hands won't move. I try to sit up, but something holds my body down, my arms and legs, a heavy weight on top of my chest. It is like I am inside of one of my old nightmares, back on the houseboat with my family when I was younger. All I had to do was wake up, and I would be safe. But this time, the nightmare is real.

There is no waking up.

"I asked you a question," the voice says.

I groan, lift my head as far as I can. I am strapped to a metal table. Around me are gray walls. And thick bars.

Movement shifts behind my head, and someone steps into view. It is a man, pale faced and dark eyed, wearing the all-black uniform of the Initiative.

"Where is your mother?" he asks me. A name tag on his chest says *Interrogation Expert, SPC. Scientific Population Control.* "Where is Patient Zero?"

"I . . . don't know," I whisper. The fragments of my nightmare are still dancing around me, making me shiver and shake.

"Where is the Resistance?"

"I have no idea." My voice trembles, my teeth chatter like rattling bones. The man dumps another bucket of cold water over my head.

I gasp. The pain draws forth a memory, flashes of a mission, gunshots, a dying dark-haired girl.

My little sister Peri, *stolen*. My brother Koi and my father, *gone*.

My mother . . . *a murderer.*

And suddenly the truth comes back to me, I remember exactly where I am. *What* I am.

I am a prisoner of the Initiative, with a connection to the Murder Complex in my brain. I came here to destroy the Motherboard, shut the system down for good, until I discovered that *I* am the only one who can end the Murder Complex. If I die, the system dies along with me.

That is the only way.

I gave myself up so that Zephyr could escape and set my family free. I wanted to die fighting the Patients, die so that the Murder Complex would die, too. A brave death, something my father would be proud of.

My plan failed. My mother escaped, my partner Sketch is nowhere to be found. The last time I saw her, she was bleeding out, close to death.

I look around the room at the dirty walls of the cell, the ceiling tiles overhead, now patched with bars that weren't there before. The details fall into place.

I am stuck inside of the very same room that holds the very same cell where my mother was once kept.

Now I am a prisoner, behind enemy lines.

And I am completely on my own.

CHAPTER 5

ZEPHYR

Lark's voice is in my head.

This is the Murder Complex.

I reach for a vision of Meadow, her lips against mine, her calloused hands on my shoulders. I'm angry that I'm not with her. I try to fight the system, try to force my way out of it.

I have flashes of here, and now. The rain falling from the sky, splashing onto my face.

And then I am sucked away again, back into the Murder Complex, unaware of what I'm doing. Where I'm going.

Back and forth, in and out, and I can't get free, can't fight it.

But then I remember the words that Rhone told me, weeks ago, see flashes of memories, us hiding out in the Graveyard, practicing. My body, chained to a steam tower, screaming at the world.

You can choose your victims, Zero. Just channel the power of the system. If you can't fight it without Meadow, then use it to your advantage. Bend it to your will.

I have to kill, feel the need and want deep down in my soul. I can't stop the Murder Complex inside. But I can angle it, turn it around.

Now I can *choose* my victim. I can be aware of my surroundings. I can focus and choose who to kill.

I imagine I'm a boy again, standing in the mirrored room in the Leech Headquarters where Lark used to work with me. I picture the Motherboard is there with me, a giant screen of numbers and codes and lines, beating in time with Meadow's heart.

"I choose my own victims now," I say to the screen.

It flashes bright red. Catalogue Numbers flash by, but they're all citizens. And this time, I want Leeches.

I try to change the numbers. Beg the system to give me someone I *really* want. It fights back against me, and I hear Lark's voice again, commanding me to follow orders.

But her orders are to *kill, destroy, no escaping, no turning back*. As long as my night ends in blood and bones.

"I choose my own victims," I say again. I shake the vision away, come back to the here and now.

I whirl around, look for Lark.

She's gone, somewhere in the trees. Her blood trail disappears in the shadows of night. She won't resurface again, not after I've come this close.

I run toward the city instead. People sprint past me, heading for the shadows. They don't know that there's no place to hide. If a Patient wants to find someone . . . we will.

We always will.

Weeks ago I'd have gone after anyone in front of me. Innocents. But tonight, I'm going to do what Meadow would do.

Take out the Leeches. I grit my teeth. Focus, hard, until I taste blood in my mouth. "I . . . choose . . . the Leeches," I hear myself say. And then I feel the freedom. I feel the system release a part of me, the part that begs to listen to its every order. The release is only for a second. A lightness in my skull, like a breath of fresh air.

But it's enough, and it's like I flip a switch in my head. The hunger for killing citizens becomes a hunger for Leeches, and suddenly the Murder Complex agrees.

The train rattles past. I leap, grab a hold, and hang on tight. It drops me off in front of the Rations Hall, right in the middle of the Shallows. I roll to my feet, then run for the alley.

Kill. Destroy. No escaping. No turning back.

There's a Leech locking the door, probably some ChumHead who came to steal rations for himself. Like he doesn't have enough already. *Kill,* my brain tells me. *Obey.*

I'm silent. A predator. I pick up a piece of pipe, broken on the cracked pavement.

Then I slink up behind him, a shadow in the night, and thrust it through his back, so hard it breaks the skin. Pierces his black heart. The guy drops, and I know I've won.

I stoop down and grab the rifle from the Leech's lifeless body.

Purge the Earth.

This is the Murder Complex.

I can't stop. I have to kill. I have to spill blood.

I turn and run down the alley, past two citizens huddled on the ground. Too obvious. The Leech Compound is just ahead. Stupid, to think they're safe.

I stop outside the gates. Touch my hands to them, and

I'm shocked backward, blown to the ground like a bullet from a gun.

I stand up, body wobbling, but I don't feel pain. Not when the Murder Complex has a hold of me. I'm strong. Stronger than ever.

I aim the rifle through the gates, look through the scope until the red dot lands right on the second-floor window. I breathe out. Steady. My heart rate slows. I squeeze the trigger.

The window shatters, and I keep shooting. Lights shut off, exploding from fired rounds. Screams come from the inside. I keep shooting, until the trigger clicks beneath my finger. I'm out of ammo.

I drop the rifle.

"You can't control me!" I scream, even though I'm wrong. They still control me; I just have a new way of dealing with it. "Screw all of you!"

I'm seeing Meadow in my head, drenched in blood as we tried to escape the Leech Headquarters together, and it makes me go crazy. I beat the fence with my palms. It blows me backward again, and I can see Leeches pouring out of the building, sprinting toward me. A part of my mind whispers that I need to run, hide. But I shake it away. I snarl, ready for the fight, *needing* it.

Someone tackles me from behind. I feel something wet, over my mouth. I try to get away, but there are too many hands, and then there's the feeling of . . . falling.

Slowly.

I sink backward, the world disappearing into a funnel of black, until all I can see is a girl's face hovering over me. Dex, Rhone's little sister, the only light in my world right now.

"Too easy," Dex says. "Take him."

My eyes close, and I'm gone.

CHAPTER 6

MEADOW

My father taught me how to be strong.

He gave me a lifetime of lessons in how to kill with a hardened heart. Peri and Koi and Zephyr taught me how to love, how to reel myself back in, to be soft again.

It is my mother's influence I will rely on now.

Because she taught me how to lie.

"Tell us where the Resistance is," the Interrogator says. He stands above me in my cell, pacing back and forth, arms clasped behind his back.

He has been doing this for twenty-one days.

I have marked the time with twenty-one gashes on my calf, using my fingernails to carve a bleeding line into my skin with every day that passes. Twenty-one perfect, solid scars. They remind me of how long I have stayed strong.

Today, the Interrogator's hands are clean. Soon they will be stained from my blood again. A part of me wants it. I deserve to be tortured. I deserve to feel pain, for messing up, losing my family when they were so close. I remember Peri, screaming for me as an Initiative soldier dragged her away. I remember the fear in her eyes, the way she looked so small. So helpless. The memory hurts more than the torture ever could.

Pain is good, my father's voice tells me. *Use it to become stronger.*

I look up at the Interrogator and give him my coldest smile. "The Resistance?" I ask. The Interrogator nods. I think of the Cave, the underground facility where the Resistance is hiding out.

We failed to destroy the Motherboard, because I was the Protector. I *am* the Protector, and I feel it inside of me like a curse. It is because I still live that the Murder Complex lives on, too.

I think of Zephyr, his eyes the color of the outside. The tiny glimpse of freedom I saw as Peri was carted away. I hope Zephyr has gone back to the Resistance. I hope they are working up a new plan to take down the Initiative.

Then I hope he will escape the Shallows, go and save my family from the Ridge up north.

I gave myself up for the cause.

I will give nothing else away today, or tomorrow, or however long they keep me here.

"I don't know who the Resistance is," I say. "But if there is a Resistance, it sounds like you have bigger problems than interrogating a sixteen-year-old girl."

"Oh, you're much more than that." The Interrogator grins. "And I guarantee, you'll spill all of your secrets in due time."

He turns to a metal table. There are all kinds of devices on it. Things that should be in a hospital, not in a dirty cell in the belly of the Initiative Headquarters. Sharp things that I don't want anywhere near me.

"Do you know, Miss Woodson, what the heretics fork method is?"

I do not speak.

"No, you wouldn't. Uneducated, as all the Shallows citizens are. Worthless mutts without any real importance to this dying world."

"Is that how you justify the mass murder of thousands of innocent people?" I ask.

He ignores me. "This is the heretics fork," he says,

holding up a metal fork with two red prongs on each end. A collar is attached to the center of the fork, as if it were made for being strapped around someone's neck. "A beautiful device, used all the way back in the Medieval Era. Do you know what that is, Miss Woodson?"

"Does it matter?" I cannot look away from the fork. The prongs are as sharp as knives.

"Everything matters," the Interrogator says. "You see, this clever little invention is something your mother would've loved to use. I'll show you how it works, in just a moment." He holds it up to the light, tilts his head. "Unless you want to tell me where your mother is?"

"My mother is dead," I say. I look right into his cold, black eyes.

"That, my dear, is where you are wrong."

I refuse to look away. He continues.

"We know about your mother's fail-safe. If she dies, the Initiative dies, too." He paces back and forth, shiny black boots on pale gray pavement. "Just as we know about the connection in *your* brain. We're working to reverse the connection your mother has to the system. But your connection, Miss Woodson, is something beautiful."

"So you know that you have to keep me alive." I hide my fear from him. I refuse to be weak. "How long are you going to torture me, Interrogator? How long are you going to try to make me scream, beg for you to stop until I give you the information you want?" I swallow, then laugh the way my mother would have. "It's been far too long. I haven't bent. I haven't broken. You can burn me with fire and pierce me with knives, but I will *never* tell."

"Our doctors are working on a surgery," he says. "We might not be able to remove the connection from your brain. . . . Your mother's work was beautiful. Brilliant." His eyes glitter, like he worships my mother. I imagine most of the Initiative does, in a way. "But in due time, Miss Woodson, we might be able to control *you*. Patient Zero, as you may well know, could use a perfect counterpart. You are in our top group of candidates."

I stop breathing. Stop feeling fear.

Now it is only hate.

He kneels down in front of me and puts his hand on my cheek. I will not flinch. I will not show weakness. "They said you were a strong one, and you've proven them all right." He taps the tip of my nose with the fork. It's cold. "This method isn't for you."

The Interrogator stands, lifts his arm to his wrist before he speaks again. "Bring her in."

Cold sweat trickles its way down my back. I wait, and

as minutes pass, I hear commotion outside of the room. A voice shouting, and the sound of Initiative boots on hard ground.

The door outside of my cell swings open, and two guards drag a hooded, writhing girl into the room.

"Just wait till I get my hands on you, you fluxing ChumHeads!"

I recognize that voice. I haven't heard it in . . .

I press my face to the bars as they rip the hood from her head, and the sight of her, *alive*, is enough to bring a smile to my face.

It's Sketch.

CHAPTER 7

ZEPHYR

When I come to, it's dark.

And wherever I am, it smells like crap.

The Graveyard.

I sit up. My head wobbles like crazy. I have flashes of what I think are memories from my time under the Murder Complex. *Lark's laugh, her wild eyes. Blood on my hands, a trigger squeezed, a scream splitting the night.*

Somewhere in the distance I hear voices, a twang and a smack that sort of sounds like someone throwing knives. Then footsteps, coming toward me.

I lie back down and pretend like I'm still out of it, because I don't want to talk right now. I don't want to explain myself.

Someone flips on a lantern.

"You can stop pretending," a voice says. It's light and airy, a young girl. Dex.

I groan and open my eyes. Dex has blonde hair, in dreadlocks that hang to her shoulders. She's small but strong, and she might be half insane. She's several years younger than me; maybe fourteen at the most. And she has two different colored eyes. One blue like Talan's, one green, like mine.

Dex sits down next to me and sets the lantern right by my head. It's too bright.

"Get that thing out of here," I groan.

"So the kamikaze awakens," Dex says. She bites her bottom lip, tilts her head sideways. "You know, I warned Rhone that you weren't ready to go out so close to the Dark Time alone. You think you've got a hold on the system, Zephyr, but you're wrong. You're getting weaker, the longer you're away from Meadow." She sighs, cracks her knuckles. "Ah, whatever. You're back to normal now, I guess. It's all in the eyes."

I've been living with Dex for weeks and it only now hits me that she reminds me of Talan. A mouth that just won't quit. "Where's Rhone?" I ask. My head feels heavy. "I need to talk to him."

I can see now that I'm back in what we call the Shack. Rounded tunnel walls, water dripping down the sides. The awful smell of sewage. And in the distance, the sounds of the Graveyard. Seagulls cawing, the hisses and clicks of cockroaches, and sometimes, faraway screams.

I relax. At least I'm safe. For now.

"How did you find me?" I ask.

Dex smiles. "I'm always watching you, Zephyr."

I laugh. If anyone else said something so creepy, I'd be freaked out of my mind. But Dex is just . . . *Dex*. There's something sort of comforting, something Talan-like, about the crazy side of this little girl. It shows up at random and usually inappropriate times. She's the comic relief in the middle of such a dark, screwed-up world.

Dex points beside me, on the concrete floor, where there's a half-eaten chunk of bread. I scoop it up and devour the thing. It's dry and it tastes terrible, but as soon as it's gone I want more.

"Anyways . . ." Dex says, giggling at me, "I'll get Rhone."

"I'm already here," a guy says from the shadows. He comes closer to the light. Black hair. Piercing blue eyes. Solid Leech-like shoulders.

"Rhone," I say, and I try to stand but my legs buckle. Dex helps me back down, pats my head like I'm her pet dog. "I controlled it. I finally got to choose my victim, like we've been practicing."

Rhone chuckles under his breath, runs a hand through his dark hair. "Yeah, that's great and all, Zero, but you chose the entire Leech Compound as your victim."

"I . . . *what*?"

I try to piece together what happened last night, but it's all fragments. That's something that will probably never change. I think I remember. . . .

"Lark," I whisper. "She triggered it a second time on me. It was like she used some sort of remote trigger on me. Some sort of phrase or something."

Rhone nods, scratches his chin, and in reality that means he's thinking, *Yeah, okay, Zero. Suuuure.*

Dex giggles again. "It's lucky we found you before the Leeches did. I wasted my last ounce of chloroform on your sorry self, you know."

"How did you even get that?" I ask. Then I remember Lark again, our encounter on the beach. "Did you find Lark?"

Rhone shakes his head. "I would have. But your little episode sort of took the lead on the mission, Zero." He shrugs. "You should rest. We'll regroup later today."

He's wrong.

I don't need to rest at all. I have a rescue mission to plan. I have Leeches to kill, and Lark, the creator of the system, to find.

"We have one week left," I whisper, as Rhone turns to leave.

"Actually, we have six days," Dex corrects me.

Rhone throws her a look that could kill.

I think back to weeks ago, when Meadow was first lost to me. I barely made it back to the Resistance, to their Headquarters underground, with a gaping hole in my head. Dex, and the nanites in my system, nursed me back to health, and when I was ready, I recounted everything that happened inside of the Leech building.

How our partner, Sketch, was left behind, bleeding out. How Lark escaped, and is nowhere to be found. How Talan died. The way the light in her eyes went out, the way she shouted her daughter's name with her very last breath.

But I held one detail back.

I didn't tell them what I still hold close to me now, the one thing I swore to myself I'd never tell.

Meadow is the Protector of the Motherboard. If she dies, the Murder Complex dies, too. That's the only way.

"We're running out of time," I say.

"I know, Zero." Rhone sighs.

I asked for an army, for a chance to attack the Leeches and get Meadow back.

I remember Orion's words. *One month,* she said.

One month for what? I asked.

She looked at me like I was an idiot. *You can take some of my people. A small group, and go to the surface. Search for Lark . . . Find her and bring her to me. If you do that, I'll have the entire Resistance help you.*

It is her final words that still stick with me now, because I'm afraid she is right. *Do me a favor, would you, Zero? Don't screw this up.*

Now I try to stand and fall back down.

"Rest," Dex says. She puts her hands on my shoulders and forces me to lie down.

"Okay," I say. "I'll rest. But once I wake up, we're going hunting again."

Rhone nods. There's that look in his eyes, the one that says he doesn't believe it will really happen.

And I'm starting to think he's right.

I fall asleep thinking of Meadow, a girl with moonlight in her eyes.

But in my dreams, they turn a deep, bloody red.

CHAPTER 8

MEADOW

The Initiative is going to torture Sketch in front of me.

I am surprised she's still breathing. The last time I saw her, she was unconscious on the floor of the Motherboard room, wounded from some perverse red knife my mother invented. It was supposed to make her bleed out.

But Sketch is strong, and there is fresh skin on her arms and legs, almost as if the Initiative patched her up on purpose. To keep her alive.

"Sketch," I say. I am not alone after all, and seeing her is such a relief that I almost break down. I want to reach through the bars, grab her hand, feel the warmth of another person who is on my side. But I can't. I must stay steady, and still, and pretend like this girl does not matter to me.

They won't hurt her if they think I don't care.

Right?

"Don't just stand there. Bring her in!" the Interrogator barks. The guards haul Sketch to her feet and drag her inside of my cell, dump her on the floor across from me. I wish I could crawl to her, but I'm bound to the bars.

They do the same to Sketch, circling her wrists with MagnaCuffs, then attaching them to the metal bars behind her back.

Up close, I can see how swollen her face is. I wonder if they've already been beating her, letting her heal, then starting it all over again.

"Don't tell these asshats anything," Sketch says. She spits blood on the floor, so close to the Interrogator's boots that I smile.

"There's nothing to tell," I say.

Sketch winks a swollen eye, and the Interrogator bursts into laughter.

"Look at the two of you. Comrades, all the way to the end." He snaps his fingers, and another guard scurries forward.

"It's warm in here, soldier," he says. "Why don't you

turn the air down a bit?"

The soldier nods, crosses to the wall and taps on a little screen embedded there.

There is a beep and a hiss, and suddenly the air vent overhead turns on. Cool air blasts my face, makes me feel a little more alive.

"Colder," the Interrogator says. "Bring the winter to us."

The soldier obeys.

For a while, the air reminds me of fall mornings on the beach, like the wind rolling in from beyond the Perimeter, raising the hair on my arms. Peri used to love the cool air.

But then it gets colder.

And colder.

So cold that my teeth begin to rattle and my fingertips begin to shake. The torn, bloody rags I am wearing are not enough to keep me warm. Soon, I can see my breath forming in puffs in front of me. Sketch trembles across from me. Our eyes meet. We simply sit and stare.

The Interrogator laughs again, claps his hands. "This is more like it, girls." A soldier brings him a coat, and he shrugs it on over his shoulders, nestles into it and sighs. "Do you know what a Cold Cell is?"

He looks to me, then Sketch.

"No, I didn't think so," he says. "We used it back during

the Fall. A simple way to break a man, when the room is so cold his blood threatens to freeze." He makes a show of shivering, pulling the coat tighter around his body. I look away. "You'll enjoy this tactic for the remainder of your stay."

I think he is going to turn and leave, but instead he pulls the heretics fork out of his coat. I prepare myself for the pain, open my heart up to it the way my father taught me to.

But the Interrogator turns to Sketch, kneels in front of her. "I'd say I'm sorry about this, but . . . that would be a lie."

He grabs her by the chin, thrusts her head up so she's staring at the ceiling, her throat fully exposed. She tries to fight him, but he's too strong. He takes the fork, and levers it so that one end of the prongs is positioned beneath her chin, the other end pointing down, against her chest. Then he straps the collar around her throat and buckles it tight.

"Now be a good girl, and don't move an inch," the Interrogator says. "Because if you do . . ." He pushes down, hard, on top of Sketch's head. She screams as the prongs break through the skin on both ends of the fork. The Interrogator laughs, presses harder, until Sketch's blood drips steady and bright. He looks over his shoulder at me, a snarl on his face. "You see, Miss Woodson? You see what the Initiative can do to those you care about?"

Sketch's eyes find mine. They are wide, full of tears that splash down onto her cheeks. She shakes her head, the movement so small I hardly catch it.

But I know what she means.

I take a deep breath and smile at our torturer. "She means nothing to me," I say. "You can kill her right now, if you'd like."

His smile falters. He releases Sketch. Her gasps are so terrible I almost can't take it.

But I do. I must.

He crosses to me. Leans down, grabs me by the hair, and pulls. I force my groan down to the pit of my stomach. "I'll do whatever I can to hurt you," he promises. "And you *will* hurt."

I look right into his eyes. "Go ahead. I dare you to try."

"We're only just beginning," the Interrogator says. "You'll break soon enough."

He stands, and as he passes, I make a promise to myself, and Sketch.

The second I get a chance I will kill this man with my bare hands.

CHAPTER 9

ZEPHYR

The Graveyard isn't bad in the morning.

Sometimes, if you can get past the smell and the flies and the fact that you're standing in the middle of a pile of crap, it's kind of peaceful.

Rhone and I are making our daily rounds, searching for food, items to trade.

Before the failed mission, I came here with Meadow.

I kissed her for the first time.

As Rhone and I walk side by side in silence, looking for something worth gathering, it kills me. Because it's like I can see Meadow in everything that moves.

A little girl who practices fighting moves with her dad,

like a younger Meadow.

A boy who carries a dagger on his hip. The sunlight catches it, reminds me of how she used to flip her weapon across the tops of her fingers.

We pass by one of the steam towers, and I swear I can actually *hear* her voice in my head.

You can kiss my ass, Zephyr James.

Stars, I miss her so much it hurts. It wasn't supposed to end up this way. We were supposed to be together and free, and now the Leeches could be doing anything to her.

I clench my fists and shove her face from my mind. It doesn't do anything but piss me off right now, because a part of me hates her for what she did. The other part loves her even more.

And sometimes, love really sucks.

"There," Rhone says when we reach the edge of the Graveyard. It's not much, an old hunk of metal sticking out of the trash pile like an arm, but it's sharp. We could shape it into a weapon, something Rhone is good at. He can turn anything useless into something lethal.

And the Gravers like lethal things.

We take it, spend a while searching for a few more bits and pieces.

In a few hours' time, Rhone has fastened a blade. He

whirls it in his hand, slices the air with it.

"Not bad," I say.

"Genius, actually," Rhone corrects me. "Let's go dig up some Gravers."

They usually only come out at night. Unless you're crazy enough to summon them, and Dex is the perfect sort of crazy.

We're in the middle of the Graveyard, by one of the steam towers. Dex stands in front of me and Rhone, holding the new blade high over her head.

"Gravers! Come out, come out, wherever you are," Dex says, in a singsongy voice. It makes me shiver, feel like there are bugs crawling under my skin.

"I don't like this," I whisper. "What if they just . . . kill us?"

"They know things," Rhone tells me. His fists are clenched, and he looks side to side, staring into the alleys of trash. "We're running out of time. We need to do something drastic."

"Attacking the Leech Compound wasn't drastic enough?" I say.

"Just shut your mouth and keep your eyes open, Zero."

While we wait, there's a buzzing overhead. A black orb

comes into view, floating overhead, like a bird without wings.

"Cam!" Dex shouts.

We all dive for cover, bury ourselves in the trash, cover ourselves with whatever we can find. I play dead, a body lying facedown, my hand over my Ward Mark on my neck, a bold, black *X*.

I can hear the whirr of the Cam as it spins in place, recording. The Leeches started sending them out only hours after we attacked their Headquarters.

They're looking for Lark. For the Resistance. For me.

They won't find any of us.

Finally, the Cam disappears, soars away into the outer parts of the Graveyard. We come out of hiding, regroup together in a cluster. I rub dirt from my eyes, and when I turn to look at Dex and Rhone, something catches my attention.

It's a man only a few feet away.

He wasn't there before.

His body is covered in the armor of the Gravers. Pieces of trash, woven together to make a breastplate. His long dark hair is laced through with coins and beads, like tokens.

"You called," the Graver says.

Behind him, two other Gravers emerge from the trash, holding spears made of old metal pipes. They could have been there all along, perfectly disguised, and we never would have noticed them. The Gravers have become one with the trash, wasted parts of the world that they've found use for all over again.

"We want to make a trade," Rhone says. He motions for Dex to hold up the blade. She lifts it high. The sunlight glints off of it, gleams like fire. It's a good blade. Surely the Gravers will want it. "The blade for information. We're searching for someone."

The Graver man laughs, but it comes out more like a wheeze. He is probably in his fifties, but his arms are strong. I bet he could put up a solid fight. "We know who you seek," he says. "The songbird woman. Lark."

"You know?" I ask.

Dex giggles. "The Gravers hear everything and watch everything. Sometimes, they talk to me at night."

Rhone puts a protective hand on her shoulder, then addresses the Graver leader. "Do you know where Lark Woodson is hiding?"

"We can offer more than just a blade," I say. "We can offer food. Stolen Leech items, when we come across them."

The Graver points to my good ear, where the Leech earpiece sits. He points to Rhone, too, who has the other part of the pair. "The machines," he says. "We want them."

I look at Rhone, raise an eyebrow. He nods. We remove our earpieces and throw them across the gap. They roll to a stop in front of the Graver leader's feet. His two companions rush forward, scoop them up.

"The blade, too," the Graver says.

Rhone tosses it.

We wait.

A cloud covers the sun for a second, and in the shadows, the Gravers look even more haunting. I clench my fists, hope for answers.

"We don't know where Lark hides," the Graver says.

"What the hell? Then give us our stuff!" Dex takes a step forward, but Rhone pulls her back.

The Graver laughs again, that same horrible wheeze. "You should join us, little one. You would do well to learn patience from the Gravers." He stares at Dex for too long, before looking back at Rhone and me. "We don't know where Lark Woodson is. But we have something else, *someone* else, that might be of interest to you."

He clicks his teeth, lifts a hand.

The Gravers behind him disappear into the tunnel

between two trash mountains. Minutes pass. Finally, they reappear, but this time they aren't alone. They're dragging a body between them, one that fights weakly to get away.

"You will find good use for this one," the Graver leader says. "She thinks she can steal from the Gravers. She is wrong."

The Gravers hauling the body come closer, until I can see it's a woman, bound in chains.

Her hair is dark, matted to her head, and when they throw her to the ground, she lets out a horrible whimper that sounds like an animal on the verge of death. The woman's limbs are too thin, way too weak for fighting. What use could someone like her be to us?

"Who is she?" Rhone asks. "Why would we want her?"

The Gravers laugh, all of them together, and it sounds like the hissing of the cockroaches that scurry among the trash.

"Her face," the leader says. "Look at her face, and you'll know." He clicks his teeth again, and one of his men stoops to one knee. Grabs the prisoner by the chin and forces her to look up.

At first, all I see is the scar. It takes up half of her entire face, the skin to the left of her nose puckering so bad that it makes her look like she came right out of a nightmare.

Her left eyes is missing, and part of her hair, closer to that side, has burned away, leaving wrinkled, reddened skin in its place.

"What's your name?" Rhone asks.

The woman opens her mouth, and when she speaks, her voice is so familiar that it shocks me down to my core.

"Sparrow," she says. Her one eye meets mine, and I gasp.

It's gray.

Gray like a storm cloud, gray like an angry sea.

Gray like Meadow's, and Lark's, and everyone else in their family. An unmistakable color.

"My name is Sparrow," the woman says again. She grimaces when she speaks the next words, spits them out like they're full of poison. "Lark Woodson is my sister."

CHAPTER 10

MEADOW

We have not eaten in two days.

At first, Sketch and I made a game out of our growling stomachs, laughing every time it happened, seeing whose would growl louder and longer.

But now the laughter has faded.

And a desperate hunger has taken its place. It reminds me of when I found my mother, how she was skin and bones, sunken eyes and cheeks.

If I were to look at my reflection, is that what I would see? A younger version of my mother, staring back? Sometimes, I feel a darkness lurking beneath the surface of my soul. Sometimes, I imagine I hear voices, whispering in my ears. They tell me that I am weakening. They tell me that soon, I will lose this fight.

Sometimes, I almost talk back.

It is my mother's insanity, the same force that once took ahold on her. And now it is after me.

I am carving another line into my calf when the Interrogator comes. He brings a whip with prongs on the ends, and lashes Sketch's back until she bleeds into unconsciousness. The next day, with another line carved, he turns on me.

Sketch and I wake, hours later, healed from the nanites, but broken down a little bit more.

Now, we sit in darkness.

"It's so damn cold," Sketch groans.

"Ignore it," I say, even though everything has become numb. My lips, my toes, my ears, and I long for the warm sand, the sun on my skin, the ocean water in the afternoon heat. "Just pretend we aren't here."

But she is right.

The chill of the air has begun to seep its way into my bones. I am afraid that if I move, I will shatter like glass.

Sometimes, Sketch falls asleep. I keep her awake by mumbling her name or singing songs that my mother used to sing when I was only a child. Back when we were on the houseboat, safe and sound.

Now, that safety has burned to ashes, buried beneath the sea.

"I'm gonna die in here," Sketch says. "They'll keep you alive because they have to. But me? I ain't worth *nothing*. They'll kill me soon."

"Don't say that," I whisper. "That's what they want you to believe. You have to be strong."

"Strength is just an illusion, Protector."

"Don't call me that." I shake my head. I want to tell her what my father would tell me: that strength, in the face of fear, is the only thing that will keep us alive. But the Initiative is always listening, watching.

I will not give them my father's words.

"Can you keep a secret?" Sketch asks.

"Yes. You should know that by now. I think both of us are pretty good at keeping secrets, Sketch."

"Prisoner humor," she says. "Nice." She swallows, and I can hear it, like rocks grating against each other. The heretics fork is still stuck to her throat. Dried blood has crusted on her skin. When she starts to drop her head, I remind her to stop, remind her that she's strong enough to keep her head held high, because I know the pain that will come if she lowers it is my fault.

Sketch is only here because of me.

"I want to die," Sketch says. She doesn't sound sad or upset. It is an honest admission, a brave thing to tell. "I wish I *were* dead."

"Then you're lucky. Because I have a theory that we're already in hell."

I think of Zephyr, the time I found him lying half-dead on the street. He wanted to die so badly he tried to kill himself. Sketch has killed countless people while under the influence of the Murder Complex. I guess every Patient welcomes their own death at some point, and now, I understand.

Because I want to die, too.

The Murder Complex is connected to my brain. Every second I live and breathe, it thrives along with me. Every time my heart beats, I imagine the system sucking the life out of me.

A leech.

The Wards are right to call the Initiative that.

The door swings open behind me, and the Interrogator walks in. He unlocks the cell and glides in, then removes the fork from Sketch's neck.

She gasps and drops her head, sucking in gulps. "I was just starting to like it," she groans, defiant as ever. She lifts her head and gives the Interrogator a glittering smile.

"Where is the Resistance hiding?" he asks. Sketch does not answer, does not move an inch.

He slaps her face. She laughs.

He turns to me, black eyes dark as coal. I wish I had my father's dagger. I don't know what they did with it, but I feel naked without the solidity of steel against my thigh.

"Where is the Resistance hiding?"

"There is no Resistance," I say.

He throws his head back and laughs. "You have your mother's humor, I see. Where is she hiding?"

"My mother is not my concern anymore," I say, and it is the same answer I will always give him, no matter what he does. Because in my heart, she died years ago. If she were still the mother I used to know, she would have come to save me by now.

She would never have left this building until she watched me escape first, until she knew that I was safe. She would have given herself up before anyone touched me.

But she didn't.

She ran, like a coward. And she's not coming back.

"You'll get nothing from us," I say. "Never."

"We'll die before we tell you anything," Sketch adds.

The Interrogator shrugs. "You'll probably die," he says to Sketch. Then he leans up against the bars so he can look right into my eyes. "But you, Meadow Woodson, will *never* get the luxury of death."

He leaves, slamming the door behind him as he goes.

He thinks he can win. He thinks that, battle after battle, he is peeling away the tough layers that surround me, forcing my answers out of hiding.

But there is something the Interrogator did not account for.

In this war, I am the strongest soldier.

I am my father's daughter, and I refuse to break.

CHAPTER II

ZEPHYR

I can't look at the woman.

Sparrow.

Lark's *sister.* Because a memory hits me as Rhone and I drag her back to our camp. It was something Meadow said, a long time ago. About her aunt being the one who put Meadow's name into the system.

Sparrow is the one who sent me after Meadow.

Sparrow is the one who tried, time and time again, to get me to kill the girl I love. She passes out by the time we've made it back to our camp. Rhone and Dex force me to leave her, say I can come back later, when she's awake.

And I will.

I'm going to get my answers from this woman.

CHAPTER 12

MEADOW

I know how to deal with pain.

My father taught me how to take it and twist it to my advantage, to fuel off of it the way a soft wind can stoke a fire.

They took Sketch away, and now, I am the only prisoner here, hanging upside down by my ankles, on some sort of table. The Interrogator asks me a question, and when I do not answer, he touches a scalding hot knife to my bare skin. The room is still freezing, and when he puts the blade to my neck, I see a trail of smoke, hear the sizzle and pop of my cold skin touching hot steel.

"Where is Patient Zero?" he asks me.

The same questions, the same answers.

It takes too much effort to speak. My heart is in my throat, and every swallow is fire.

"Patient Zero," he says. "Zephyr James. We know you have information on his whereabouts. Cooperate, tell us, and you'll live like a queen."

Zephyr. He knows their secrets, all of the inner workings of the Murder Complex. As long as he's out there, the Initiative will search. With what he knows, he could incite a full-scale rebellion.

I wish he would.

I imagine him saving me, dropping from the sky in the same way that I did for my mother. Shooting everyone down, pulling me to his chest. The two of us, finding freedom together outside of the Perimeter.

I push the dream away.

Sometimes dreams are impossible lies.

"TELL US!" the Interrogator screams. He whips me across the face with the back of his hand. The sting is so strong that I almost don't feel it.

"No," I groan. *"No."* Hanging upside down, I feel small. The Interrogator's hideous face towers above me. My vision grows spotty and dim.

"Very well," he says. "I can do this all day, Miss Woodson."

He presses the blade of the knife flat against my fore-arm, right above my *fearless* tattoo. The pain is so intense that I start to see the world in green. I pretend the pain is only Koi's knife. He is scratching the tattoo into my arm, back on the houseboat. We are together and safe. I don't want to scream. My father would tell me not to. But still, I cry out.

"Had enough?" the Interrogator asks. "Where is the Resistance?"

"You'll never find them!" I say. He presses the knife to my other arm.

"Where is your mother?"

"I . . . don't . . . KNOW!" I scream. "I don't know any-thing about anyone!"

He pulls the knife away. My skin peels back with it, and I want to sob, scream, curl into a ball. Instead, I focus on the wideness of his shoulders, the way that he favors standing with his weight on his heels, how he uses his right hand more than his left.

The Interrogator stoops to one knee, his face even with mine. I see the dark lines under his eyes, smell his rancid breath. He makes me want to puke.

He doesn't see that I've gotten one wrist loose, that I've twisted and turned and done the tricks my father once showed me. I have to keep him distracted, so I can free my other arm. "Go to hell," I whisper. I spit in his face.

He punches me in the nose. Twice. Blood drips from my nostrils, into my eyes, staining my hair. I long for a weapon, for something to thrust through his gut, stop his heart. But I can't do that. I can only use words.

"That's all you've got?" I ask, still working on my wrist. He turns his back to me. "You can do better than that, Interrogator!"

He turns, eyes wide. "Not impressed, Miss Woodson?"

"Barely." I force myself to laugh, to act like I am completely unfazed. "I was hitting people harder than you as a toddler." I close my eyes and take his next hit.

And the next.

I keep laughing, channeling the insanity I learned from my mother. If I act out of my mind, they might let up. I laugh through the pain, and I do not stop. I only laugh louder, harder, until I realize that maybe, this insanity is not a ploy. In this moment, it feels alive and real, like a beast inside of me.

The Interrogator lets out a frustrated growl.

I smile. He can't take it anymore.

He steps closer.

So close I can imagine how I will kill him.

I just need him to take one more step.

"You're as insane as your mother," he says. "You'll live in this cell for the rest of your life, until you rot."

"I won't," I say. "Someone will come for me. And they'll make sure I'm the one who gets to slit your throat."

He walks right into my trap.

I smile, as wide as Peri does. Then I reach out, lightning quick, and grab his neck with both hands. I put all of the strength I have into the twist, and when I hear the snap, I scream for joy.

The Interrogator's body drops.

"You will *never* win!" I yell, and laugh. I want the others to hear me. I want them to know what I've done.

That I've beaten them today. And I will tomorrow, and the next day after that.

It doesn't take long. Guards rush into the room, rifles aimed at the ready. Men hold me down. I scream and writhe and try to get away, but it's no use.

"She killed him!" one of the soldiers says. A young boy, too young to be working for them, maybe only a few years older than Peri.

"I'll kill you, too," I hiss, and I know that with all of the blood in my body now gathered in my head, I must look wild.

Red as fire.

"Get him out!" a guard barks. "And page the doctor. It's time!"

They drag the Interrogator's body from the room. There is a rush of movement, footsteps and voices, as more soldiers flood the cell.

"Move over!" a woman shouts. More footsteps, the clacking of heels on hard ground. A woman shoves her way between the guards. Her red hair is tied neatly back in a bun at the nape of her neck. She wears white nurse scrubs, and her blue eyes are locked on to mine.

"Miss Woodson, I'm Doctor Wane," she says.

"Go to hell," I whisper.

"I *had* hoped it wouldn't come to this, my dear." She kneels down to my level. It's then that I notice the shine of a syringe in her hand.

There is nothing I can do to escape it.

She moves too fast, and the needle is in my neck.

A pinch of pain, and suddenly the world starts spinning.

In a matter of seconds, I leave everything behind.

CHAPTER 13
ZEPHYR

Sparrow wakes up hours later, when the sun is close to setting.

I sit with my back up against the wall, watching. Staring at the horrible scars on her face. I shiver, even though it's hot as hell in here.

I don't trust this woman.

"Who are you?" I ask.

Sparrow sits up. Even in the light of a single lantern, I can see her gray eyes. It's like staring at Meadow, or Lark, and I bounce between feeling a surge of hope, of warmth, to a horrible, deadly cold.

"I told you who I am," Sparrow says. She sounds too

familiar. "The real question is who are *you*?"

I open my mouth to speak, but she raises a hand. "Oh, I already know, Patient Zero. I'd recognize that Catalogue Number anywhere. I rigged your name to Meadow's in the system. Several times, after my monster of a sister kept removing it."

If it were Lark speaking to me, I'd sense the anger in her voice. But Sparrow is different. Instead of a fierceness that borders on insanity, it's like she's lost all hope.

She's a dry husk of a human, inside and out.

"I should kill you right now," I whisper. "You ruined my life. Do you know how hard it is to love a girl, when all you want to do is murder her?"

She sighs, runs a hand over her scar. "I didn't ruin your life, Patient Zero. My sister did. I was simply trying to find a way to reverse what she'd done."

"By continuing the killing," I say.

I clench my fists. I breathe through my nostrils, in, out, in, out, to get ahold of the rising anger.

Sparrow shakes her head. "It was the only way," she whispers. She leans her head back against the wall, closes her one eye. "I remember Meadow, when she was a baby. She used to squeeze my fingers, you know, the way babies do. Except Meadow was always the kind you had to force to let go. She was strong. She didn't cry. She grew and she watched things and she was eager to learn." She swallows, hard. "I used to work for the Initiative, right alongside my sister. She was always the smarter one, always the star. And I wanted to be like her. Until . . ."

"Until what?" I ask.

She opens her eye, stares right at me. "Until the day she linked the Murder Complex to Meadow's brain. She was an infant. Just a *baby*, and Lark . . . did what she did, and I knew. I knew I'd lost my sister to the science."

She coughs into her sleeve, sinks slowly back toward the ground. She looks so small and frail, like a Ward child. She looks like she wants me to believe her.

But if there's anything I've learned, it's not to trust the people in this world.

"Why should I believe you?" I ask. "How do I know that any of this is the truth?"

Her eye looks wild for a second, like she's just seen someone come back from the dead. She takes a deep, shaky breath. "The things I did back then . . . I'll never be able to run or hide from them. I barely made it out of the Leech building alive. If it weren't for my training, I wouldn't have survived." She points at her scars. "Lark did this to me, when Meadow was just a baby. My own sister, when I tried to tell her that what she was doing was wrong."

I can picture it in my head, hear Lark's cackling laugh, see her swaying on her feet as she chases her sister down.

"I begged the Gravers to bring me to you. I want to help, Patient Zero. I want to do something good."

"Good?" I ask. "What good can come from being Lark Woodson's sister? What good can come from anything in the Shallows? Meadow is gone. If anything, all you want to do is help so that you can get to her and kill her yourself. End the Murder Complex forever."

Sparrow sighs, then shakes her head. "I do want to kill someone," she says, lowering her head. "But it's not Meadow. I was wrong about killing her. Sure, it would end the system, but the Initiative would still be in charge. They'd still have their weapons, and their strength. There's another way, a better way, to solve all of our problems."

What's left of Sparrow's Catalogue Number wrinkles as she frowns, and for a moment, the lantern flickers. Her burns come to life, like worms squirming across her face. She stares at me, and I stare at her, and the fire in her eye matches the fire in mine.

"Who do you want to kill?" I ask.

Before she even speaks, I know the answer.

"My sister," Sparrow says. "I want to kill Lark Woodson."

CHAPTER 14

MEADOW

Waking up is the hardest thing I have ever done.

I feel like I'm stuck beneath the waves, getting pummeled left and right as they break over the top of my head. I want to breathe, want to break free, but the water keeps pulling me back under. A voice calls out to me from the surface, muddled and far away.

"How do you feel, Miss Woodson?"

Someone pries open my eyelids. A light shines, too bright and too close, and I flinch away.

"She's responsive. Give her a moment."

"We don't have a moment, Doctor."

"She's under my care, and I'll be the one conducting

business in this operating room."

Feet shuffle. Someone takes a deep breath. "The Commander wants her now."

The Commander.

The Initiative.

It's a name that strikes fear into my heart, a hammer pounding relentlessly. And then I remember where I am, what just happened to me, why there are bindings across my body and a ceaseless tingling in my limbs.

I open my eyes and scream.

I thrash. My head is loose, so I'm able to sit up enough. A nurse tries to settle me back down, but I bite her hand, hard.

Blood gushes against my teeth and I refuse to let go.

It's chaos. Screaming, feet pounding.

I want to get out.

I want to break free.

It takes two people to pry my jaw from the nurse's hand. I spit blood in their faces, still thrashing like a fish onshore.

And that's when I feel it.

Heaviness, in the back of my head.

Sort of like there is something latching on to my skull, refusing to let go.

I freeze, eyes wide. "What did you do to me?"

Doctor Wane comes over, her surgical mask hanging from her neck. "Meadow, it's best not to stress yourself out after such an invasive surgery."

"Invasive?" I'm breathing hard, heavy. There's a beeping behind me somewhere, and it pounds in time with my heart. Loud, louder, so loud I want to scream and shut it out but I can't move. "What did you *do* to me?"

Doctor Wane clicks her tongue. Her eyes are soft. They tell me I can trust her, like windows to her soul.

Liars.

"We did what we had to, to salvage the mission of the Murder Complex." She motions for someone to assist her. "Help her upright. But don't unbind her."

A male nurse scurries over. His eyes widen as he unfastens my neck and presses a button, lifting my bed so that I'm almost upright on my feet, secured by the bindings.

"I'll kill you for helping them," I whisper to him. "You deserve to die."

He trips as he stumbles backward, lands on his butt. I laugh like my mother.

I laugh because I feel insane, and I laugh so hard that soon tears stream down my cheeks.

Doctor Wane waits until I get ahold of myself.

"We've installed a Regulator into your central nervous system," she explains. She stands just across from me, a sick smile spreading across her face. "It's a beautiful thing, really. A way to control you, without threatening the life force of the Murder Complex. We can speak to you at all times, give you orders through the system. . . . Would you like to see it?"

No.

I don't want to see it. I don't want to look. If I see it, it will mean that this is real.

But then Doctor Wane turns a mirror toward me, and I catch the reflection of myself in the mirrored wall behind my hospital bed.

I am staring at a girl who isn't me. Cannot be me.

My hair has been cut short, chin-length in the front, buzzed away to nothing in the back. It reveals a small black box that connects to my neck, right at the base of my skull, so seamlessly connected to my skin it is as if the machine is growing right out of me. Thin black wires slither out of the sides of the box, snaking down toward my spine, disappearing beneath a hospital gown.

"No," I whisper. "Get it off of me."

"We can't do that," Doctor Wane says.

"Get it *off*!" I scream. My voice is ragged. I want to

kick, fight, scratch out her eyes. "Get this thing out of my body!"

"Control her," Doctor Wane says over her shoulder. "The black button, Adams."

And suddenly there is pain. A shock, vibrating through my whole body, jutting out from my spine, stretching to my toes and fingertips.

"Test the connection to the girl," the doctor says.

And then . . . impossibly . . .

I can hear Peri's voice. Peri's *scream.*

She is sobbing. Calling for *Mommy, Daddy, Koi, Meadow.* And I can't reach her, can't talk back to her, but I know that this is not fabricated. Fear this extreme has to be real. What if it's a recording? What if they have already killed her?

"Stop it!" I scream. "Make it stop! Don't you touch her, don't you ever touch her!"

Doctor Wane holds up a hand. "She's had enough for now," she says.

Peri's screams disappear.

I'm sweating, tears streaming down my cheeks. My whole body trembles.

"This Regulator is connected to an identical one, across the country, that is installed in your sister's body," Doctor

Wane says. "Brings you closer together in a way, yes?"

"You're a monster," I whisper. "I won't let you get away with this." I look up at Doctor Wane. There is murder in my eyes, bloodlust seeping from my soul.

"We've already done it, Meadow," she says, smiling. She reaches out to stroke my hair, her hands lingering on the Regulator. "We've broken you," she whispers. "Now, you will do anything that we ask."

CHAPTER 15

ZEPHYR

The Night Siren goes off. Rhone and Dex go out to search for Lark.

They leave me behind, because of my last episode. Instead, they tie me up in chains across from Sparrow.

We're prisoners together. The Patient and the Creator's sister.

I fall asleep, and in my dreams, I visit Talan.

It's early morning.

Talan is sitting on the shore beside me, dark hair waving in the wind. Her daughter Arden runs in circles behind her, chasing a tiny crab as it paces sideways, claws raised to attack.

"I like the sunrise," I say. "It feels like a fresh start."

"You're such a girl." Talan laughs and sticks her tongue out at me.

"Real mature," I say. "I'm being serious."

"That's your problem." She leans back onto her elbows. "You're always too serious. Life isn't about that."

A wave rushes up and tickles my toes. "Yeah? What's it about, then?"

"Sex," Talan says, and when I laugh, she waves me off. "Smiling, and laughing, and stealing from people. Putting the first bite of food in your mouth after a hard day of Collection Duty. Curling up next to your daughter at night."

"Those are your favorite things," I say. "Not mine."

Talan nudges me. "It's all the stuff that makes me feel alive, Zeph." She lets a handful of sand run through her fingers. "Tell me about yours."

"I don't feel alive," I say.

"But you are," Talan growls.

"Fine." I watch the waves. I hate the ocean. But I like the world above it. "The sun. The moon. The stars. Things that are far away from here."

"There's one other thing," Talan says, "that makes me feel alive."

"Arden?" I ask. "Does Arden make you feel alive?"

We both turn to look at her daughter. She's splashing in the waves, giggling her head off.

"Yeah." Talan nods.

But just as a wave crashes, I see her eyes turn toward me. They look different than normal. They look soft. And I swear I hear her say, "And you."

CHAPTER 16

MEADOW

I have been a prisoner for days.

And now, suddenly, I am free.

I am sitting in a plush red chair inside of a circular room that is adorned in gold. It does not belong in the Shallows. It belongs in a storybook, far away from here.

Somewhere beautiful and new, without death and lies.

I look down at my wrists. There are no MagnaCuffs, no guards standing behind my back, tranquilizer rifles aimed at me, ready to take me out the second I make a wrong move.

Instead, there is a Regulator in my skull and my spine. The threat of my sister's torture hangs over me, heavy as a storm cloud.

This is the Commander's office. The man who runs the Initiative.

His portrait is across the room, hanging on the wall. Staring down at me, exactly like the one that I saw of my mother just a few short weeks ago. The Commander has jet-black hair oiled to his head. Strong bones, an angular face that is just as sharp and untouchable as I imagine his heart must be.

"I hate you," I whisper to the portrait.

The door behind me slides open, and he walks in.

"Miss Woodson." His voice is just as oily as his hair. I do not give him the satisfaction of turning around. I hear his boots *clack-clack* on the hard floor, and it takes me back to the day I found myself in the secret Initiative building in the Everglades.

The day I discovered the Murder Complex.

The day I discovered who my mother really was.

The Commander moves past my chair, takes a seat across from me on a pristine white couch. He takes a moment to sit and stare. I feel like his eyes can see through me, see everything I want to hide but no longer can.

Because he holds the key to controlling me now.

Peri.

"How are you feeling?" he asks. He laces his hands

together and settles them into his lap. He could be an uncle, asking me about my day.

I want to peel the skin from his face.

"It's quite rude to ignore your elder, Miss Woodson," the Commander says. "I'm afraid we'll have to work on your manners."

He taps a silver bracelet on his wrist.

The pain comes like lightning in my veins.

No! Please, no! NO! It's Peri's voice again, inside of my head. I imagine her face, her wide gray eyes turned red from tears. From terror and torture and everything she never deserved.

Daddy! Daddy!

"Peri!" I scream, but I know she can't hear me. I slam my hands against my ears, curl into myself. "Make it stop! Make it STOP!"

"Fascinating," the Commander says. "All right, that's enough for now."

Meadow! I hear her scream my name just as her voice cuts off.

The pain fades. But the anger only gets hotter and hotter.

I am left gasping for air. Holding my arms against my chest like it can keep my heart whole, when in reality, it is crumbling to pieces inside of me.

My sister.

My *sister.*

"How does it feel?" the Commander asks. He kneels right in front of me, and I want to hurt him so badly. I want to destroy him, see him hung from his ankles, see him turn to ashes in the middle of an inferno.

But all I can do is sit silent and still.

If I move, if I do *anything at all*, Peri will be punished.

"How does it feel to have something you love under attack? It is exactly what you've done to the Initiative. Your Resistance came into my home, my world, and tried to destroy it. Do you see what happens, Miss Woodson, when you hurt something I love?"

My breath comes out in a low hiss. I meet his eyes, and in mine, I hope he sees the fire. "You'll burn for what you're doing to her. She's just an innocent child. Take me. Take me and hurt me, but leave her out of this." I do something my father would never do.

I beg.

"*Please.* I'll do anything. Anything you want. Just take me instead of her."

The Commander throws his head back and laughs.

It echoes off of the round walls, slithers through my ears.

"The fearless Lark Woodson's daughter, begging for mercy from her enemy." He paces, back and forth, laughing as he goes. "Your sister is much more than a child, Meadow. She's an asset. A very valuable one, and the Initiative intend to use this new connection to your sister as a way to get you to do our bidding. Anything we ask, you'll do. Anything we need, and you'll fall at our feet, begging to help us."

I clench my teeth. I grip the chair as hard as I can, force myself not to lunge from my seat and grab his throat. "What do you want from me?"

He sits back down on the white couch, legs crossed, poised and proper. It cannot hide the madness inside of his soul. "Your mother is quite the inventor," he says. "This Regulator you have, it was one of hers. An original option, before she and her team discovered the connection we could make with the Murder Complex. But we've found uses for her old inventions. The Initiative is sentimental, wouldn't you agree?"

Breathe in. Breathe out. My father's voice. *Don't move, don't speak, don't do anything at all.*

"We used to be great friends, your mother and I. But then she turned her back on the Initiative. She decided that she couldn't handle the pressure of the job. And of course, she lost her mind, the crazy wench."

Deep breaths, calm and even. My father's voice guides me. *You can control your anger. Reel it in, and save it for later, when you will need it the most.*

The Commander continues. "She eventually did give in, you know. Gave us the codes, showed us the workings of her system. But there's a problem, Miss Woodson. Do you know what that problem is?"

I shake my head. I don't know, and I don't care.

All I want to do is kill him, save my sister, and die, so that no one ever again will be affected by the Murder Complex.

"Your mother's system is rebelling."

That gets my attention. I look up, and he smiles. "How?" I ask.

"A virus, of sorts, and quite complex in its coding. Naturally, we have plenty of people on the job, working around the clock to repair it." He sighs, and for a second I catch the dark circles beneath his eyes. "It came from somewhere inside of the Shallows."

"What do you need me for?"

He licks his lips, then gives me a smile that chills me to my core. "You're going to find your mother, of course! You're going to bring her back to us and convince her to retake the system. Repair it, renew it, and run it all over again."

"And if I refuse?" I ask. "Or if I bring her in, and *she* refuses?"

He raises an eyebrow. "Oh, I think you'll find that convincing you, the both of you, will be quite the fun little game."

He reaches into his jacket and pulls out a NoteScreen. He stands, places the device onto my lap, and heads for the door.

"You'll leave first thing in the morning," the Commander says. "A quick tap on the screen should be all the convincing you'll need." He shuts the door behind him, and I am alone.

I stare at my lap.

The NoteScreen stares back.

I don't want to touch it. I don't want to know what horrors will lie on its face the second it comes to life.

But I reach out and tap the screen.

It is my nightmare, come true.

It is my world, crumbling away like ashes or dust.

It is an image of a wooded area. Trees tower all around, and somewhere in the distance, I think I see a flickering fire. There is movement, near the base of a tree.

There is a trembling child. Lying against the trunk, curled up in a ragged blanket. The child's back is to the camera, so I can see all of their hair is shaved away. I gasp as I see the same black device as mine stuck to the back of the child's neck, and I know.

It's her.

"Peri," I whisper. I press my face so close to the screen that my breath fogs it up. I wipe it away, and I see Peri roll over onto her side, so that she's facing the camera. Her face is smudged with dirt. Her bald head is covered in cuts. Her eyes are dim, like fading lights. There is a metal cuff on her wrist, the color of the springtime sea. It shows how thin she is, how small. She trembles, and I see her breath come out in thick fog. She moans, just once, and then she goes still.

"Peri, hold on. Just hold on," I hear myself say. "I'm sorry. I'm so sorry. I'll come for you. Daddy will come for you. Koi will help."

She's crying.

"You're okay," I say, wiping tears from my own eyes, and I wish she could hear my voice, know that I'm here, I'm watching, and I'm going to make it all better some-how. "You're okay. . . . You have to be okay."

Suddenly, the image fades, pulling her into darkness. I

tap the screen again, but it does not light back up. She's gone.

"Peri?" My voice cracks. "No. Come back. Just come back to me."

I tap it again, and again, and again, but her image does not return.

The fury comes from out of nowhere.

I don't have control of myself anymore. I stand up and throw the NoteScreen across the room. It shatters against the wall, bursts into a million pieces. I grab the chair I was sitting on and launch it against the door. The sound is deafening, a roar that mirrors the blistering hate inside of my heart. "Let her go! Just let her go!"

I scream my sister's name.

I scream for her brokenness, and for mine.

I grab a shard of the NoteScreen's glass, the sharpest, longest one, and aim it toward myself.

I could end this now. If I die, *everything* the Initiative has built will die, too. It's worth it. For the first time in my life, survival is futile. Dying is the key.

But the second I thrust the shard toward myself, right over my throat, I hear a voice.

The Commander. *I wouldn't do that, Miss Woodson. If*

*you kill yourself, rest assured that your sister would soon join
you in death.*

There's a jolt of pain.

Peri screams again.

I drop the glass. "Get out of my head!"

I curl into a ball on the middle of the floor. I can feel
the pieces of myself tumbling around, breaking into fragments with every second. Soon they will be as tiny and
worthless as grains of sand.

I rock back and forth, whispering her name.

"I'll do it!" I scream. "I'll do whatever you want!"

That's a good girl, the Commander says.

The door of the room slides open. I can't live for myself,
and I can't die. Everything I do goes back to her, and I
will do it. Whatever they ask, I will do it, because Peri is
worth the worst deeds in the world.

Sometimes, we have to give up everything, throw our
lives into the line of fire, if it means saving the ones we
love.

CHAPTER 17

ZEPHYR

I wake up, drenched in sweat.

I'm breathing hard and heavy. I feel like I'm going to puke.

It wasn't a dream. It was a memory.

"No," I say to myself.

And then I really do puke.

Because it hits me. All this time I didn't know. I didn't *know*, and now she's dead, because of me.

She loved me.

Talan *loved* me. And not as just a friend. She loved me as more than that, in her own way, and she didn't have much love left to give, but she gave it to me.

How did I not see it? How did I not know?

The last few days of her life, I just ran off. Left her alone, chased after some girl I barely even knew. Then Talan came, and she gave her life away so I could keep mine.

And I'm just sitting here, hiding like a ChumHead in the Graveyard, not doing anything to avenge her.

I puke again, emptying my stomach. Sparrow's snores cut off, and she wakes up.

"What happened to you?" she asks.

Our eyes meet. And that's when it starts.

Welcome back to the Murder Complex, Patient Zero.

Initiate Termination.

"No," I gasp. I look at Sparrow for help, but we're both in chains. "RUN!"

"I can't run," Sparrow says sadly. "We'd better hope those chains hold."

Initiate Termination.

"Stop it!" I scream, wish I could put my hands to my head and squeeze it hard, but I can't. I think of Meadow, because she's the one who helps me fight the system. She's the one who saves me.

But then Talan's face pops up. She's crying.

You chose her over me, she says.

The guilt comes.

I lose my strength.

The Murder Complex sucks me under.

CHAPTER 18

MEADOW

Doctor Wane escorts me back to my cell.

We walk side by side, as if we are old friends, but the entire time, all I can think of is my father, telling me to run. *You can fight anything off, Meadow. You can find a way out of any situation. You just have to be resourceful.*

I must ignore his voice now.

Escape is impossible.

I swallow hard, imagine my father fading. The sunspots on his face, the wrinkles at the corners of his eyes. *I'm sorry,* I think to him. *I've failed you.* He slips from the surface. Sinks deeper and deeper away, locked in the back of my mind. A prisoner, like me.

"You'll notice you feel stronger," Doctor Wane tells me. She pats me on the back. "We replenished your system with nutrients, gave you muscle enhancers. You're brand new!"

I look down at my arms. The muscles look ropier. Stronger than before.

Funny, how opposite it is from how I feel on the inside.

"Get a good night's sleep," Doctor Wane says, when we reach my cell. "First light, you'll begin the search for your mother."

"I'm thrilled," I say under my breath.

"You should be, dear!" She grabs my shoulders, whirls me to face her. "After this, you'll be the Initiative's darling!"

She unlocks my cell and ushers me in.

It is still freezing. Sketch is back, curled into a ball in the corner, trembling the same way Peri was. "I want you to make it warmer in here," I say, curling my fingers around the bars. "I may not be able to fight you, but I can make this new relationship a pain in your ass. And you'll need me at my best, should anyone attack me outside. It's dangerous out there." I stare hard, refuse to blink.

Doctor Wane smiles. "Of course, dear. Of course." She taps the little box on the wall outside the cell, and I hear the air vents overhead shut off. Silence, finally.

"I want food," I say. "Before I leave. For Sketch."

"You're pushing it, Miss Woodson," Doctor Wane says. Then she nods. "I'll have some delivered. You see? I scratch your back, and now you will scratch mine. Tomorrow, you have a job to do. Do it well, and you'll be given more than this."

It is a small gift, the only thing I can offer Sketch. Doctor Wane leaves, and we are left alone. The second the door shuts I rush to Sketch's side and turn her over. I gasp when I see her face.

Swollen features, eyes so hidden beneath bruises and fattened skin that I can hardly tell if she is awake or not. Her arms are nearly shredded, skin hanging off of them, revealing bits of muscle. She lies in her own blood.

"Sketch," I gasp.

They have forced me into wearing the Regulator. Why would the Initiative still need to torture her, when they can control me?

I put my hands over her heart, touch her neck to feel for a pulse, but there isn't one.

"Please don't do this," I whisper. "Not now. Don't leave me. Come on, you're fine. Not you, too." I hold my fingers beneath her nose, see if she's breathing, but there's no air. I pound her chest with my fists, so hard it hurts me. "Come *on*!"

Seeing her like this . . .

I am not mad. I am not angry.

I am made of fire.

I hit her harder, a final punch to her chest. "You can't just *leave* like this!"

She gasps. Her eyes widen as far as they can, and she sits up, flailing her arms in front of her.

"Thank God!" I scream, and I crush her to me, wrap her in my arms. "You were dead!"

"I was sleeping, you ChumHead," Sketch says, but I can hear the tension in her voice. The fear of doubt.

"What happened to you?" I ask. "What did they do?"

I help her sit with her back up against the bars. I take her hands in mine and rub them, warming her as best I can.

"More Resistance questions," she says. She leans close, her lips touching my ear. "They know about Orion. I couldn't. I tried . . ."

I shake my head and whisper softly, "You didn't tell them where the Resistance is, did you?"

"No," she says. "No, I held on to that."

And that's when she sees that I look different now. My hair, short in front, buzzed away at the back. The black Regulator protruding from my skin.

"Damn," Sketch breathes. "What . . . is that thing?"

"The Initiative's backup plan," I groan. "They have one connected to my sister. It hurts her when I don't obey."

She lets out a low whistle, then winces in pain. "Patients don't have choices. Only dirty Leech chores. They got into your head. We're pretty much the same now, Woodson."

I don't answer.

"Thanks for saving my ass," Sketch says. "But next time . . . let me die. Let me go in my own way. It's all I have left."

"What is?" I ask. I move to her feet, try to rub heat back into them as well. They are as chilled as ice.

"The choice to die," Sketch says. "I'm ready, Meadow. I've been ready for a long time."

"But . . ." I swallow, hard, and that is when I realize it. "I wasn't ready for you to go."

She nods, then smiles, if only for a moment. "You've gone soft. It's pathetic." But then she grabs my hand and squeezes it tight. "I needed you, too, I guess."

We fall asleep side by side, our heads leaning against each other.

And even though I feel impossibly alone, for the first time in my life, I think I have made a true friend.

CHAPTER 19

ZEPHYR

There's no one to kill but Sparrow.

I writhe against my chains. I have to get to her. I have to spill blood.

"Stop," she says. "Control yourself."

She's so close. I can almost reach out, almost touch her. I could slit her throat or crush her skull and feel her wet blood on my hands.

"Patient Zero, you *can* fight it," I think I hear her say.

But the Murder Complex needs me. Wants me.

I have to kill.

"Control your breathing. Remember who you are."

"Do . . . not . . . resist . . ." I hear myself say. I want to swallow the words, fight the system, but it calls on me, sings to me like a song.

"Remember who your enemies are. It's not me, Patient Zero. It's them," Sparrow says. "Breathe with me. In, out. In, out. Do it."

Somehow, I force myself to breathe.

I force my body to react to *my* commands, even thought the system begs me not to.

"In, out. Good," Sparrow says. "Keep going. You are Zephyr James. You are a person, not a machine. Say it."

"I'm . . . a person," I gasp, and my head is pounding, and all I can think is, *Kill, destroy, no escaping, no turning back.*

"Say the rest," Sparrow commands, and her voice sounds so much like Lark's that it hurts.

"I am not a machine," I growl.

I breathe deeply in, slowly out. I do it again, and again. And then I realize that it's quiet.

The system fades into the background. I keep breathing, keep doing what Sparrow says, as she guides me from darkness to light.

When it's over, we stare at each other in silence.

A drop of blood slides from my nose, splashes onto my leg.

"You can't keep this up much longer," she tells me.

"You're exhausting your brain. It wasn't meant to handle this amount of stress."

"I don't really have a choice, do I?" I whisper.

She smiles. It's horrible, tugs at her scars in a way that makes me want to look away, but I don't. "You can keep up this charade, searching for Lark, hoping she'll surface," Sparrow says. "But the longer you wait, the weaker you'll become."

"So what do you suggest we do?" I growl.

She opens and closes her mouth. She's probably been looking for a way to kill Lark for as long as I, or anyone else, have.

But the answer comes to us, when Rhone and Dex sprint inside the tunnel.

"She's . . . she's coming," Rhone gasps.

Dex leans over, tries to catch her breath.

"Who is?" I ask. Sparrow and I both lean forward against our chains. "Lark?"

"Is it her?" Sparrow asks. "Tell us!"

Rhone looks at me when he speaks. "The Leeches announced it all over the place, probably so Lark would see it. She's coming outside, tomorrow." He leans against the wall, takes another deep breath. His final words send a shock that rolls through me, inside and out.

"They're setting Meadow free."

CHAPTER 20

MEADOW

The Initiative releases me when the sun comes up.

With a fresh cut mark on my calf, I follow Doctor Wane through the outer halls of the building. She places her hand on my shoulder, weaving me through the halls as if I am her pet. The Regulator is as heavy as ever, sucking on my soul.

I'd cut my own head off if it meant getting rid of it. But there is Peri.

I have to stay alive, or they'll kill her. The Commander said so himself.

I think of Peri, covered in blood, and another piece of me breaks away. A flicker of my mother's insanity swims through me, emerges as a laugh that bubbles from my lips.

Doctor Wane looks sideways at me. "I see the truth," she whispers. "I see your mother in you, Meadow. And I don't mean the way you look on the outside." She sighs. "It's a pity, really."

I don't argue.

Because I am afraid she might be right.

We stop at the front entrance, where the walls are covered in old Pins.

It is a sign of so many citizens' deaths. The last time I saw this, I was breaking in to this very building, thinking I had a chance to destroy the Motherboard. It would make me shiver, if I had any feelings left inside. Guards line the walls of the room, weapons at the ready. Probably positioned here around the clock, in case of another Resistance attack.

It will not come.

It may not ever come again, not after our failed attempt.

Standing before the doors is the Commander.

His oily hair shines like the Pins, and I want to slit his throat. "Miss Woodson," he says, when he sees me. "The finest Initiative soldier we have."

"I'm not a part of your disgusting little fantasy," I hiss.

"Oh, but you are." He smiles and taps a silver bracelet on his wrist. One single button on that bracelet controls my little sister's fate.

His barcode is bold on his pale skin. He wears the usual Initiative uniform, black and pressed clean. I see the patch on his lapel, the Initiative eye.

Doctor Wane pulls out a black device from her lab coat, presses a button, and waits. Seconds later, a black Orb floats into the room. It stops, hovers in front of me.

"This is a Cam," she says. "It will be our eyes while you carry out your mission."

It isn't human. But I know the Cam is watching me. When I move, it moves.

The Commander nods in approval. "Go on, then. Your mother is waiting."

"You'd better hope the Resistance doesn't come while I'm gone," I say. "I'm sure they'd love to slaughter you like the pigs you are."

Before he can slap me, I turn on my heel, shoulder past the two guards, and march right out the front door.

Sunlight.

The second it hits my face, I feel a little more alive. It may not be real freedom, but it is a taste. I blink away the brightness, let the warmth settle on my skin.

I will go along with the Commander's plan to find my mother. But I won't try too hard. I will stall, take him in circles, waste as much time as I can. If I could get a message to the Resistance . . .

The Cam bobs along at my side.

No. The Initiative will see, whatever I do.

I hop the train as it comes past. There are three others, standing in the shade of the car. When they see the Regulator on my neck, and the Cam at my side, they recoil.

"You're her," a woman says.

"Who?" I ask.

She leans closer, peers at me. "The soldiers, they said you'd come today. Said if anyone touched you, they'd lose rations for a month . . . or worse." She whistles and backs away. She is quiet as the train soars past the Reserve.

I see the marshlands fly by in muddled colors, flashes of white from the Wards' tents. I imagine Zephyr is there now, safe and sound, but the image brings forth a hot surge of jealousy.

I gave myself up so he could get away and free my family. I wonder if he's done it yet. I wonder if he has found them all, far away from here.

If only the world was nice enough for that to be true.

I wonder if I will ever see any of them again.

When I reach the edge of the city, I leap. I join the pressing crowd, a wave of people surging as one. The Cam soars into the sky, out of reach. But when I look up, it's still following.

She won't be out in the open, the Commander's voice says in my head.

"You can't just pop in when you feel like it," I growl. "If you expect me to concentrate, and do this job right, get out of my head."

The crowd moves me toward the Rations Hall. I long for the old days, working side by side with Orion. How different life would have been, if I hadn't met Zephyr. If I'd gone on, working day in and out, not knowing that the entire time, she was on my team. Maybe she would have recruited me eventually. Maybe we would have had more time to plan and do things right from the start.

I duck right, head for the alley, stepping over a dead body.

I look behind the Dumpster. There is a sleeping person, but it isn't my mother.

You're wasting time. Do you think I'm a fool?

"Give me access to the Rations Hall," I say.

I can almost hear him sigh.

Then the door across from me pops open, and I rush inside.

I check behind the crates, look inside the empty ones.

I see faces pressed up against the glass barrier. Wards and other citizens, starved and desperate. A fight breaks out, and Initiative guards end it with a bullet to a woman's brain. Blood splatters against the glass, bright crimson.

There is nothing in this building, Miss Woodson. Move on.

"Get *out* of my head!" I growl.

I leave through the alleyway and cross the street, head for the beach. I press through hundreds, thousands of people. Everyone pushes and shoves. Someone knocks my Regulator, and pain radiates through my body like shards of ice.

I gasp. I feel like I can't breathe, so I push harder, then almost tumble into the alley. I run, leap over another body that is missing an arm.

The second I hit the jungle floor I'm sprinting. My body takes over, needing to run, to *move*. And being lost in nature makes me feel, for a second, that I am just heading back home.

The houseboat will still be there.

Peri will be waiting on deck, her curls dancing in the wind.

Koi will be carving on a slab of wood, and my father will train me before the Dark Time comes.

I hear the roar of the ocean. I stop on the edge of the trees, see the waves crashing onshore. The ocean is angry today. The shipwrecked boats dip and dive, tossed about by the current.

I have a flash of a memory. *Smoke trailing to the sky. The last bits of my houseboat, sinking beneath the waves.*

Zephyr's hand, touching my arm as I wake up. Me throwing his body to the sand, threatening to kill him if he comes near me again.

How badly I want his touch now. How badly I want his soft words, and his foolish belief that things will always be okay.

I sit down in the sand.

The Commander speaks to me, but I interrupt him. I have a small ounce of power, and I am going to use it.

"My mother won't come to me here," I say. "She'll come to me in a place that matters."

And that's when I realize it. *Our first home. The place we were last happy, a real family.*

"I need paint," I say. "Bring me paint, by the old apartment complex on Main."

As you wish, the Commander says.

I have never heard so much darkness in a single man's voice.

CHAPTER 21

ZEPHYR

I hate the Resistance Cave.

I stand at its entrance with Rhone, Dex, and Sparrow, preparing myself for the argument that I know is soon to come.

The Cave is shaped like a dome, an arching ceiling with water dripping down the concrete walls. It's hidden under the Shallows, a patchwork of tunnels and concrete caverns that are perfect for hiding out.

"This isn't going to work, Zero," Rhone says beside me.

I swallow. "It has to work."

We step into the Cave as a team.

Tunnels jut off into different areas, leading to places

all over the Shallows. People are scattered about. Some of them sit by a crackling fire. Others practice fighting.

I see some new faces, some old.

The last time I was in the Resistance Cave, I was hoping for help that I knew Orion wouldn't be happy to give.

The time before that, I was with Meadow.

Memories rush for me and grab ahold. *Meadow teaching me how to fight, how to harness the power of my training from when I was only a child.*

Talan is here, glowing with life, making jokes that make me laugh until I feel like I can't breathe. Sketch paints our faces before we head into the Leech Headquarters to shut down the Motherboard. Kill the Protector, and end the system for good.

Three weeks ago, we were a family. An army.

Now, we're broken, scattered across the Shallows. Some of us are dead.

Some of us might as well be.

And some of us . . .

"Zero!" a voice shouts from across the Cave. I'd recognize it anywhere, because I've hated its owner since the very first time I saw her. Sparrow tenses beside me, though I don't know why.

"Orion," I say. The Resistance Leader, who once posed

as a Leech Officer. She's the reason we got into this whole mess in the first place.

I hate her.

I also need her.

She's seated by the fire. Her bald head, covered in tattoos now, shines an eerie gray in the dim light. She waves us over.

Dex squeals and sprints past me to join the other Resistance kids as they chase a rat like it's a toy.

"I'm telling you, Zero, this is a no-go," Rhone warns.

"I've heard enough," I say. "We're out of options."

We cross the Cave with Sparrow in tow, and I get ready to beg for the cause.

CHAPTER 22

MEADOW

I stand on the steps of my old apartment building, a can of bloodred paint at my feet. This is the last place where my family was happy together. This is the last place in the Shallows that might still hold a special place in my mother's heart.

If I am right.

And I could be horribly wrong.

The windows of the building are boarded up. There are plenty of them that I can paint a message on, large enough for my mother to see.

I dip my fingers into the paint and lose myself to the motion.

I start on the far left windows, the first-floor ones that I can reach.

And I spell out the time, and I spell out her name, in large letters, one on each window. My heart cracks a little more with each letter, but finally, I step back and admire my work. The wet paint drips down the sides of the old brick, and the moonlight illuminates it. Like blood.

6 a.m.

For Peri.

If somewhere, deep down in my mother's heart, she still feels for us, and somehow, a part of it still beats for her family, when she sees the message . . .

She will come.

CHAPTER 23

ZEPHYR

The second Orion sees Sparrow, she freezes.

"You," she gasps. She takes a half step forward. "Sparrow?"

Sparrow reaches out with trembling hands. "Orion," she whispers. "It's been a long time."

They stare at each other like they're both seeing something beautiful, something that couldn't or shouldn't exist in the Shallows.

I didn't even know they knew each other. Rhone shrugs when I look at him, like he didn't know either. We help Sparrow walk forward.

Orion closes the distance in two quick strides, and I

think they're about to both fade into one sobbing mess, when Orion suddenly goes bright red. Not from embarrassment. From fury.

"I thought you were dead!" Orion screams. "We all did!"

She leaps.

And tackles Sparrow to the ground.

It's all screams and curses, and Sparrow's flattened on the concrete floor of the Cave. Orion rolls her over, puts her thighs on either side of Sparrow's body. Then she starts beating the hell out of her.

"Stop it!" I yell, but no one moves.

A crowd gathers.

Sparrow screams, and Orion keeps hitting, and finally Rhone and I step forward and yank them apart.

"You *liar*!" Orion shouts. Rhone and I hold her back as she fights to get away.

"I'm sorry," Sparrow sobs. She's lying on a heap on the floor, gasping for breath. Dex helps her sit up, rubs her back in circles, wipes blood from her face with her T-shirt. Sparrow sobs. "It was to keep you safe."

"We were best friends," Orion says. "You never came back. You abandoned me. You were the closest thing I ever had to a sister, to a family."

It's then that Sparrow's head pops up.

She blinks through the blood dripping down her one good eye, and she looks like she's just killed a person. "Don't ever say that word to me again," she whispers. "You and I are *not* family."

"We were once," Orion says.

She shakes away from Rhone and me, then stomps down one of the darkened tunnels and disappears.

Orion comes back an hour later.

Rhone and Dex and I are sitting by the fire, with Sparrow beside us.

I tense, as Orion approaches.

"If you attack again, we'll leave," I say, but she holds up a hand.

"Stop. It was my mistake." She glares at Sparrow, then sits down across from us. "This ChumHead here . . . She was one of us, once. I mean, after she left the Leeches' side."

I spin to look at Sparrow. "You were in the Resistance?"

She pulls down on her shirt collar. Three stars are tattooed low on her collarbone, morphed from her scars. The Orion's belt. She shrugs. "You didn't ask, so I didn't say."

"That's how she's always been," Orion groans. "Doesn't

give the details, and even when you ask, she gives half the whole truth." She sighs, picks a strand of fabric from her pants. "Just like the night she went on a kamikaze mission to shut down the Motherboard herself."

Dex giggles. "That's *awesome.*"

Sparrow went to shut down the Motherboard?

"You died in there," Orion says. "You *had* to have died in there. We waited, and we searched, and there was never any trace. Why didn't you come back to us?"

"Because I didn't want to be found," Sparrow says.

"We were . . ." Orion swallows her words. "It doesn't matter why you didn't come back. What matters is that you're here now. And I swear to the stars, if you don't explain why, Sparrow, I'll make you wish you really were dead."

They glare at each other. Two of the most messed up women in the Shallows. It makes all the sense in the world that they'd be friends. Dex watches with wide eyes, like she's enjoying the show.

"I tried to shut it down," Sparrow says. "But my precious *sister* never told me about the Motherboard's Protector."

"Who is it?" Orion asks.

No.

No, no, no.

"Sparrow, stop," I say suddenly. I beg her with my eyes. *"Please."*

She gapes at me, and for one second, I think she's going to keep the secret. I shake my head. She nods.

I shake my head again. "Don't."

Everyone looks back and forth between our silent battle.

Finally, Sparrow makes the choice. "I couldn't march into town and slaughter my own niece. I'd be just as bad a person as Lark was. So I simply put her name into the system. Allowed fate to take control and the Lottery to choose her. It's not my fault Patient Zero became the one programmed to kill her. It's also not my fault that he failed to do so."

Orion stares, mouth open.

"You . . . your niece is the Protector?"

Sparrow nods.

"*Meadow Woodson* is the *Protector?*" Orion's eyes turn to slits, and Rhone gasps, and every head turns to look at me.

"Well, hell," I groan. I put my head in my hands.

Sparrow shrugs. "They deserve to know the truth. They deserve to make a choice. To kill Lark, or to kill Meadow."

"No one is killing Meadow," I hiss. My hands ball into

fists. The fire is suddenly too hot, and too close. "She didn't want this life."

"No one does, Zero, but we're all in hell anyways," Orion says. "We should kill the girl."

I'm on my feet before I realize it. "You will not *touch* Meadow. If you lay a finger on her, I'll kill you myself."

Orion throws back her head and laughs at me. "And why should I listen to you, Zero? What have you proven to me?"

I take a step forward. The fire is hot on my ankles, but I don't care.

"I brought Sparrow to you. And she agrees with me on the solution to our problems. We want to kill the system, but we also want to get free."

"And?" Orion asks.

"And the best way to do that is get revenge on the woman who put us all in this mess in the first place. We're going to kill Lark Woodson. And you're going to help us do it."

Orion laughs. "You're funny, Zero. The woman can't be found. You know it, and I know it, so her daughter is the next best thing. We all heard the announcements. She's out in the Shallows, free. We can find her. Kill her quick and painless."

"Orion." Rhone speaks up for the first time. "Listen to what Zephyr has to say."

She stares at him.

Annoyance flashes through her eyes. Then the calmness of respect.

I speak before anyone else can. "If we kill Lark, there's a fail-safe. She'll die, and as soon as she does, every Patient in the Shallows will react."

Sparrow nods, joins in. "The moment Lark's heart stops beating, the Patients will follow her revenge order. And you'll love this, Orion, I know you will. Their Target is the Initiative. The Patients will take out the very people that have controlled them for *years*."

Orion's eyes light up.

"That's all good and well, Zero," she says, ignoring Sparrow, "but you can't find Lark Woodson. I've already told you that."

"That's the best part of the plan," I say, smiling. "We won't have to find her. Because Meadow is going to draw her out."

That gets Orion's attention.

"We should kill them both," she whispers.

"No," I hiss.

"*Yes*. I'm in charge here, and if you want my army's

help, you'll listen to me. You'll kill the girl, and end this all for good."

That's when it hits me.

"I don't need you," I say to Orion.

She laughs, but I cut her off. I stand up, cross to the pile of weapons that the Resistance has, in the center of their building. I choose a crossbow, a quiver of arrows, and sling it over my shoulder. Then I turn back to the fire.

"I don't need you, Orion, because I'm a Patient of the Murder Complex. And the second Lark dies, my army will come. And I'll be the one to lead them."

"Zero, you're making a mistake," Orion says.

"No," I say. "I'm doing what I should have done this entire time."

I hoist the bow higher on my shoulder, look to my friends. Dex and Rhone help Sparrow to her feet. Dex comes to my side, but Rhone holds up a hand.

"You can't go with us this time, Kid."

Her eyes look like they're going to pop out of her head. "What? Of course I'm going. I'm not staying *here*"—she looks over her shoulder—"with *them.*"

Rhone's voice is sad, like he's looking at his little sister for the very last time. "I'll be back for you, when it's safe. For now, you'll stay here with the others your age."

"I'm not a child!" Dex shouts. Her voice rings across the Cave. "This is my fight, too!"

I step forward, kneel down to her side. "Stay, Dex. For me." I feel guilty as hell, because I know she'll do whatever I say. She always has, since the very first day we met.

Tears fill her eyes.

Then she falls forward and body-slams me with a hug. I'm about to say what I always say. *Thanks, Kid.* But then I realize Dex isn't a kid, and she never has been. She's been forced to grow up fast, forced to forget the years of being young, where everything is happy and careless and safe.

I have a fleeting memory. Something my dad used to do with my mom, and even though I know it's a fabricated memory given to me by the Leeches, it seems like the symbol it stands for is true. I reach for Dex's hand, take it in mine. She looks up as I press my lips to the back of her hand. "Thank you," I whisper. "For believing in me."

Her face grows as red as the sunrise. "Be safe," she says. And then, in normal Dex fashion, "Give those Leech bastards a good show."

She stands on tiptoe and kisses my cheek. Then she turns to Rhone and sticks her middle finger up in the air.

"I love you, too, little sister," Rhone says, chuckling.

Dex turns and runs away to join the other kids.

"Let's go," Rhone says.

We head down the tunnel, back the way we came.

It's when we're almost out of earshot that I hear Orion's voice.

"You'd better look after Meadow, Patient Zero. Stand in my way, and you'll both end up dead."

We see the message on the way back to the Graveyard.

It's in bold red letters, still dripping like blood down the bricks.

6 a.m.

For Peri.

I know that name. It's Meadow's little sister.

A Leech Cam soars by overhead, scanning the streets. We all dive into the shadows as it passes by.

"This is where she'll be," I say. "I'm sure of it."

Sparrow squeezes my shoulder. "Then we'll stay," she says. "I'll do it. I'll kill my sister."

At first, I want to say yes. How will Meadow ever be able to look at me the same, once she sees what I've done? Lark is her mother. I saw the love in her eyes when we found Lark in the Leech building. Saw the brokenness, when she discovered what a monster her mother *really* was. But she loves her, still. And as long as Lark lives, Meadow will hold on to that.

I hate it.

I realize deep down, for the first time in my life, that I truly want to kill.

This is the only death, and the only victim, that I won't ever regret. "I'll do it," I say. "I have to be the one."

"I was afraid you'd say that," Sparrow says. "Go ahead. Do it for the both of us. Make her bleed."

We hide in the shadows and wait.

CHAPTER 24

MEADOW

I search the Shallows all night.

I go through the Graveyard, look in all the places I think she might be. I check the old storage units, the locks on them now replaced from when Zephyr and I were hiding here, the time we found my mother's secret unit, all of her information on the Murder Complex.

She is nowhere to be found.

I take the train to Cortez, walk the boardwalk. This was the place Zephyr almost kissed me. The place where he first turned on me and tried to kill me. I run the streets, and memories flash by with each step. *Zephyr, grabbing me by the hair and slamming my face into the sand. Me, stabbing him in the shoulder. His eyes, cold and black.*

I don't know where my mother is.

Because the more I think about her, the more I realize I hardly knew her at all. The articles I found in her locked storage unit, about her science and her beginnings, are the biggest truths I ever got from my mother.

I don't know her childhood. I never asked her questions, and she never spoke about herself. She told me stories. Imaginary ones, of nonexistent worlds, with characters that weren't real and never could be.

Everything, even our time spent together, was centered around a lie.

And she *knew.* The entire time, she knew, that I was the key to keeping her precious creation alive. It makes me hate myself.

It makes me wish that I could dive into the sea and sink to the sand, forever forgotten from the world.

When dawn is near, I take the train back to the city. It soars over the bridge where I once leapt from the roof of this very train, dove into the waters below, and boarded an Initiative yacht to escape Zephyr.

So much has happened.

And now, I am back to chasing things again, except instead of chasing my mother's ghost, I am actually chasing her.

Once I find her, I won't be alone in this anymore. We'll be together again, prisoners.

A part of me hates my mother. The other longs to see her again, to share in the fact that we are both pawns of the Initiative, and we always have been. She made it that way.

The train slows as it closes in on the main strip. The night has passed, and the sun is rising from the sea, shedding its light on the early morning. I pass the Graveyard, remember the moment when everything went bad. When I lost my family.

The train is nearing the old apartment building. I hop off, roll to my feet, and run toward it. And as I get closer, see the little concrete row of steps leading into the building, my heart drops to my toes.

She isn't here. It is exactly 6 a.m.

I wait, pacing below the steps.

Two minutes pass.

Three.

I slam my fist into the brick building. Either my mother didn't see the message, or she didn't care. I am not sure which is worse.

It destroys me. I stand up, scream into the morning.

"LARK!"

I hear the wind blowing, see the sun rising in the distance, throwing the color of blood into the sky.

"YOU'VE KILLED HER! YOU'VE KILLED PERI!"

I throw my head back and scream, so furious that I'm reacting only on instinct now. Then the screams fade to laughter, and for a moment I forget who I am. Tears slip from my eyes, roll down my cheeks. My father's voice doesn't come to calm me.

Instead, I hear only whispers of ghostly screams that sound like Peri. I don't want to gain control of myself.

I want to be empty.

I want to be free.

When my voice fades, I drop to the steps.

That's when I see it.

Movement, a person walking out of the shadows of the nearest alleyway.

Silver hair.

That's all I need to see to know it's her. I stand up and run, sprinting across the street, until my mother and I are standing face-to-face.

"Meadow," she says, and it is the sound of the past.

The sound of safety.

I do what I never thought I would do, ever again. I fall into her arms.

And I sob.

She wraps me up, holds me close. Her hands find the Regulator at my neck, and she gasps. "I knew it. I knew they would do this to you." I hear her voice as she whispers into my ear, as she strokes my hair, holds me tighter. "My god, look at the precision on this. Who did they match you with?"

I bristle, start to pull away, but she reaches out.

"It's all right, Meadow. I'm here now. I'm here."

"Peri," I say. "They've been torturing her. . . . She's in pain."

"My poor child," she says. I hear her holding back a sob. She swallows it. "Your sister is fine, I promise. The pain is real, but it will not kill her. If anything, it will teach her to be strong. I designed the program myself, years ago. Beautiful thing, isn't it?"

I gasp. "No, it's not *beautiful*." For one second, can't she just be the mother I need her to be? The mother who brought comfort to me, so many years ago? "They showed me a video. Her hair is gone, her body is . . . I have to get to her. Before it's too late."

My mother stumbles. "There's no way out, Meadow."

"So we'll make one," I say, but she is already shaking her head.

Tears well up in her eyes, and she presses her hands to her temples. "I did this, my god, it was all *me*."

She reaches out to touch me, pull me in for a hug, but I take a step back. "You're coming with me," I say. "The Initiative needs you. You can tell them what they want to hear, and they'll get rid of the Regulators. Peri will be okay again."

"She'll never be okay," my mother whispers. "Pain like that is something you don't easily forget. My daughter, my littlest daughter. She never was strong, Meadow. Not like you."

She laughs, stares at the sky.

It sounds exactly like the laughs that have come from *my* lips recently.

"We'll start over," my mother says. "We'll make the Shallows a better place, together. It was always meant to be this way."

"You're wrong," I say. I wrap my hand around her wrist, start to pull her away.

"Wait," she says. "Meadow, you must know the truth."

"The truth can wait. It's time to go. For once in your life, stop trying to get out of doing the right thing. You *will* fix this. If not for me, then for Peri. For my father and Koi."

She holds steady. "This is the right thing," she says. "Please. You have to know, Meadow, you have to understand my mistake."

Footsteps come from the darkness.

I hold tighter to her wrist, assuming it to be Initiative guards. Soon they will come and bind her with MagnaCuffs, take her back to Headquarters. She doesn't run.

She stays by my side. There is a sudden change in her eyes, a sadness that wasn't there before, as she looks at me.

"I'm sorry," she whispers. "I'm so sorry, Meadow."

"Sorry for what?" I ask.

She opens her mouth, leans in to whisper. I hear her words, *beg* them not to be true.

What she is saying *cannot* be true. My world shatters.

"Meadow . . ."

"Stop," I say. I shove her words away. Lock them deep in my heart and choose to believe they are false.

She opens her mouth to speak, and for one moment, I think she is going to apologize for *everything*. Everything she's done to me, to my family, to the world, for the secret she just told me. I need this moment. To truly begin to forgive her, I need to hear her apology.

But she never gets the chance to say it.

Instead, she lurches forward, like she has been pushed from behind.

She gasps.

A trickle of blood slides from her lips.

"No," she whispers. "No!"

Then she falls.

I see it all happen in slow motion, hear myself screaming, feel myself drop to her side. "Mom!"

There is an arrow protruding from her chest. Blood blooms like a fresh rose on the fabric of her shirt.

I don't have to see the wound to know it was a perfect hit. I know she has seconds before she dies. I know that everything around me is a blur, and I can't focus on the hidden killer.

All I see is my mother.

Dying.

Again.

She coughs, gasps for breath. She opens and closes her mouth like a fish. "You have to . . ." she gasps. "Stay."

"I'm not leaving you," I whisper. "You're going to be okay." I rip the arrow out, push my hands to her chest, but blood bubbles through my fingertips.

A gushing river.

It's too much. Too fast.

She is going to die.

"No!" she yells, and her eyes go wild, like she's staring into bright light. About to cross over. "The revenge order," she gasps, and suddenly she's gripping my wrists so tight that I cry out. *"Stay!"*

"I will," I promise. She is leaving the world behind. Leaving *me* behind. I thought I'd gotten her back. I thought I wouldn't be alone in this any longer. She could have taken control again, sent me to the Ridge, set Peri free, removed our Regulators, or demanded my family to be sent home. She could have fixed it *all*.

Tears splash down my cheeks, onto her forehead, as her grip goes slack. I can't stop the bleeding. "Don't. *Don't go.* Don't leave me again. Not now. You can't!"

A tear rolls down her cheek. "Forgive me," she says. She reaches up to touch my Regulator.

She takes a deep, sputtering breath.

Then her eyes glaze over. Her hand drops, leaving a trail of blood on my cheek.

I am vaguely aware of a voice that sounds like Zephyr's, calling my name, and the footsteps of many, racing toward me.

But none of that matters.

Nothing in this world matters, not even me.

My mother is dead.

CHAPTER 25

ZEPHYR

Lark Woodson is dead.

The Creator is finally, finally dead.

And I shot the arrow that killed her.

It's the only thing I can think. The only thing that comes to mind.

I should be happy. I should feel my entire body relax, my heart grow so full it's about to burst. The woman who ruined my life has finally gotten what she deserves. I see Sparrow hobbling next to Rhone, rushing from the shadows.

Rhone reaches Meadow, tries to pull her away from Lark's corpse.

Meadow is sobbing over Lark's dead body. There's something black and unnatural sticking out of Meadow's skull. I freeze as I look at her.

This *can't* be Meadow. A sobbing, shell of a girl, covered in cuts and bruises, half of her hair cut away. She screams, and the sound rocks me backward a step.

What did the Leeches do to her?

Meadow shakes Lark's body, shouts curses at her.

I want to explain myself. I want to tell her why I killed her, that it was for *us*, for everyone.

But suddenly there's a flash. Blinding white light behind my eyes.

A horrible ringing pierces my thoughts. It's worse than the Night Siren, worse than Meadow's scream.

I can't hear anything but the ringing.

I can't see anything but the white light.

And then there's a word. A single word in Lark's voice, that surfaces through the chaos. The word comes again, over and over and over, the sweetest one I've ever heard.

Revenge.

CHAPTER 26

MEADOW

My mother is dead.

My mother came for me, came to help me save Peri, and she tried to apologize, and now she is . . .

She is only asleep.

She is dead.

She is asleep, right here in front of me, waiting for me to wake her up.

She is dead.

"Get up, Meadow! Leave her!" A man's voice, and I think I feel hands tugging at my shoulders, trying to pull me away.

I throw them off.

I need to hear my mother's apology, to know that she was truly sorry for everything that she had ever done. She asked me to forgive her. I have to tell her that I want to, that I want things to be the way they always could have been.

First I need to hear her say she's changed.

"Say it!" I shake her, but she won't move. Her eyes roll back into her head, and her mouth flops open in a silent scream. "Say it! Wake up!"

It's only when Zephyr's face appears in front of mine that I look away from her.

"Zephyr," I gasp.

He is *alive*. Here, in front of me.

"We have to run," he says.

He grimaces, like he's in pain, like he's fighting the Murder Complex, but how can anything be more painful than the reality that my mother is dead?

"Meadow, now!" he growls. He tears me from the ground with such strength that I gasp. "She's dead. It's time to go."

I nod through my tears.

I take his hand.

My fingers are covered in blood.

We stand up, and together, we run.

CHAPTER 27

ZEPHYR

Revenge.

It's the call of the system. It's her fail-safe, just like Sparrow warned me about, tried to prepare me for.

I breathe deep, in and out.

I hear the word screamed over and over again. I fight as hard as I can. Meadow's hand in mine is the only thing steady, the only thing holding me here and now.

We make it halfway to the marshes, almost to the edge of the city, when I can't control it any longer. The Night Siren goes off, even though it's early morning. Leech soldiers rush into the streets, their eyes wide like they don't know what's going on.

I see others like myself. Patients, sprinting forth into the new light of day.

We look into each other's eyes, and we know.

REVENGE.

I dive for the Leech closest to me and tear his throat out.

CHAPTER 28

MEADOW

The Patients turn into monsters, killing with a grace that only comes from years of training.

The Night Siren wails, out of time and place in the daylight, a screech that normally sounds like a mother mourning her child.

Not today.

Now it sounds furious, like a vicious monster.

Mixed in with it is the sound of the Commander's voice. *You did this,* he says.

The pain comes. Peri's screams ring in my ears, and I tell myself this isn't real, this isn't real, this Is. Not. Real.

I focus on the world around me, fight through the pain,

hold on to it like an anchor to keep me in this moment.

Zephyr's hand leaves mine.

He leaps, and lands on top of an Initiative soldier. I watch as he rips the man's throat apart. Blood sprays and hits me, warm and thick on my face.

This is real. My father's voice comes to me from the deep. I free him. I let his voice flood into me, and it is so beautiful, so alive. *Hold on. Focus, Meadow. Stay alert. Don't lose yourself yet.*

Someone runs up beside me and touches my shoulder. I whirl around.

I stare into my mother's eyes.

"Meadow," she says, but she is mutilated, half of her face scarred and her hair has turned dark. She is *not* my mother, but a broken, twisted copy of her.

And of me.

"Who are you?" I gasp.

I tear my hand away, stumble backward, but someone comes up behind me. I whirl, see it is Rhone from the Resistance team, whose father knew my father. He is solid and steady, and he wraps his warm hand over mine.

"Come with us!" he begs. "We have to escape here."

I look for Zephyr in the chaos.

"I won't leave him," I say.

"Zero will find us," Rhone says back.

The streets are a blur, as people sprint past, pushing and shoving and crying out for loved ones. Patients are attacking the Initiative, all around. Guns fire. Knives are thrown.

Soldiers drop to the city streets, and the citizens trample their bodies in their rush for cover. It's all happening too fast, out of nowhere.

And then I realize why.

My mother is dead.

The Patients are reacting to her fail-safe. Soon, the world will burn to ashes around us. This is the only chance to escape from here. Now there is nothing left for me.

I let Rhone and the strange, broken woman lead me away.

It's only when we make it to the edge of the city that I see Zephyr again.

He is leading a wave of Patients toward Headquarters.

CHAPTER 29

ZEPHYR

Dust and smoke and death.

The revenge of the Patients is in full swing.

It's different from the Murder Complex.

This is the Creator's order, and we know exactly what we're doing.

We march in a solid line, taking out Leeches as they try to run away. When they shoot us with their rifles, some of us drop.

But then something amazing happens.

A group of citizens emerges from the city. They follow in our wake, with pipes and sticks raised over their heads. I can't hear them over the sound of *revenge, revenge*, but I can see the anger in their eyes.

The hope.

We reach Headquarters, hundreds of Patients and citizens of the Shallows.

We're showered with bullets.

My leg is hit. I know it, but I can't feel it. The sound of *revenge* only gets louder, fueling me forward. I have to kill the Leeches.

I have to make them pay, because Lark Woodson is dead.

CHAPTER 30

MEADOW

The citizens of the Shallows have joined the war.

In this moment, I know that I should be with them, fighting for freedom, fighting for justice against the horrors my mother and the Initiative caused.

Instead, I am running.

I sprint with Rhone and with Sparrow, who holds my hand and tells me to go, keep going, and don't look back.

I listen, because I am tired of thinking. Because everything is happening too fast, and this moment all feels like a dream.

Or a nightmare.

I go from smiling about my mother's death, to horrible,

heart-wrenching feelings of loss. There's no time to think, or process, or worry about her secret.

I can only drown in the feelings.

"Get down!" Rhone shouts.

We dive in the grasses just fifty yards from the building. A group of Initiative soldiers sprints past us, heading into the battle.

"Which way?" Rhone asks. Sparrow is lying beside him in the grass. "Perimeter?"

"We can't climb the Perimeter. It's impossible. Go for the building, side door. It's a coded entrance, but I can hack it."

Her voice is painfully familiar, the sound of an old memory, an old, near-forgotten dream.

And then, as Rhone calls the all-clear, and we start to run again, I remember.

She is my aunt.

She is the woman who once held me as an infant, who gave me presents every year on my birthday. She is the woman who put me into the system, who tried to get me killed so that the Murder Complex would die with me.

I follow her, but not because I trust her.

It's because it's my turn to be the killer.

My turn to get revenge on the woman who I am sure murdered my mother.

CHAPTER 31

ZEPHYR

A bomb goes off.

Bodies drop, others are thrown to the air. Some are blown to bits. I feel hot blood on my face, a gash running down my temple. Screaming that I think might be my own.

My good ear rings. I can't focus.

Punish them, Lark says in my head. *Make them pay for my death. Revenge. Revenge. Revenge.*

I scream the word.

I lift my fist into the air.

Behind me, an army of voices responds. It's the final wave, the final war cry.

We push forward, and the Leeches pull back.

They can run, but we will chase them. They can hide, but we will find them. They can fight, but we will fight harder.

We are the Patients of the Murder Complex.

And we will win.

CHAPTER 32

MEADOW

My body is drenched in blood.

Guards lie dead at my feet, just outside the Headquarters building.

"Hurry up," Rhone hisses.

"Shut up, and maybe I will," Sparrow says, as she leans against the building, working. Trying to break through the codes that hold the door in place. The NoteScreen embedded in the wall shows a series of numbers and symbols, soaring across the screen.

"We have minutes, maybe, to get out of here," Rhone says. "If the Patients fail, and the Leeches gain control . . ."

Sparrow whirls on him. "They *won't* fail. That's the

beauty of it. They can't fail, because my sister programmed them not to. Now shut the hell up and get inside."

The NoteScreen turns green.

The door hisses and soars up into the ceiling, just as there's a horrible pain in my skull. *You cannot escape me, Miss Woodson,* the Commander says, and his voice is rushed, breathless, like he's been running.

I have to find him and kill him.

Peri's voice starts screaming in my head. She is sobbing uncontrollably, and her cries no longer form words.

I drop to my knees, press my hands to my ears, but it cannot drown out the sound. "Make it stop!" I scream. "Make it stop!"

I can see Rhone and Sparrow leaning, trying to speak to me, but I can't hear anything they are saying. All I can hear is my sister, drowning in pain that mirrors my own.

My sanity is cracking, slipping through my fingertips like fresh hot blood.

Rhone lifts me, hauls me inside the building. He is about to shut the door behind us when I shove my shoulder in the way.

"Zephyr" is all I can manage. Rhone nods, runs back outside. Sparrow says something to me, puts her hand on my shoulder, but I can't hear her.

The pain intensifies until it's too much. I throw my head back and scream.

I have to stop this.

I turn and run down the halls of the building.

I am going to make the Commander bleed.

I am going to make him beg for death.

CHAPTER 33

ZEPHYR

The Leeches set off another bomb the second we breach the building.

It happens so fast. I'm in the air. Then my breath is gone. I'm lying on my back, staring up at the sun, and I don't know if I'm dead or alive.

There's a ringing, everywhere. A hand grabs mine in the chaos, holds on tight. I roll over, see a Patient girl with tears in her eyes. Holding me while she dies.

More gunfire goes off, and people scatter, dive for cover. I want to scream at the Leeches, kill them all. Because they're not just shooting at adults. They're shooting at kids.

The anger helps me to my feet. The command keeps speaking to me, the only thing that pushes me on.

I use the hatred that I used when I first found Lark outside of this building, near this very spot.

I'm about to sprint forward when someone tackles me. We go down.

I spin, growling, ready to snap the Leech's throat.

But it's Rhone.

"Zero, come with me!" he shouts. His face is flecked with blood and sweat.

"Revenge," I gasp, because it's the only word that makes sense. The only word I can form.

"Meadow is waiting," he says. He rolls off of me, and I try to sprint away.

I have to fight. I *have* to kill.

"Just stop!" Rhone screams. "Don't make me do this!"

I don't listen, because I can't.

Something smacks me in the back of the head.

Lark's voice calls for revenge as the darkness takes me away.

CHAPTER 34

MEADOW

Sparrow trails after me, shouting my name.

A guard steps out of a room to our right. He sees us, spins with his rifle. I kick the barrel hard, and it falls out of his hands.

No, please, no. Peri's screams don't stop.

I harness the pain, fight through it, but I don't know how much longer I can hold on.

I dive for the guard, grab the back of his hair, knock his head against the wall so his nose shatters. I take his rifle, shoot him twice, then sling it over my shoulder. He has a dagger tucked into a sheath on his thigh.

I grab it, whirl it around, and tuck it into my waistband.

I run, and the pain is so bad I am seeing flashes of white. I wonder if soon, I will pass out.

I can't. I have to keep going.

Daddy! Meadow! Koi!

I turn left, down a hall. I know this route and will never forget it.

Two soldiers are stationed in front of his door.

Two squeezes to the trigger, and they are down.

I reach the door, but of course it is locked.

You will never reach me, the Commander says. *I'll kill your sister before you ever get to me.*

I fire the gun. One, two, three times, then in rapid fire. The door does not buckle or break. It is made of thick, unbending metal.

It is only when I see Sparrow arrive at my side, see her typing codes into a NoteScreen on the wall, that I know I'm close.

"You'll never touch my sister again," I say to the Commander. I know he can hear me.

The door slides open as the NoteScreen turns green, and I see him sitting at his desk.

He looks up, his face a mask of horror, his mouth hanging half-open, his eyes as wide as the fullest midnight moon.

I shoot him once, in the shoulder. He screams, as blood

explodes in a spray of crimson, the brightest, most beautiful color.

He presses the button on his wrist, and Peri's screams get louder. So loud that my whole body trembles. I cross the room at a staggering walk. My breath comes out in hitches, and I hear a low, rumbling laugh coming from deep in my chest.

The Commander crawls underneath his desk, tries to hide and block me out, like a child.

I sling my rifle back over my shoulder and grab the dagger instead.

"Don't do this!" the Commander shouts. "I'll give you anything, anything you want. It's yours!" He's cowering, shivering like a wounded animal, and it makes my lips curl into a cold, deadly smile.

He screams as I stoop down to his level. Laughter leaves my lips, escapes like a breath of fresh air. I wrap my hand around the back of his head, hold his face steady, so he's forced to look at me.

"I'll see you in hell," I whisper.

Then I plunge the knife right through his eye.

Sparrow is silent as she follows me back to the doorway, where hopefully Rhone and Zephyr will be waiting.

I wipe my blade clean on my shirt, tuck it into my waistband again, and for a hint of a moment, I feel like the old Meadow again.

But then I pass a mirror that hangs on the wall, and I catch a glimpse of my reflection. The Regulator, the blood staining my shortened curls, the wild look in my eyes.

I am not the same Meadow.

I will never be the same again. Not until I have my family back.

"Your father trained you well," Sparrow says behind me. She is out of breath, hardly able to keep up.

I can't look at her. If I do, I'll kill her. All these years, she wanted to kill me. And yet, she helped me attack the Commander, get my revenge.

And I need her to help us get out of the Shallows, first. We reach the small door that leads to the marsh. Sparrow slides to the floor, gasping.

"You have to understand, I wasn't always this weak," she says. She sighs, rubs her hand across her ruined skin. "I'm not the woman I used to be."

A flash of memories slides through me, flickers of my torture, Peri's pain, my mother dying in my arms. "Neither am I," I say. I look at the NoteScreen on the wall. "Can you program it, so I can see Peri? The

Commander did it once, and made me watch."

Sparrow's one eye darkens. "I'm sorry. The system is down."

The door behind us opens.

I spin with the rifle at the ready, but it's only Rhone.

Zephyr is slung over his shoulders, unconscious, but I can see him breathing.

He's alive. I give Rhone a nod of thanks.

"Well, now that the gang is back together, can we move on?" Sparrow says. She rises unsteadily to her feet.

"Which way?" Rhone asks. He looks at the blood all over my shirt, my hands and arms. "What did I miss?"

"Payback" is all I say. "Let's go, back of the building. The exit is through the cell room."

Rhone shrugs, Sparrow nods, and we rush forward into the halls.

Behind us, there's an explosion that rocks the building. The ceiling trembles. Dust falls over our heads. Then I hear voices and shouts. Zephyr starts to moan, lifting his hands like he's stretching out for something.

"Not yet, Zero," Rhone says, and slams Zephyr sideways against the wall. Zephyr's head hits it with a smack, and he goes still again.

"Damn." Sparrow whistles. Then she laughs.

Rhone looks up at us with wide eyes. "What?" he says. "Someone has to keep him under control, otherwise he'll go crazy on the Leeches. We don't have time for that. Come on."

We keep moving.

A bullet soars past, whistling, and lands in the wall to our right. I dive, then turn, and fire.

An Initiative guard drops.

"For the love of god, would someone watch our backs?" Rhone asks through gritted teeth.

"I'm on it," I say.

I walk backward, trailing them and taking out guards as we go. Two, three, four. I hit them all square in between the eyes. Their heads explode, and I smile. I can't feel the pain of the Regulator anymore. Peri's screams have disappeared. But something new has taken their place, a darkness that creeps into me, cold and heavy and unlike anything I have ever experienced before.

I welcome it. I let it steal me away.

We reach the cell room. Rhone kicks the door open, and I sprint ahead of them.

I shoot two guards, one right after the other.

I'm out of rounds. I drop the rifle and reach for my dagger, but there's no one left here. Only prisoners huddled inside cells, and the smell of dead all around. I cough, cover my nose with my shirt.

"Sketch," I gasp.

I nearly forgot about her.

And suddenly I'm running up and down the cells.

"Set them free!" I scream, and behind me, Sparrow must have tapped something on the wall, because the cell doors spring open.

Prisoners rush out, stumble past each other in their hunger for escape. I shove past them, check all the cells, but I don't see her.

Not until I reach the very last one.

She's cuffed to the iron bars of the cell, waiting.

"It's about time you came for me, Woodson," Sketch says, with a smile on her beaten face. She's covered in blood and bruises, and she's so thin, too thin. "I was starting to think you'd forgotten me."

The building trembles again. Another bomb must have gone off.

I can hear screams now, footsteps coming closer. I don't know if they belong to Initiative soldiers or Patients or citizens. I know we have to leave, now.

"Help me get her free!" I shout.

Sparrow hobbles closer, drops to her knees. She starts to

work on the MagnaCuffs, and as she does, she's gasping for breath.

I see red staining her shirt, mixing with the mud and grime. But she hasn't killed anyone. She's not strong enough. Was she hit?

"When you get out, follow the tracks," Sparrow says. She breaks Sketch's left wrist free, then moves on to the right. "But don't get caught. The trains run up and down the tracks. Search parties, collectors. Stay smart. The Ridge is on the other side of the country. You can't walk there. Find another way."

"You aren't coming?" I ask.

She looks down at her stomach. "I won't make it half a mile before I'm dead."

"I wanted to kill you myself," I whisper.

Sparrow's head snaps up. Her gray eyes, so much like my mother's, stare back at me.

"I know you've been trying to kill me for years," I whisper.

Sparrow nods. "It isn't personal. It's the only way to end the system."

"I know," I say. She is almost done with Sketch's other wrist. "I hate you."

Sparrow smiles, a gruesome look that makes her scars

squirm. "You're a lot like your mother. I can see so much of her in you, you know. Even when you were younger, I had a feeling you'd turn out just like Lark."

"I am *not* my mother," I hiss. I swallow, hard. "You killed her. She might have been a monster, but . . ." I hold out my dagger. My wrist shakes, but I steady it. I can finish Sparrow off now. I can get my revenge for my mother's death.

"I didn't touch her, Meadow," Sparrow says. "Someone else took my sister's life."

The MagnaCuff pops free. "Flux, that feels good," Sketch says. "Woodson, come on." She stands to leave the cell.

But I stay, staring at Sparrow.

"Who?" I ask. "Who killed my mother?"

She's about to answer when the door to the cell room bursts open. I hear commotion, shouts. I stand up, move into the hallway between cells.

Orion is here.

"Ah, just in time," Orion says. She looks nearly the same as she did when I last saw her. But her eyes are darker, somehow, like they have seen too much they cannot forget.

"Be careful, Meadow," Sparrow sighs. She stands up

and hobbles away, starts working on the codes to the out-side door.

"What are you doing here? Are you coming with us?" I ask Orion.

She smiles when she looks at me, but the light doesn't reach her eyes.

"Blondie," she says. "You're exactly who I came to see. I know your dirty little secret."

"Orion, no," Rhone says. Zephyr is slumped in the corner, next to him, finally waking. Rhone stands, and moves toward Orion, and I don't know why.

Not until she swings a gun forward.

She aims it at me.

And shoots.

CHAPTER 35

ZEPHYR

I wake up in time to see Orion talking to Meadow, and Rhone moving toward Orion, and Orion smiling a cold, deadly smile.

It happens in slow motion.

The gun in Orion's hand.

The bullet being fired.

The casing shooting out of the side of the gun, and the actual bullet soaring toward Meadow.

It hits her.

Meadow drops, and I scream.

And then I'm leaping to my feet, diving on top of Orion.

I hit her again and again. Revenge is still calling my

name, begging me to go after the Leeches, but right now, Orion is a Leech.

A bloodsucking, life-stealing Leech, and she deserves to die.

Crimson stains my hands.

I punch.

And punch.

Someone hauls me off her. "Zero, stop it!" Rhone shouts. "It's over! She's gone!"

Orion is a bloody mess, lying on the floor of the cell room.

Meadow.

I shove away from Rhone, sprint for Meadow, and I don't want to see her body, as lifeless as Orion's. But I *have* to. I have to say good-bye.

I skid to a stop. Meadow is doubled over, groaning as she leans against the bars of a cell. Blood drips down her shirt, splashing into a small puddle on the stone floor.

I gasp when she looks up.

"Meadow," I say. "You're . . ."

The bullet hit her in the shoulder. Orion *missed*.

"She's fine, Zero," Sketch snaps. "Now shut up before you start crying. And help me walk, will you? Leech bastards busted my knee and it's time we get out of this hellhole."

Meadow smiles and laughs, but there is a twinge of something new behind that laugh. Something unsteady, and dark.

"It's time to go," Rhone says, from the exit door. He's holding Sparrow up, as she tries in vain to type the final codes.

She's dying, fast.

The NoteScreen by the door turns green, suddenly. It opens with a hiss, and I see the way to freedom. The bright green on the other side.

"The Perimeter will be open for sixty seconds," Sparrow hisses. "Go." She waves a bloody hand. *"Go!"*

Rhone helps her to the ground. She leans her head back against the wall. She's smiling, and for once her face doesn't look so bad. She almost looks pretty, in her own twisted way.

"I'm out of here," Sketch says.

She goes through the door.

I follow, but stop when Meadow kneels beside Sparrow.

"Thank you," Meadow says. She leans down, whispers something into Sparrow's ear.

Sparrow's eyes widen. "I can't help you with that," she whispers. What are they talking about?

They see me looking.

"Just go before I change my mind and finish you off," Sparrow says to Meadow. "Forty-five seconds left. Go."

Meadow nods.

I turn to Rhone. "Are you coming?"

"No," he says. "I'm staying here. If the Patients win, the Shallows will need a new leader."

I want to argue with him, but there's no time. And he's already made up his mind.

Instead I hold out my hand.

He takes it, and his grip is firm. Solid. He'll be a good leader, if he's able to take control.

"Give 'em hell, Zephyr," Rhone says, and I realize it's one of the few times he's used my real name.

"You, too," I say.

I turn and grab Meadow's hand.

She holds it tight.

We take our first steps toward freedom, out into the afternoon light.

CHAPTER 36
MEADOW

A groaning noise comes from the Perimeter. A trembling in the ground that I can feel in my toes.

"Thirty seconds," I tell Zephyr.

Sketch is ahead, hobbling toward the exit. The Perimeter slides open, and suddenly, as my feet carry me away, my oldest dream comes true. The one I used to have on stormy nights, when the boat wouldn't stop rocking. The dream that chased my nightmares, left me with enough hope to go out and look at the sun in the morning.

I push my legs faster, harder, because if I don't, I might stop. I might turn back to the only world I have ever known, feel the fear that came with my mother's dying secret. Tears slide down my cheeks, and as we cross over, and our toes hit cool green grass, and we see train tracks that lead into an endless, open world . . . I smile.

I am outside of the Shallows.

And I am never going back.

PART TWO
THE OUTSIDERS

CHAPTER 37

MEADOW

We run for hours, following the tracks like Sparrow said.

We stop for breath, and I am staring out at a world I have never known. It finally hits me. Freedom.

I am free.

Free.

Zephyr takes my hand, squeezes it tight. "We made it," he breathes.

"Holy balls," Sketch says from my left. She turns around, stares at the Perimeter in the distance, holds up both middle fingers. "Flux you! Flux all of you!" She laughs, and Zephyr and I join in, and we all laugh until we can't anymore.

"What now?" I ask, when everyone calms down. And reality hits us.

No one answers.

So we simply stand for a while, watching the world. Most of the landscape looks like the Reserve. Marshlands, with the beach to the far left. The train tracks cut across the marsh, jagged as stitches. The wind blows across the tops of palm trees, bending them at their middles, making them bow like they're welcoming us to the outside. There is a small brick building, crumbled and forgotten, half of it blown to bits by the Fall.

I turn around, stare at the Perimeter in the distance.

From here, I could cover it up with my thumb.

But it still separates me from the only world I have ever known. Inside are my people.

My memories.

My mother. Her secret.

And here . . . there is only open space.

Suddenly I feel alone. I feel the tug of doubt, whispering to my soul. Not in my father's voice, but my mother's. *You'll die out here. You'll never save your family.*

I feel a flash of a memory. Pain from the Interrogator. The ghost of Peri's screams. The pressure of the knife in my hand, tearing through the Commander's eye.

I need the sand on my toes, the waves tugging at my ankles. I can see the ocean in the distance, beyond the palms, calling me home.

I drop Zephyr's hand and run.

"Meadow!" he screams.

I don't stop. I just sprint, arms pumping, breathing in and out, until my feet hit the sand. The waves crash onshore, and there's trash just like there was in the Shallows, floating with the waves as they explode against the beach. I run a few steps into the water, then dive headfirst into silence.

Here, I can breathe.

Here, I can pretend I am myself again, the Meadow before the Initiative. The Meadow before the Murder Complex.

I can feel the touch of my father's hand on my shoulder, the softness of Peri's cheek as she leans against me in sleep. I can hear my mother's old lullaby, and the scratching of Koi's knife on driftwood. I could stay here forever, in peace.

But hands grab me from behind and haul me to the surface. I gasp, water dripping from my eyes.

"Meadow!" It's Zephyr. He whirls me around and pulls me to his chest and holds me tight. "What are you *doing*?"

"I felt lost," I say.

"You'll never be lost," he says. "I'm here now. I'm here."

"But my family isn't," I say.

"Meadow," he whispers. "We'll find them. I promise."

There is beauty in every part of him, and sunlight in his smile, and the softness of a summer rainstorm in his voice. So why can't I feel the way for him that I once felt?

A lifetime has passed since we last saw each other. I have secrets from him, and from Sketch, and I wonder if he holds secrets from me, too. I look away.

He touches my chin, lifts my head up so that our eyes meet again.

He smiles, and the wind blows the hair away from his face. All of the fear, the doubt that I would never see him again, fades. He touches my Regulator gently, moves a curl from my face.

"You're . . ."

"Mutilated," I whisper. I move so that he can't see the machine on my skull, but he steps closer.

"I was going to say more beautiful than I remember," he says. "But mutilated works, too."

A laugh escapes me.

He rushes forward.

And kisses me.

At first, I want to pull away. But he presses harder, kisses stronger, and suddenly I am in his arms, being lifted from the sea.

"Meadow," he gasps, and my name on his lips is so sweet. I kiss him like he is air and I need so desperately to breathe. The world fades away.

His breath, my breath.

His arms around my waist, my fingers in his hair.

I never thought I'd feel his lips again, never thought I'd be here with him.

Outside. Free.

"Hey, ChumHeads!" Sketch screams from the shore. "That's enough! Stop it before I puke!"

Zephyr laughs against my lips. I can feel him smile, and it radiates into me. But he pulls away, and the darkness settles back in, wraps itself around my heart.

"We should get moving," he says.

I nod.

He kisses my forehead before he sets me down.

Then he takes my hand, and together we head for the shore.

CHAPTER 38

ZEPHYR

We spend the rest of the day hunting for food.

There's nothing.

No fish, no crabs. Not even coconuts in the palm trees.

The sun melts into the sea. The three of us stand onshore, watching. It's the same sun we've always seen in the Shallows. But now it sort of looks . . . different.

"It goes on forever," Meadow says. She's right. In the Shallows, the ocean ended with the Perimeter. But now, it just stretches on and on.

I nod. "It's like it never ends."

"What if it doesn't?" Meadow asks.

Sketch tosses a shell into the waves. "Everything

ends, Woodson," she says.

They share a meaningful look that reminds me of two old friends. Not two killers.

But I guess they've been through hell and back together.

"We should find shelter," I say.

Even though we're free, and there are no Patients after us, and no Leeches hunting us down, I feel like we're being watched. I feel like these train tracks are leading us somewhere dark. Somewhere dangerous.

It's like a chill in my spine. A weird, tingling feeling that raises the hair on my arms. I wonder if the Murder Complex can still reach me here.

We haven't talked about it yet, and I'm afraid what might happen, if Sketch and I both turn on Meadow in the night.

"Let's try that building up ahead," Sketch says.

We make our way inside, crawling over piles of broken glass and brick. It looks like it might've had stuff a long time ago. But now it's been picked clean.

All that's left is an old chair, the stuffing ripped out of it.

Meadow uses a brick to bash it to pieces, and we make a fire from the wood.

"Who's going to take watch?" Meadow asks. In the

firelight, she's got dark circles under her eyes. I wonder if she's slept, *really* slept, since the Leeches took her.

"There's no one out here," I say.

Sketch laughs. "That's where you're wrong, Zero." She spits into the fire. "The whole reason for the Murder Complex is because there's *too* many people out here. Right?"

"That's what my father always told me." Meadow nods. She holds the dagger in her hands, twirling it the way she used to. But now, her hands shake a little. She drops it, and her eyes widen. She scoops it up, then tucks it into her waistband. "Do you think . . . Does the system reach you here?"

So she's wondering it, too.

"Zero and I should sleep somewhere else," Sketch says. "Just in case."

"No," Meadow says. She glares at us both. "We stay together."

Sketch sighs. "Fine, Woodson, but if we turn on you, it's your death."

"No one is dying," Meadow says. Her voice turns to a whisper. "Not until we find my family."

"Unless we *do* die first." Sketch laughs. But she sees the look on Meadows face, like there's fire in her eyes. Sketch sighs. "It'll be fine, Woodson. We made it this far. We'll make it all the way if that's what it takes."

Meadow swallows, hard. She stares straight ahead. "I guess so."

"I'll stay up," I say. "You two rest."

"Don't have to ask me twice," Sketch says.

In seconds, she's snoring, twitching every few minutes. Mumbling in her sleep. I watch her, waiting for something to happen. I try to reach out and touch the system in my mind. But it feels emptier now. Like I could sleep, and I wouldn't see the faces of people begging to be ripped from this world.

Meadow lies down beside me, just out of reach. "Come closer," I say. "You've been far away for too long." She hesitates, then scoots over and lays her head in my lap. I can feel the machine on her, cold and hard against my legs.

"What does it do?" I ask.

She stiffens. "It's a Regulator. It controls me," she says. Then she changes her mind. "Or it used to, at least. Peri has one just like it."

When she says her sister's name, her voice cracks.

"Can we remove it?" It's solid black, thick and heavy.

"No," she says. "At least, *we* can't. They put it in surgically."

My stomach whirls. "We'll worry about it later. Get some sleep."

"I don't want to sleep," she says, even though she yawns.

"Why not?" I ask.

"I have nightmares," she whispers. "They're too real."

"Don't worry." I smile down at her, even though her eyes are already closed. "I'll keep them away."

"My mother," Meadow says. "I know she was a monster."

"She was," I say, and I'm about to tell her that it was me, that I was the one who fired that arrow into Lark's chest.

But then I see the look in Meadow's eyes. The pain of loss.

I wait for her to speak.

"When she . . . when she *died*," Meadow says, like she's testing the word on her tongue, "she was apologizing for something. But she didn't get to finish. What if she was trying to change, Zephyr? She could have escaped with us. Or fixed things. She told me . . ." She trails off, shakes her head. "It doesn't matter anymore what she said. Because now she's dead, and it's my fault. I lured her out. And for *what*? A sister I might find? A father and a brother that may or may not already be dead?" She takes a deep breath, and I notice her fingers have gone back to her dagger.

"We'll find your family, Meadow. They aren't dead."

She takes the tip of the dagger, moves it toward her ankle. I see lines carved there, numerals that have turned to scars.

Before I can stop her, she turns the knife to her ankle and carves another line in her skin. Fresh blood drips down like a river.

Then the cut turns to a scab, as the nanites stitch it back up.

"You shouldn't hurt yourself," I say. I reach out, try to take the knife from her, but I stop myself. Meadow isn't Meadow without a weapon, and right now, I'm seeing a girl that's not the same as she was before.

I wonder if she'll ever come back.

"I'm not hurting myself," Meadow whispers. She sits up, trails the tip of the knife on the dusty floor. "I'm marking the days they've been gone." Her gray eyes flit upward to meet mine. There's a trickle of moonlight coming through a hole in the roof, and she looks ghostly pale.

Dead.

"You promised me you'd find them," Meadow whispers. "I helped you escape so that you'd find them. And you're still *here*."

There's a hitch in her voice.

The darkness again.

"Meadow," I say, but she stops me by holding up the knife.

"You wasted time waiting on me," she says. "You waited around for nothing, Zephyr. And now my mother is dead. I have a Regulator on my spine, and I'm . . ." Her breath hitches. "It doesn't matter what I am. What matters is finding them. Nothing more."

"I stayed for you," I say. "Because that's what you do for love, Meadow."

"Love is a joke," she says. "I loved my mother, and now she's gone, and all I'm feeling is pain. I'll kill the person who killed her. If she's dead, they deserve to die, too."

I can't tell her.

"If we don't find my family," she whispers. "Then her death will have been for nothing."

There's this horrible guilt in her eyes. Like she really believes she's the one who killed her mother. But it's me. I've got Lark's blood on my hands.

The guilt should be in *my* eyes, the same way it's been all these years of waking up with people dead at my feet. But not tonight.

I can't tell her.

"Kill or be killed," Meadow whispers.

Oh, stars, I can never tell her. I just got her back.

I say nothing. She turns away from me, lies down with the Regulator against the hard ground. I hear her voice, whispering horrible things to the darkness. The whisper in her voice isn't Meadow's.

It's Lark's.

I will kill you.

I will find you.

I am already dead.

When she wakes up screaming, hours later, I go to her. I hold her tight, kiss her forehead, tell her it's not real.

But we both know it is.

I wish I could've saved her sooner.

Because I can tell that a part of her is already dead.

CHAPTER 39

MEADOW

In the morning, we walk along the tracks. They lead toward the coast, cutting near the sand. I think of Koi, how he prepared me for the day I'd jump and try to make it onto the red or blue train. I stop looking at the tracks, because the memories hurt too much.

Sketch counts our steps, and announces when we've hit another mile. I walk alone in front.

Sketch and Zephyr speak in hushed voices behind me.

I'm not listening, because I don't care.

The heat of the day is like fire, making it hard to breathe, hard to concentrate, hard to keep going.

But I won't stop. Not until I know my family is safe.

Sometimes, I imagine my mother's ghost is walking beside me. Whispering the last words she ever said.

I don't want them to be true. But if anything, when it came to her science, my mother never lied. What I know haunts me, and when the wind blows, I shiver. I whirl around at every noise. I stare into the trees, and I think I can see faces.

I think I can see Peri.

I think I can hear her screams.

"MEADOW!"

It's louder than it's ever been.

I slam my hands against my ears, claw at them with my fingernails. I cry out, and suddenly Zephyr and Sketch are rushing for me, trying to calm me down.

They hold my arms to my sides. I thrash and fight, but I'm exhausted.

I can't get free.

Zephyr kneels in front of me, looks into my eyes.

"It's not real," he says. "*I'm* real. Look at me, Meadow. Right here."

I see two pools of endless green, hear a voice that's calm and gentle and safe.

My breathing slows.

Peri's screams fade, but the looks on Zephyr's and

Sketch's faces do not.

They think I am insane.

And I realize, as I swallow back tears and force myself to focus . . . they are right.

CHAPTER 40

ZEPHYR

It's halfway through the day, and Meadow's losing her mind.

We force her to rest, for five minutes. Because with every step, she's getting worse. I tell myself she's hungry, thirsty, tired. I tell myself this isn't Meadow.

I wish I believed that.

She sits beside me on the sand, in the shadow of a mossy tree. She's running her fingertips across the cuts on her legs, whispering the numbers of the days she's been without her family.

"Too long," Meadow says.

I look sideways at her. "What?"

She doesn't move, just keeps staring down at her scars. "They're been gone for too long."

I can't sit here any longer. "I'll go find you some water," I say. "Stay here."

I stand up and cross the sand. Sketch is sitting by the water's edge, tossing trash into the waves.

She tenses when she hears me coming. "What do you want, Zero?"

"The truth," I say. I sit down beside her in the hot sand. "What happened back there?"

"Woodson lost herself for a second," Sketch says with a shrug. The wind blows onshore, but her dreadlocks stay motionless, heavy as hell.

"I don't mean today," I say. "I'm asking what happened in the Leech building? What did they do to her?"

It's a long time before Sketch answers. She sighs, leans back on her elbows. "I didn't know Meadow before the torture, not like you did. They tried like hell to hurt us, Zero, and they did. Cutting us. Burning us. Beating us until we blacked out, and then doing it all over again. But Meadow didn't break, not from any of that. She laughed in their faces. She killed one of them."

I shut out images that come from Sketch's words. Meadow, bleeding, screaming, but never begging.

"Then what?" I ask. "The Meadow I know would never act this way. The Meadow I know is too strong."

Sketch nods. "She's strong, yeah. We were strong together, until they took her away. Because Woodson has a weakness that I don't have."

I look at her, raise my eyebrows. "What weakness is that?"

"Love," Sketch says.

Love makes us weak.

Meadow said that to me, once, in the Shallows. She didn't realize she was a victim to that already.

"She whispered her sister's name in her sleep," Sketch says. "Every night. The Leeches might be bastards, but they aren't idiots." She turns to me, and I notice for the first time that she has amber eyes. Like a sunset. "The Initiative saw someone strong, someone willing to fight back. They took what means the most to her in this world. They used it against her."

She stands up, brushes sand from her thighs. "Meadow is broken from the inside out. And until she finds her family again, no one in this world will be able to put her back together. Not even you."

"And if they're dead?" I ask. "If we make it there, and they're already gone?"

Sketch's voice is barely a whisper. "Then we can say good-bye to Meadow. Because she won't live in a world where her family no longer exists."

She leaves me.

I sit alone by the shore, watching piles of trash drown in the waves.

Wondering, for the first time, if following Meadow is really worth it.

CHAPTER 41

MEADOW

You're strong enough, my father's voice says to me. *Don't give up. Not now, Meadow. Not ever.*

I cling to him. Beg him to keep speaking to me, because I am tired. I need him to lend me his strength, so that I can feel whole again.

We move on. I tell myself that soon, I will be able to hear my father's real voice. I will be able to lean against him and let him scold me for falling apart.

I will grit my teeth and nod, and I will be the daughter he trained me to be.

Not now.

Now I know that to be the Meadow I once was, I have

to find my father alive. All of them, alive.

"Thirty-seven miles," Sketch says from behind me, when the sun is high in the sky. "We've been walking all day and there's nothing."

It's empty. The train hasn't passed by yet on the tracks, and we haven't seen anyone. Where are the survivors from the Fall? Where are all the people my father talked about? The millions . . . billions? The reason for the Cure? He said it made us live forever, that there were too many people out here. That the world was being crushed under our weight.

"Smoke," Zephyr says. He points into the distance, a few miles away, where the shore breaks up into a pile of rocks. "You think there're people over there?"

He's right.

A trail of smoke rises from the other side of the rocks. And as we get closer, walking in silence, we hear voices, people laughing.

I tighten my hand over my dagger.

We are not alone.

No one can be trusted, Meadow. My father's voice. And he is right. This is not the Shallows, where people are weak, and starved, and fight with the sloppy moves of a child.

This is the Outside.

I know nothing about the people here.

"We should avoid them," I say. Sweat drips down my neck, and I wipe it away.

"We could kill them all and take what they've got," Sketch adds, grinning like the madwoman she is.

"We're not killing anyone," Zephyr says, putting his hand on Sketch's scarred arm.

She shrugs him off, then kicks up a spray of sand. "Relax, Zero. I didn't say we *had* to kill them. I said maybe we *could*."

"We could scout them out. Figure out who they are, what they're up to. If there's a fire, they're at least surviving," I say. "Maybe we'll figure out what they're eating, how they're staying alive out here."

Zephyr puts a hand on my arm. "Are you okay? Can you . . ."

"Can I what?" I ask. "Can I handle this? Is that what you're going to ask me?"

He takes a half-step back.

"I can handle anything," I say, my voice rising. It feels good to say it, because I need it to be true.

My mother's secret is toying with me, tugging at the back of my mind, a constant whisper that begs me to be weak.

"I'm fine," I say.

Sketch and Zephyr nod, but then we hear a crack. We whirl around, and there are two men, walking across the sand toward us. They are tall and bony, with sunken cheeks and eyes. The one on the right twitches every few seconds, as they get closer. "Maybe," he says, pointing a sharp three-pronged weapon at us, "you three should just shut the crack up and come with us."

"What's in it for us?" Sketch calls out. I want to tell her to stop talking.

I want to throw my dagger at the strange men, then turn and run, because no one is safe, and they walk with a purpose and strength that can only mean one thing.

This is their territory. And they want us to know it.

"You come with us, dark one"—the other, taller man nods at Sketch—"and you live."

His friend smiles. Black teeth. Some of them are missing. It reminds me of my mother.

I'm about to throw my dagger, tell Sketch and Zephyr to run. But then the man says something that stops me.

"Your faces. You have the Mark."

I reach up, my fingers skimming my Catalogue Number.

"Yessss." He nods, his voice as slithering as a snake's.

"We know about your kind."

"You've seen more of us?" I ask, wasting time. Trying to think of a way out.

The man whirls his weapon, and I know in an instant that he could kill us from where he stands, if he wanted to. And his eyes say that he does. "The train runs along the tracks. Once every few months. But you didn't come on that train, now did you? No, if you had, you'd already be dead. They shoot them. Soon as they leave the walls. No one escapes the guns."

I have always wondered what happens to those people on the other train, on the Evaluation day. The train that leaves the Shallows behind, packed with citizens.

Now I know.

The man grins again, but it isn't a welcoming grin. It sets my bones on fire.

"How did you escape? We want inside the walls."

Sketch barks out a laugh behind me. "Trust me, ChumHead, you *don't* want inside those walls."

"You're new here," he says. "You don't know what you're facing."

What could be worse than the Shallows?

Nothing, my gut tells me. *Nothing at all.*

But his eyes are hungry. He does want inside the

Perimeter. Maybe he thinks safety is on the other side. He doesn't know the Shallows is full of darkness and death.

He shrugs. "I'll offer you a choice, right now. You either tell us how to get inside of those walls . . . or you come with us."

"We don't answer to anyone but ourselves," I say, twirling my dagger, and in this moment, in the face of fear, I find my strength. "There are three of us, and two of you."

"You counted wrong." The man's eyes fall on to mine, and he laughs, just as three more men emerge from the tree line.

They have rifles.

"We can run," Zephyr says with a gasp, beside me.

I take a deep breath. "They'll shoot us, Zephyr. You can't outrun a bullet. Our best option is to wait. Then take them out at close range."

"This is their land," Sketch says. "Not ours."

I frown. We are at the disadvantage, even if we do run. Others could come.

"We'll go with them," I say, clutching my dagger tighter. "Wait for me to move first."

I take the lead, walking forward into what I pray is not our first and last mistake.

CHAPTER 42

ZEPHYR

The men take us across the beach.

Two in front, three in back.

The whole time, I keep waiting for Meadow to use her father's psycho training on them, use her dagger to break us out of this. But she walks with her eyes straight ahead, her face totally calm. It scares the crap out of me, seeing her this way.

We reach the rocks, scramble up to the top and peer down. I gasp when I see the people on the other side.

Men, women, a few kids. About twenty people in total, and they all look well fed enough. They sit around a fire, laughing. A few boys wrestle in the back of the crowd, and two older women are stitching clothing. It looks strangely normal. Like a family.

I smile sideways at Meadow. "Maybe this won't be so bad," I whisper.

But she shakes her head, so subtle I almost don't catch it. "The smoke," she says, her eyes set in slits as she stares at the bonfire. "It's black."

"Black?"

"It shouldn't be so dark," she whispers.

I don't get what she's talking about, and I don't have time to ask, because the men prod us with their weapons, and we start the climb down the other side of the rocks.

Everyone cheers when they see us. It's like some weird welcoming committee. Two little kids run up to us—a boy and a girl—both small like Dex, and for a second the pain of missing her hits me in the gut. I wonder what happened to her, when I left. I wonder if Rhone took control, or if the Leeches regained their power.

The kids touch our foreheads, stare at our Catalogue Numbers.

There's a woman who comes out of the crowd. Her dark hair almost reaches her toes, and as she walks forward, everyone stops. They bow at her feet.

Meadow and Sketch and I stand in front of her like ChumHeads. Not knowing what the hell we're supposed to do.

"I am Medin," the woman says. Her voice is silkier than the men who brought us here. She lifts a hand, touches my forehead. "Welcome to my family."

I want to flinch away from her for some reason. But I sit still as she strokes my Catalogue Number.

"A Marked one," she says. She looks at me like I'm holy, her eyes wide. "How did you cross the wall?"

I look sideways at Meadow and Sketch. "We're looking for the fastest way to the north," I say. "Do you know how to get there?"

"Maybe." Medin smiles, then touches my forehead again. Her fingernails are sharp, and for a second, there's a pinch of pain. "But you must earn the answer. How did you cross the wall?"

"We . . ."

She pulls her thumb away. A drop of my blood sits on her skin, bright red in the sunlight. She lifts it to her mouth, and my stomach whirls.

She licks my blood.

That's when I realize that her eyes are tinged with red.

And as she signals for all the people to come closer, I

notice that their eyes, too, are red. Their hands shake. Some of them twitch.

"Black smoke," Meadow says. "I remember the story now. Koi told it to me, when I was little, to scare me . . ." Then her gray eyes go wide, and she flips her dagger out, holds it in front of her. "They're cannibals."

"What the hell is that?" Sketch asks.

"*Cannibals,*" Meadow says again. "They eat . . . people."

"Get them!" Medin hisses to the crowd. "Get the Marked ones!"

The group screams, hands reaching. They rush toward us, too many of them to beat. I'm pulled away from Meadow and Sketch. I can hear Meadow's scream as she lashes out with her dagger.

She takes out two people with her hands, then lunges for Medin, but the crowd surges around the woman. It takes three men to hold Meadow back. She uses her Regulator to smash one's nose in, but others take his place.

Sketch curses as they tackle her, and soon the three of us are lying facedown, side by side in the sand with our hands and feet tied up.

"Well, we're fluxed," I hear Sketch breathe beside me.

It's such an obvious, stupid thing to say that I laugh.

Meadow laughs, too, and Sketch joins in, and it feels good, the three of us in this together.

But it also really sucks.

Because we're about to be eaten.

CHAPTER 43

MEADOW

The fire blazes hot and high. The crowd chants.

I wish now, more than ever, that my father were here.

Find a way out. Find a weakness in your enemy, and crush them.

My mother's voice takes his place. *You can't win, Meadow. You will never survive out there.*

Peri's screams drown them both out.

I bite my tongue hard enough to taste blood, to force myself back to reality. I have to think. I have to find a way to escape.

They took my dagger. There is nothing sharp to cut my bindings with, and even if there were, Sketch and Zephyr and I are in the middle of the crowd. They watch us all with hunger in their eyes, stomachs growling.

It makes me want to retch.

To take a human life is one thing. But to devour one, crave the taste of one . . . It is far more evil than anything I ever experienced in the Shallows.

And suddenly I miss it. I miss knowing that the darkness was my greatest enemy, that the ocean would keep me safe, that I knew every street and alley so well I could run with my eyes closed and make it back home.

The man who captured us, the one with the trident, approaches. "We're ready for the blonde one," he hisses.

His eyes fall on me.

He stoops down, runs the blades of his trident across my neck. It touches the Regulator, makes a screeching noise. "Medin wants the black box first."

I spit up at him, and he cackles. The crowd joins in as the man lifts me by my bound wrists, then starts to drag me across the sand.

"I'm sorry!" I say to Zephyr and Sketch, but I can't see them anymore. I can only hear commotion from behind me.

Zephyr's voice, screaming, "Take me! Take me instead of her!"

The man dragging me stops for a second.

"Quit it, Zephyr!" I yell back. He needs to shut his mouth. He needs to stay alive, and let me die, because he is too good for death.

"Yes, let them take him, Meadow!" Sketch yells, as they drag me farther away. "Take the boy! He tastes way better!"

"Sketch!" I glare at her. "What the hell?"

The three of us start arguing, yelling at each other, and the crowd is rising with their cackles and chants.

But it all goes silent when an arrow comes from the sky.

And lands itself right in the middle of my captor's forehead. He drops me. I watch from the ground as he staggers for a second. It almost looks fake, as if there were a target right in the center of his head. He gasps, and deep-red blood trickles from the wound, down his cheek, then splatters onto the sand.

He falls.

The crowd's chanting turns to screams, as more arrows come, one after the other, taking out every man, woman, and child. The people who aren't hit scatter, sprinting across the beach, chasing the train tracks into the distance.

By the time the sand is stained red from blood, Zephyr and Sketch and I are alone.

And then, from the trees, comes a monster.

CHAPTER 44
ZEPHYR

I don't know what the thing is.

It looks like a walking mass of plants.

"What the hell is that?" Sketch growls. She rolls across the sand, trying to get closer to Meadow and me.

"Just shut up for a second, Sketch!" Meadow hisses.

She's able to sit, hands still bound behind her back.

The creature comes closer, walking on two thick legs. It steps into the sunlight, and I almost laugh. Because it's not a creature at all. It's a person covered in palm fronds, overgrowth, ripped branches.

They could have been there the entire time, hiding in the tree line, and no one ever would've noticed.

Stars, it's amazing.

It's also totally creepy.

Meadow scoots backward and puts her wrists against the dead man's trident. She's able to cut her bindings, grab her dagger lying forgotten on the sand. She sprints right for the person.

They're holding a bow, and when they whirl it around and nock an arrow into place, Meadow dives. The arrow barely misses her. She flings the dagger. The person reaches up.

And *catches* it. By the blade. Blood drips from their skin. They drop the dagger to the sand.

"That was a warning shot!" It's a man's voice. Deep, rumbling. Probably someone old. "And now Martha's gonna rip me a new one for this hand."

Meadow freezes, kneeling in the sand. "Who are you?"

The man reaches up, takes off a mask of palm fronds. We see his face.

He's old. Wrinkled, tan, his face covered in sunspots. And he's smiling.

"You're from the Shallows," he says, still standing over Meadow. He's the first person to actually know the name. He nods at her barcode tattoo. "You have Catalogue Numbers. All three of you. Only reason I'd stick my

neck out to save a bunch of idiots that fell into the Eaters'
hands."

"You know about the Shallows?" Meadow tightens her
fists like she's about to snap.

"What's it to you if I do?"

Meadow stands up, brushes sand from her thighs.
"What do you want?"

"For you to trust me." The man laughs when Meadow
snarls and backs away a step. "If I wanted to kill you,
you'd already be long dead."

He shoulders past her, toward Sketch and me. When he
gets close, he pulls out a hand-carved knife.

"Touch us and die, old man!" Sketch screams. She tries
to stand up, but she wobbles, then falls to the sand again.

The man sighs and leans down to Sketch's level. She
spits in his face, and that only makes him laugh. "Oh,
Martha's gonna love you," he says. He flips his knife
around and points it at her.

He cuts her bindings loose.

He moves to me and cuts mine off, too.

"Strange group, you three," he says, over his shoulder
to us. He puts his face mask back on, then heads up the
beach, toward the trees, passing Meadow as he goes.
"You're lucky the Initiative ain't come by yet today. You'd

already be right back to where you came from."

"You know about the Initiative?" Meadow asks.

The man shrugs. "'Course I do. They got outposts, too. Closest one's 'bout a hundred miles down the tracks." He sighs. "They'll find you, if you ain't got a place to hide. You may as well come with me. Eat some real food. Get some rest. The three of you look like hell."

He stoops down and picks up Meadow's dagger. That's when I see behind his ear, a small tattoo.

It's an eagle, with outspread wings. The same kind of bird on a coin that Talan once found.

"An eagle," I whisper. "What does that mark mean?"

The man smiles. The first real smile he's given us. "You can decide that for yourself, once we get to where we're goin."

He flips Meadow's dagger around, handle out. "Name's Ray," he says. "You?"

Meadow doesn't answer. Instead she takes the dagger, her eyes on him the entire time.

"Suit yourself. There's more Eaters out here, too. This is their territory, and I ain't gonna save you twice. And keep up. It's a long way home."

He disappears into the trees.

It might be a death wish. But we follow.

CHAPTER 45

MEADOW

Ray runs the whole way.

We follow, breathless, and the landscape changes from beach to marsh, then marsh to dry grasslands. We come to a wall made of wood timbers, held together by thick bands of metal. A trail of smoke rises from the center, and voices carry over the top of the wall.

"You want to survive out here, you gotta stick with the strong ones," Ray says, pointing at the wall. "They're strong. Which is exactly why we need to keep moving. Come on."

We head into tall grasses that sway past our hips.

"Where is everyone?" I ask. "My father said that the

Outside was overrun with people."

"Oh, we're overrun, that's for sure," Ray grunts from up ahead. "This is the outskirts, Chickadee. That big wall that surrounds the Shallows . . . It's got rumors. Some say it's cursed. Lots of people have tried to climb it, and bad things happen. Paralysis. Death. Besides, Initiative Collectors come this way all the time."

Crickets leap from the grass, hitting our faces. I swat them away.

Soon we come to a patch of trees. They are thicker than the ones in the Shallows, and moss hangs like curtains from their branches. There is a fence of sorts, laced around the outside of the trees.

A sign hangs from the entrance, carved out of old wood. For one moment, there is a pang in my gut.

It reminds me of something Koi would have done. Only his would have been so much more beautiful, alive with life.

This sign has only words.

THADICUS.

"People crave the way things used to be, ya know?" Ray explains. "They try to create things from the past. Cities. Governments. It's all good and well till the stronger ones come and take what ain't theirs."

206

We enter Thadicus.

Or what is left of it.

There is a small natural clearing in the trees. Once, this might have been a good place for a camp. There are remnants of shelters made of wood and sticks. Some of them have fallen over like broken limbs. Others have been seemingly picked clean of the strongest branches, perhaps taken for shelters elsewhere. An old, headless doll sits in the leaves, and scattered all around are the remains of burned-out fires, like scars on the earth.

Something catches my eye, at the far side of the clearing.

A rope swings from low-hanging branches.

A skeleton hangs from the rope. My stomach lurches. It is missing its hands.

"What happened here?" I whisper.

Ray stops next to me. "Death," he simply says, and then he shrugs. "This is nothing. Welcome to the Outside, Chickadee. It only gets worse from here."

CHAPTER 46
ZEPHYR

One second we're walking in the trees, shoving through moss and sticks, and the next, we're standing on a concrete road. Miles away, the outline of a city towers into the sky like a ghost.

The camps start here.

It's like the Reserve back in the Shallows, just tons and tons of tents everywhere. Shelters made up of whatever people can find. Old metal cans, sticks, doors ripped from houses, window screens, tarps. We pass, and no one pays us much attention. At first there's only a few here and there. But the farther we walk, the greater the number becomes.

It's like the Shallows, countless faces and voices that rise all around. The only difference is that here, the land goes on forever. There's no Perimeter surrounding this place.

Which means that there's probably far more people than the Shallows ever could have had. I imagine that the Murder Complex can still reach me here. I imagine all of these people with Catalogue Numbers, just waiting to be picked off by Patients like me.

But so far, the system hasn't come.

So far, I feel stronger. Better.

If it weren't for Meadow's mission, I'd be free.

Sketch is walking beside me, and Meadow is out of earshot from us.

"You realize this could be our new world, right?" I ask her.

She kicks a chunk of rubble out of the way. "What do you mean?"

I sigh. "I mean it would be already, if we didn't have to go to the Ridge."

She stares straight ahead, taking in the packed streets. "What are you getting at, Zero?"

"We're following Meadow like homeless mutts, giving up our freedom for a mission that isn't ours to begin with. Doesn't that bother you?"

"No," she says automatically. Then she swallows, hard. "Don't tell her I agree with you. Don't even tell her we talked."

Here I am, in this open space, a world without walls. And I'm marching toward a new Perimeter. A new cage to close myself in.

But then Meadow looks back over her shoulder at us. I realized we've slowed down. "You okay?" she asks. There's a hint of concern in her eyes, a wrinkle in her Catalogue Number that lets me know she cares.

And that makes my chest constrict.

Because sometimes, you do stupid things for the people you care about.

And stars, even when it hurts, I care about that broken girl.

"We're fine, Woodson," Sketch says, waving Meadow off. Then she looks back at me.

"I wasn't asking because I wanted to stop this," I say. "I was asking because I had to know that if I'm in this, you're in this." I lower my voice. "It's obvious she's not . . . not herself, lately."

She laughs. "That's the understatement of the century, Zero."

I look into her amber eyes. "I need to find a way for

us to keep going, when it gets tough. When we feel like backing out on her."

Sketch scratches at her cheek.

Then she punches me in the face.

I stagger back, too shocked to do anything, and spit blood. "What the hell was that for?"

She laughs, a crazy sound that means she just enjoyed what she did. "You start to doubt, you get decked. Deal?"

I rub the burn away from my brow. Then I nod, walk closer to her, and swing my fist.

She dodges it.

"You gotta do better than that, Zero. Now let's keep going before we turn this into an all-out war."

The day gets hotter and hotter, and it's hard to keep track of how long we've been walking. I realize, as we go, that this isn't just for Meadow. It's for me, too. I'm looking at things I've never seen. I'm out in the world that I never thought I'd see.

The tents stretch down the road, until there's a blockage in the way.

A big graveyard of metal.

"What the hell are those?" Sketch asks.

She points ahead, where the road is packed with hunks

of metal on wheels, hundreds of them scattered, all broken and forgotten. Just like the shipwrecked boats in the Shallows. Some of them have shattered windows. Shards of glass are spilled across the road, and they catch the sunlight and sparkle like droplets of liquid fire.

"They're cars," Ray says.

He points at a green one.

And as I look at the color, a memory slams into me.

I'm just a boy, training in combat back in the Initiative Headquarters.

There's a guard standing behind me, whispering to his comrades.

"The Green, man," he says. "What do you think?"

The other guard laughs. "I think you're an idiot."

"Zephyr?" Meadow touches my shoulder. "Did you hear me?"

I blink, still staring at the green car. The memory fades away. But it was real, I know it was. I can sense the difference between the ones I actually had and the ones the Leeches implanted into me. It's like tasting salt water compared to the fresh kind.

Big difference.

"I'm fine," I say, blinking. "Really, I'm fine."

Meadow frowns, the lines of her Catalogue Number

straightening out. "I didn't ask you if you were." She watches me for a second, concern darkening her eyes. "Is it the system?"

"No," I say. "No, it's nothing."

Ray shuffles forward, explains what the cars are. "They're smaller vehicles, better than trains. But you need gas to work 'em. And we're fresh out of the stuff. Let's move. We don't want to be out when darkness hits."

"Finally, something we can agree on," Sketch says. "Come on, Woodson."

Meadow gives me a final look before following after her.

We walk toward the city, snaking around cars. I let my fingertips touch their hot metal sides. My boots crunch over wasted glass.

The entire time, I feel like I'm stuck in a dream.

CHAPTER 47

MEADOW

When I was younger, I used to think the Shallows was massive.

The buildings towered taller than I could ever be, and standing beside them made me feel impossibly small.

But the Shallows was nothing compared to this city.

There are triple the amount of buildings here, stretching high into the sky like a man-made forest. Some of them are missing their tops, and others have crumbling sides.

The sounds of life rise like the whispers of ghosts, growing louder, and clearer, the closer we get. We stop at the entrance just as darkness hits.

The colors of the city are muted at night, blacks and whites and grays, and I feel for a moment, the surge of anger that comes before every Dark Time.

But there is no Night Siren. This is *not* home.

We enter the city.

At first I think the people are corpses lying about. But then they move, they stand, they speak, and I am staring into the eyes of the living dead.

They are all skin hanging on bones.

They are sunken eyes and protruding hips and shoulders that are poking through filthy skin.

They are starving to death. I thought, in the Shallows, that we were hungry. But we had rations. We had jobs, where we could work for just enough food to survive. Here, there is no Rations Hall. There are no jobs, no payment. There is only the hope that you can find something to survive on.

This is like nothing I have ever seen.

So many people scattered about, far more than the Shallows. It seems the city streets have been made into homes. Shelters are all over every square inch of space, up against buildings, in Dumpsters, pouring out onto the fire escapes, even tarps that flap in the wind on the roofs. The smell is like the Graveyard, only this is fresh, a constant flow. In this packed city, with the buildings so tightly wound together, the wind cannot make its way clearly inside to ease the stench.

Fires burn all around. I hear infants, crying, and wonder why anyone would bring them into this world.

I think of the Shallows, with its overflowing numbers. But there, sometimes, you could find space to breathe. Here you could never do that.

We follow Ray through a pathway of sorts. Hands stretch toward him. Some voices call out to him, while others shy away. But one thing is constant.

They know him.

And they let us pass.

We reach the end of one street, turn right into another.

There's more people here, more shelters. It all melts into a blur.

I think of my mother. She did this to them, gave them a curse of life without death. And these people look like they want to die.

"Almost there," Ray says over his shoulder.

He stops before a building that has a big open mouth beneath it, disappearing into darkness underground. A thick metal gate covers the entrance, and three armed guards stand behind it.

When they notice Ray, the guards pull on a heavy chain. The gate groans, and it begins to slide up into the ceiling.

"I've never seen anything like it," I say to Zephyr as we wait.

"It's a parking garage," Ray says, turning back to us. "It goes underground a few flights, and it's . . . Aah, well, you'll see," he says, as we all stare back at him like he is crazy, or speaking an entirely different language. "You three, I swear. It's like you ain't lived a life before. I forget all you've known is that damn walled city. Come on, then. Let's go."

We follow Ray into darkness. The ground slopes down, down, and then it turns a sharp left.

Down, down, again. Walls surround us on all sides. The ceiling is low, made of concrete. I feel incredibly small, like the weight over our heads could crush us at any moment. But it is cooler down here.

Torches flicker up ahead, and there's another gate, made from scraps of metal, probably not originally a part of this place. More armed guards. Ray calls out to them, and they raise the gate, let us pass.

I see a symbol painted on the wall. A powerful bird, lit by flickering torches. An eagle. It was the symbol of our country, before the Fall. Now the bird is a thing of the past. Or it used to be, until now.

The lower we go, and the more turns we take, the more signs are painted on the walls. More eagles. A logo that reads *NEW US MILITIA*.

Ray touches the logo with his fingertips, mutters something under his breath.

We come to a third makeshift gate, and more guards that nod to Ray as we arrive.

The gate rises, slowly.

"Welcome to the Outpost," Ray says.

I hear voices. Commotion, the hum of a generator. I see a flickering light.

I only get a glimpse of what's inside. A table, with men gathered around it, deep in conversation. Computer screens, a giant map spread across one wall. Rooms, sectioned off by sheets. A stockpile of weapons, and food. Cots lining the walls. Lanterns glowing like watching eyes.

I'm about to ask what the Outpost is, what we're doing here, when suddenly I feel something hot and thick drip from my nose.

I touch it, pull my fingertips away. They are soaked in blood.

"I'm . . . bleeding," I say.

Everyone turns to look at me. The blood drips like a waterfall. My head feels fuzzy and light, and suddenly the world begins to flicker in and out of focus. My mother's whispered words sing to my soul, and I finally know that they are true.

I fall. My Regulator slams against the floor.

The last thing I see before darkness takes over, is a man dressed in white.

He stares down at me with cold, calculating eyes.

CHAPTER 48

ZEPHYR

"Stop screaming, Sketch," I groan. "You're going to wake Meadow up."

"This ChumHead thinks she can comb my dreads away!" Sketch growls. She's sitting beside me on an old cracked leather couch. Martha, Ray's wife, has been trying to rake through Sketch's dreads for the past hour.

"If you would sit still, I might be able to fix things," Martha says. She is old and gray, wrinkled as all hell, but her eyes are kind. She fed us food from metal cans. Something sweet and savory, called peaches. She let us bathe ourselves in a washbasin and gave us clean clothing to wear. New boots, probably from dead Militia members, but they fit my feet well enough.

I feel, for the first time, genuine care and concern from a stranger. I wonder if this is what it would have been like, to grow up with a real family. Not a fabricated one.

Ray sits in a chair across from us, drinking boiled water from a can. He chuckles as he watches Sketch. "We had grandkids, long time ago. Might as well let Martha get her fix on caring for ya."

The old woman digs the comb in again, and Sketch screams like a whiny Ward child.

I want her to stop.

But then again, if she doesn't, Meadow might wake up.

When she fell, Ray sent for a man he called *the Surgeon*. His hands were steady and his eyes were cold. He took Meadow away, and now I'm sitting here by the little makeshift hospital room, waiting.

And waiting.

And waiting some more.

I can hear a beeping noise in the corner of the room, where she's behind her wall of sheets. The New Militia has resources, and power. More than the Resistance in the Shallows ever had. I stare at the closed wall of sheets, desperate for an update.

"You look like a sick puppy," Sketch says. "Woodson

will be fine, Zero. Trust me."

"What do you know?" I ask. I kick off my boots.

Sketch groans as Martha pulls the comb through again. "The Leeches wouldn't have put that thing in her head if they knew it would kill her. She'll be fine."

"And if this *surgeon* fluxes up when he's removing it?" I ask.

Sketch shrugs. "Woodson wants to die, Zero. You and I both know that."

"Not until her family is free."

Martha reaches out and touches my shoulder. "The Surgeon does great work, child. Relax, and rest. You look tired."

Her words are stupid and simple, but her voice is so soothing. If I'd had a real grandmother, I imagine she'd probably have been able to calm me the way Martha is trying to right now.

I look around the Outpost. It's the nicest place I've ever been inside of, except for the Leech Headquarters. They have all sorts of technology. Generators that give us light. Maps of the Outside. Radios, weapons, food, clothing, even medicines, though I don't think there's use for that kind of thing anymore. Not with the Cure.

I want to know who they are, what they're about, and

why they took *us* in, when there's so many people they could have taken instead.

But no matter how many questions I ask, they won't answer.

"When the General comes back, he'll decide what to tell you," Ray says.

And so we wait.

Hours pass. I go in and out of sleep. I eat something called refried beans, and if I weren't so sick over worrying about Meadow, I think I'd love their taste.

Finally, the Surgeon opens up the curtain. There's blood on his hands and white clothes. His nurse comes out behind him.

I stand. Sketch stands, too.

"We couldn't get it off," he says. My heart sinks. "We could, however, remove the computer system inside of it, and lessen its weight. It's shut down now. Even if the Initiative wanted to try to reach her through it, they couldn't. I simply don't have the tools to remove it from her spine, without risking her life, or paralyzing her."

"You can't just . . . rip it out?" Sketch asks.

The Surgeon shakes his head. "She'll be fine. We think the system inside was getting to her. Hopefully, without it running, her symptoms will decrease, and eventually, disappear for good."

There's something hidden beneath his tired eyes.

Something that looks like a lie.

"You sure that's all?" I ask.

The Surgeon shuffles his feet. "That's all there is." Then he goes to clean up.

Sketch sits down on the couch, shoves me with her boot. "Go see her, Zero. I'm sick of your face."

I sweep the curtain aside, and step into Meadow's tiny room. I pull an old metal chair next to her bed, and hold her hand. Stars, she's beautiful in her sleep. With her head against the rough flour-sack pillow, it's hard to imagine the Regulator is still attached on the other side of her. At least it's shut down. They can't hurt her anymore, not with that.

I hope.

Her lips are full, half parted.

I stand up, quietly, and lean down to kiss her. "I missed you," I whisper. My lips are about to touch hers when her eyes fly open.

She gasps in shock. Before I can move away, she smashes her head against my skull.

CHAPTER 49

MEADOW

I knocked him out.

I literally knocked Zephyr out with a head-butt.

It's a tactic my brother Koi always begged me to try, but I never wanted to, afraid it wouldn't work. I guess it does.

I leap out of bed to help Zephyr as he groans and sits up.

"I was trying to *kiss* you!" he gasps. "What the flux?"

There is already a purple lump on his head, over his Catalogue Number, but he doesn't seem worried about himself. He stands, brushes himself off. Then he reaches out, moves a stray curl away from my face.

"Meadow, you just had surgery. Shouldn't you be tired?"

I shake my head. I feel stronger than ever, like I could

run for hours and not stop. My mother's words sing to me from the deep. *Only a few days* . . . I swallow them back, force them to hide.

There is heaviness at the back of my head and neck. The Regulator, still attached to me like a parasite.

"They tried to remove it," Zephyr says. "They couldn't. They shut it down, though. We think the system was too much for you to handle. Hopefully you won't have symptoms anymore."

I nod.

But he is wrong. It isn't the Regulator that is hurting me.

It is my mother's secret, and now I believe it, without a shadow of doubt.

Zephyr sits down in his chair again. "I was worried about you." His eyes are wide, green as fresh grass. His hand stays on my cheek, warm and soft. I lean into it and close my eyes. I could stay here forever, in the quiet.

"Why?" I ask. I realize that these moments are precious. Even if I refuse to admit it, even if he won't say so either. "I'm sorry. For everything, so far. This isn't easy, you know."

"I know, Meadow," he says. "That's why I'm still here. Well that, and Sketch can pack a mean punch."

I'm not sure what he is talking about. But right now, I don't care.

I am selfish when he is close.

"Come here," I whisper. "I want to apologize."

"There's nothing to apologize for," Zephyr says. But I feel him lean in, feel his warm breath on my face. His lips are almost against mine when the curtains around my bed fly open.

"Really?" Sketch is standing there, her hands on her hips. "I'm going to be sick, watching you two."

Zephyr groans, pulls away. "What do you want, Sketch?"

She frowns. "The General's back. And he wants to see us. Now."

CHAPTER 50

ZEPHYR

The first things I notice about the General are his eyes.

They're a deep, dark brown, so dark that they could almost be black.

He's seated at the metal table, waiting.

He wears army greens, and on his chest there is an old, faded patch. A red-and-white-striped rectangle, blue and flecked with stars in the upper left corner. It's a symbol I've seen before, in another pre-Fall thing Talan collected. Some stupid, worn book, but the symbol stood out to me. A flag.

"Welcome to the Outpost," he says. His hair is salt and pepper gray. It makes him look like he knows a million more things than I ever could. "Please, sit."

Meadow and Sketch take their seats. I slide in beside them, and we sit in awkward silence until Sketch opens her mouth.

"Who are you?" she asks. "And how do you have access to a place this nice when everyone else is out there in hell?"

The General looks at me when he speaks. "I'm George Jenkins, General of the New US Militia," he says. He sits straight in his chair, like there's a pole in his spine. "You three are lucky to be alive. Testing Site Three is not an easy place to survive."

"That's what we do," Meadow speaks up. "We survive. And apparently, that's what you and your people do, too." She leans forward, and even though her eyes hold the General's, I know she's watching all around us.

She still doesn't trust this place.

And maybe I shouldn't either, but it feels good to be somewhere safe. Somewhere that *feels* safe, at least, with gates and walls and weapons. And food.

"Surviving seems to be all we can do, in today's world," the General says.

"That's true." Meadow nods. "I survive for my friends, here, and my family. What I'm interested to know, General, is what are you surviving for?"

He smiles, wide. "That's the question I was hoping you'd ask, Miss Woodson."

How did he know her name?

Meadow's hands clench into fists. Her eyes turn to slits. She reaches for the dagger at her hip, but before she can go any farther, the General holds up a hand.

"No need to defend yourself here. I'm merely stating the obvious." He waves over one of his soldiers.

A man comes over, holding a file of papers. The General takes it, flips through until he finds the one he's looking for. He sets the paper on the table in front of us, swings it around so we can see it.

My breath hitches. It's a copy of the article Meadow and I saw back in the Shallows, in the old storage unit that belonged to her mother. I see Lark's face on the front page, smiling and happy, as she holds a pair of scissors. She's standing in front of the Perimeter, about to open up the Shallows for the very first time.

"You're the spitting image of her," the General says. "Which is why, initially, I was afraid of what your reaction might be, when I tell you that the reason I survive is to stop what your mother started."

Meadow sits silently, and he goes on.

"Anyone who came from that woman must be

sympathetic to her cause. But then I saw that machine attached to your skull. I saw the *X*s, tattooed onto the backs of your two companions' necks. And I wondered, why would Lark Woodson, the Creator of the Eternity Cure, the creator of the Murder Complex and the Shallows, allow her daughter to wear a machine like that? And better yet, why would she let her escape?"

Meadow looks down at her hands. She takes a deep breath, and when she answers, her voice is ice. "Because she's dead," she whispers. "And . . . I'm the reason why."

The General taps his fingers on the table.

"If that's the truth, child, and I hope it is, then you're welcome to stay here, and join us, or you may leave in peace. But first, I think we need to share stories. Then we'll decide if we are on the same side or not." He taps the paper in front of us. "I'd like to hear your story first, Miss Woodson, if you don't mind."

Meadow looks at me, then Sketch. I can see her mind working, see her calculating how much she'll tell him. Trying to gauge if he can be trusted or not.

Finally, she smiles and nods. "Of course, General," she says.

Then she leans back, folds her hands into her lap, and begins to tell our story.

CHAPTER 51

MEADOW

My father told me once that we should never share the whole truths of our lives with others.

He said that it was like giving away pieces of our souls, and if we give too many pieces away, we will eventually lose our strength.

Because of him, my entire life has been made up of half-truths and lies.

My mother was not the woman I believed her to be, because my father held a part of the story back. My past, even my own body, was never fully mine to know, because my mother chose not to tell.

Today, I continue their pattern.

I tell the General *almost* every gritty detail. I tell him about what Zephyr and Sketch are, how they've learned to fight the system. I tell him the number of people I have killed to survive, about the Red and Blue trains that run through the Shallows, about the rations job I got, and how Orion was an undercover Resistance member. I explain the truth about my mother, how a part of me smiles when I realize she is dead. How the other part of me wishes she could come back and change things for the better. I tell him about what happened in Headquarters. Sketch shivers when I mention our torture. I tell him about the Motherboard, and how when my mother died, the Patients set off to get revenge on the Initiative, because of my mother's fail-safe.

I tell him about how my family was stolen away from me. How I am trying to get to the Ridge, so I can rescue them, so we can be together and free on the Outside.

What I hold back is my mother's secret, and the truth about my mind. About my connection to the Murder Complex. About how the only way to truly kill it in the end, is to kill me. Not many can be trusted in this world, and until I know his story, I won't give that piece of me away.

I don't know how long I talk for. Sketch and Zephyr

help fill in the blanks, talk about what the Murder Complex did to them, how many countless they killed without the freedom of self-control.

When we're done speaking, I realize the soldiers have all been listening.

I realize they all look as if they have seen the ghosts of their loved ones, rising from the dead.

The General clears his throat. He motions for one of his soldiers again. This time, a man delivers a small drinking glass and a bottle of amber liquid. The General removes the top, pours a little into the glass, and chugs it down.

I can smell the pungent scent from across the table. I wrinkle my nose in disgust.

"That was quite a story," he says, as he fills the glass a second time. "And one I know to be true. We've been tracking the Initiative's moves for quite some time now. I'm sorry, for what they've done to you. I'm also sorry for what I have to show you next."

"Well, flux," Sketch says. She sighs, then reaches forward and takes the bottle of liquid from the General. She throws her head back, chugs from the bottle, and comes up coughing. "Might as well start this now."

CHAPTER 52

ZEPHYR

"Let's take a walk," the General says.

He leads us out of the room, up a few flights of the parking garage, until we're back at the entrance. The two soldiers from earlier are still standing guard. When they see the General, they stand and raise their hands to their brows in one swift motion. Then they stand still as statues.

"At ease," the General says. The soldiers relax. "I'd like to take my visitors to the Crow's Nest."

There's a door in the wall, and the General's men unlock it for us. It swings open with a puff of dust, and behind it, there's a concrete staircase, leading up into darkness.

Sketch groans. "You could've told me *before* the drinking there was gonna be so many stairs."

The General doesn't laugh. I'm starting to think he's a ChumHead, like his pants are too tight in all the wrong places. He moves past us, into the stairwell.

We follow.

It goes on forever.

All the levels are marked with bright red numbers, painted on the wall. When we reach another level, I'm dripping sweat. But it feels good to move. It feels good to climb, because we're heading toward answers.

And since leaving the Shallows, I know we all have questions we want answered. Especially Meadow.

She walks behind me, and the higher we go, the harder she breathes. It's not normal for someone who could probably outrun me ten times and only break a light sweat.

I look over my shoulder as we climb. "You okay?"

Her face is pale. Her lips are a horrible, papery white.

It's not like her.

I think of yesterday, when her nose bled, and she dropped like a swatted fly. She won't like this, but I stop and wait for her to catch up to me. She's exhausted from the surgery, probably. I wrap my arm around her waist and climb by her side.

"I don't need help," Meadow says.

"I don't care," I say back.

This is the game we've been playing since we left the Shallows. One snappy remark after another. She's too stubborn.

I can be stubborn, too.

I help her more by lifting some of her weight onto me. I'm practically carrying her up the stairs now.

"I said I'm fine, Zephyr." Meadow glares at me.

I laugh because I can't help it. "You're acting like such a . . ."

"I know," she says. She sighs and leans her head against my shoulder. "I know."

We pass flight twenty. Thirty.

The whole time, the General is up ahead of us not looking back.

At one point, there's a hole in the wall, like something was blasted through here. We scramble over rubble and keep going, until finally we reach the very last set of stairs.

It leads to a single red metal ladder that heads into the ceiling.

The General goes first, climbing on hands and feet. He shoves open a grate and disappears into cool night air.

Sketch goes after, complaining, as always.

Meadow rests heavy on my shoulder.

I help her to the ladder. She leans against it, and when she breathes, I can hear a wheeze in the back of her throat.

"Just relax here for a second," I tell her.

"I don't need to relax," she says. "I can do this." Her voice doesn't sound convincing. She looks up at me with sad, gray eyes, the same ones I've been waiting to look into for so long.

She's here now. She's with me and she's safe.

But she's not the same.

"Something is happening to you," I say. "We need to get help, Meadow."

"I'm just tired."

"That's exactly it," I say. "You don't get tired. Not the Meadow I know."

She shakes her head.

When she speaks, she stares into my eyes, and I'm haunted by what I see. "The Meadow you *knew* is dead."

She turns, grabs on to the ladder, and climbs into the sky.

CHAPTER 53

MEADOW

We are at the top of the tallest building in the city.

And if I weren't already out of breath, the sight would have stolen mine away.

Up so high, we can see for miles. Buildings go on, stretching into the darkness, and beyond, I can see other places.

Forests.

Dark, flat patches of land, and long expanses of road that reach on and on into nowhere, or somewhere, however you look at it.

The world is just so *big*. I feel as small as a seashell, as if the Outside is a wave so large it could crush me whole.

The General takes us to the edge of the building, where a woman sits, waiting.

In front of her is what looks like a long tube of metal, shining black as oil under the moonlight.

When she sees us, she stands, salutes the General. She has deep-red hair the color of blood, and on her bare shoulder, big and bold, is the same eagle tattoo that everyone else here has. A statement. For a moment, I am reminded of the Initiative's eye tattoo, open and all-seeing. They were all marked with it, and it seems that this New Militia has marked themselves with a symbol, too.

It is strange, how things constantly remind me of home.

I wonder if I will ever truly escape my past.

No, Darling, my mother's voice taunts me from the grave. *You will never escape the Shallows, no matter how fast or how far you run. It is your destiny.*

"Sasha," the General addresses the woman, pulling me from my thoughts. She's young, I realize, perhaps only a few years older than I am. Sasha smiles and nods with respect, and the Commander continues. "I need to show them the truth. Fire it up, will you?"

Sasha nods, then turns to the metal tube. It is like a giant lens, aimed at the sky.

"You ever seen a telescope?" she asks.

Zephyr and Sketch and I shake our heads.

Sasha laughs. "No, not many have, I guess. There's not much of that stuff left today. But this baby, she's great." She pats the telescope on its side. "A real powerhouse, aren't you, girl?"

Sasha lowers the telescope so that the end is pointing out into the distance, away from the city. She puts her eye up to the smaller side, makes some adjustments.

I see her shoulders stiffen. She stands, nods at the General.

"It's ready, Sir."

"Good work, Soldier," he says. He turns to the three of us, and his eyes hold a gloom that wasn't there before. "The Shallows is surrounded by a Perimeter. As is the Ridge, where you're trying to go. And the third site, at the Drop. It's a way of keeping you all in and keeping others out."

"We know that." Sketch shrugs. "We had to escape the damn thing to get free."

"'Free,'" the General says. "It's a strange word, isn't it? We all have different meanings for it, and I think you may find, after you see what I'm about to show you, that your definition of freedom will change."

He moves aside.

Sasha smiles sadly and waves us over.

I go first.

"Just put your eye here," she says. "Like a rifle scope. You look like the kind of girl who knows her way around a gun or two."

I nod, and she helps position me so that I can stare with one eye into the telescope. It's strange, like looking into a black hole, and at first, all I see is darkness.

"This is miles and miles away, out in the ocean," Sasha explains. "You see it yet?"

"It's too dark," I say, but then suddenly there is a blinking light.

It starts out as purple.

Then blue.

Then red.

Then back again.

As the light blinks, an image begins to take shape. A solid line splitting the darkness, a little lighter than the rest of the night sky.

"It can't be," I whisper. "That's not possible."

"I'm sorry," Sasha says. "But it is."

"What is it?" Sketch asks. She stands up, grabs my shoulders, and whirls me around to look at her. "Woodson, what the hell is it?"

I can still see the image burned into my head, a massive stretch of silver, standing out in the ocean, holding us in. This was supposed to be the *Outside*. But how can that be, when we're still trapped?

"It's a Perimeter," I say.

My words settle in, and I know from the horror in my voice that they are true.

CHAPTER 54

ZEPHYR

There's a Perimeter around what's left of the country.

It's miles and miles away, out in the ocean. You can't see it without the telescope, even if you're standing onshore staring until your eyes hurt.

If you can pretend it's not there, you can pretend you're free.

But what is freedom, really, if it's all a lie?

The General sits down on the roof and explains what he knows.

"A long time ago, about twenty years, this country was the United States. Big world power, if you can believe it. Damn, those were good times. We were strong. We had all the power, all the answers." The General points to his chest, where that strange symbol sits. Red and white and blue. The flag. "And then it all went to hell when the Plague hit. Huge epidemic, and it wasn't just here. It was everywhere, all over the world." He sighs, looks down at his boots. "People were dropping left and right. It was airborne. Hit the world like a storm, and we didn't stand a chance in hell."

Meadow nods. "That's why we were in the Shallows. Or why we thought, anyways. Our whole lives, we believed the Pins we had were keeping the Plague away from us. In reality, it was just my mother's Eternity Cure. The nanites are in all of us, in our blood."

The General nods. "The government couldn't do anything to stop the Plague, and it all fell apart."

"Until my mother," Meadow says. Her voice breaks. I see sorrow in her eyes. Then disgust. It's like a constant battle for her.

Will it make things better, or worse, when she finds out I was the one who killed Lark?

The General goes on. "The Initiative stepped up. They were strong, and they weren't dying from the Plague, and it'll be a cold day in hell before any dying country *doesn't* follow the new world leaders who have the answer to cheating death. The Initiative brought your mother with them, a young, brilliant woman they'd found in Florida. She created the Eternity Cure. People stopped dying. It was the answer we'd been looking for. It was sent airborne, and waterborne, to fight the Plague. All over the world, governments were distributing it."

"So the Initiative isn't just here?" Meadow asks. "Where are they?"

"The Initiative is the US branch." He shrugs. "There are others, in other countries, but we lost contact. Satellite systems went haywire, when the power went out with it. The Perimeter you saw in the ocean, it surrounds what's left of this country. Stretches from sea to sky, and it's electromagnetic. Scary as hell. Uncrossable. Those who try, die."

"So the whole country is prisoner," Meadow says. She's taking the news well.

I'm freaking out so bad I can't even find words.

"Why?" Sketch asks.

"Because the Initiative offered up the United States as one of the controlled variables in a worldwide experiment," the General says. "We're the country that's trying to reverse things. The testing sites, the Shallows, the Ridge, the Drop. It's all ways to deal with the Cure.

Murder, manipulation. They're trying to fix what Lark Woodson and her team started."

"And you want to fight that?" Sketch asks.

The General nods. "People aren't mice to be thrown into mazes. The world got sick, and the Initiative made it even sicker by eliminating death. What they're doing to our people . . . It ain't right. This is the new way of the world. We should be able to live free in it, or die trying. The New Militia has a few branches. We're gathering teams, gearing up for a fight. It took years to get to where we are now. Those people out there, in this city? They protect us. Help hide us from the Initiative. It's been a close call, and we've lost people. We've moved around a lot, regrouped. But we're almost ready. Soon, we'll stage simultaneous attacks on the Ridge and the Drop." He smiles. "You and your people took care of the Shallows for us."

Meadow nods, chews on her thumbnail.

"My mother said the Ridge was up north. Do you know where it is? What happens there?"

The General is quiet for a long time. "Your family is stuck inside of the site for Genetic Mutation. It's in what used to be Northern Washington. They're working to reverse the Cure, testing on the citizens of the Ridge." He sighs, stares out at the packed world around us. "Trust me when I tell you this, girl. The Ridge is worse than the Shallows. You don't want to go there, and you can't just walk in, anyways. You're free now. You're out of the system. Keep it that way. Fight with us and help us fix what your mother broke."

"No," Meadow says.

The General raises a brow. "No?"

"No." Meadow shrugs. "I won't help you unless you decide to help me."

Sketch chuckles and claps her hands, like she's enjoying the show.

The General stands up, brushes off his pants. "You're just a girl. What could you offer us that we don't already have?"

Meadow stands, steps closer to him until their noses are practically touching. "I'm not just a girl. I'm Lark Woodson's daughter, and if I want help, you'll help me. Get me to the Ridge. Help me get inside. I'll find my family, and once I have them, I'll help you fight back. I'll help you destroy the Initiative from the inside out."

"You drive a hard bargain," the General says. "What if you die? Is your life not worth anything?"

Right as he says it, Meadow's nose drips again.

Fresh red blood, bright even in the darkness.

That's not supposed to happen. The Surgeon said it would stop, now that the Regulator's computer is down.

Unless it's not the Regulator, and never has been.

Meadow lets the blood drip down her face. "Trust me, General. I have nothing to lose."

I can see a new light in his eyes, see him thinking, planning. "It doesn't matter. I can't simply send you into the Ridge. Do you think they'll let you just walk in there, especially with the barcodes and that Regulator strapped to your skull?"

"I do," Meadow says. "Because they'll let my mother inside."

"Your mother is dead," the General says. "By now, all the soldiers in the Initiative will know, in every testing site."

"So we'll trick them," Meadow says. "We'll bring her back to life."

"That's imp . . ." The General trails off. His eyes light up. He smiles, and nods.

I don't even have to look at Meadow to know what he sees.

She's identical to her mother, the same silver hair, the same springtime storm eyes. She's been tortured for weeks, she's lost weight, and there's a darkness, a touch of insanity in her, that wasn't there before. She might only be sixteen, but she's faced worse than most people should in an entire lifetime.

She could pull it off.

"Make me into my mother," Meadow says. "Give me a team, dress them up as Initiative soldiers. We'll hijack a train and attack their Headquarters, then break through to the Ridge from the inside out."

"And how will you explain the Regulator?" the General asks.

Meadow doesn't skip a beat. "I'll tell them you did it. The New Militia will do anything to break down the Initiative, right?"

He nods, lost in her plan.

"Just get me close to the Ridge, and I'll find a way inside. I'll find my family, and once I'm free again, I'll swear my service to the New Militia. For the rest of my life, I'll be your greatest soldier."

"Meadow, no," I hiss.

"Like hell you will," Sketch yells. "We just got free!"

Meadow glares at us with such intensity that we both shut our mouths. "I wasn't asking you for help. You're free now. You two can do what you want."

"I'm sticking with you, Woodson," Sketch says. She looks at me like she's ready to punch me. Our stupid little game.

"I'm with you, too, Meadow. I made a promise, and I'm going to keep it. But don't do it like this," I say. "We'll find another way. Don't trade your freedom, not when you just got it."

She looks down at her hands. "I was never free."

The General rubs his hands over his jaw, breathes deeply as he thinks.

Meadow looks up. "You said your reason for survival was to stop what my mother started. Let me help you do that."

They stand together and move off to the side, talking in hushed voices. I don't have to hear what they're saying to know what is going on.

The General is falling right into Meadow's hands.

CHAPTER 55
MEADOW

We eat a full meal tonight.

The New Militia has canned food, something I have never seen before the Outpost. We eat beans, and peas, and a soft orange fruit that explodes with flavor when it touches my tongue.

Afterward, we sit around the table and discuss.

I tell the General we only need seventy-two hours, starting the moment we make it inside the Ridge. We plan together in private.

We argue over whose plan is best, but I will not back down.

Finally, the General agrees to go with my ideas, and the plan is in place.

Tomorrow, I will become my mother. Tomorrow, I will be the woman who ruined me. The woman who broke the world. I will hand my freedom over to the New Militia. I will become the soldier my father always trained me to be.

But for tonight, I want to be free. One final time, I want to grasp the illusion. I want to feel the freedom my father once felt.

I want to feel the wind on my face. I want to *run*.

Everyone is asleep, scattered about the Outpost. Sketch snores from the couch, and Zephyr is curled up on the floor in front of her. Curtains are drawn around all the cots, and no one will be awake to stop me.

I tuck my dagger into my waistband. I tighten the laces on the new boots I have and leave everyone behind.

The walk up the levels of the garage is exhausting. Weeks ago, I would have been able to sprint these concrete floors, breathing evenly, without breaking a sweat.

Tonight I stumble.

My nose drips blood.

I wipe it away and force myself to keep going, to forget about the pain in my skull, the weight of the Regulator against my neck. I persevere the way that I always have, and finally, I make it to the top.

The guards won't let me leave, so I take the staircase

again, the one that leads to the roof.

I am only halfway up the second floor when I fall.

My knees crack hard on the staircase, drip with blood. I try to stand but I'm too weak. My head spins, and the world flickers in and out of focus. This isn't right.

This isn't supposed to be happening. But it is.

My mother said that it would.

I bang the back of my head against the wall.

The Regulator's thick metal rings from the impact, but it does not crack.

I bang my head again, and again, and I lose myself to the fury. To the hatred I feel for myself, for getting caught. For not being able to die in the Resistance Headquarters.

For getting my mother killed by drawing her out of hiding. For the pain that Peri felt, because of me. For dragging Zephyr and Sketch along, when they deserve to be *free*. Away from me, away from my selfishness.

You are just like me, my mother's voice says. I want her to be wrong.

But I think she is right.

Suddenly I'm furious at myself for caring about my mother's death. She was a monster, inside and out, and she will always be.

But I could never forget the way she whispered my name. *Forgive me.*

She was my mother, and I will always love her.

Love makes us weak.

I tear at the Regulator with my fingernails. I draw blood but I don't stop. I want it out. I want to be strong again.

I want to die.

I want to survive.

It's only when I feel hands on mine, gently pulling my fingers from the Regulator, that I notice Zephyr.

He kneels in front of me, soft green eyes watching mine.

"Meadow," he whispers. He says it like a song, and his eyes are so gentle, so . . .

My head spins. I slump over, and he catches me, wraps his strong arms around my waist. He pulls me up, holds me like I'm a child.

I both hate it and love it at the same time. He smiles down at me sadly, the way I used to look at Peri, when I knew she was weak, when I knew she wouldn't be able to fight back against the darkness of our world.

"Don't," I say. "Don't look at me like that."

"Like what?" he asks, as he carries me back down the stairs.

"Like I'm weak," I say.

He stops. "You think . . . Stars, Meadow. It's not because I think you're weak. It's because you've been through so much, and you still want to fight. You still won't give up." He leans his head down, looks at me closer. "Why won't you just give up?"

"Because I can't," I simply say. "Because giving up is not something I know how to do."

We reach the first flight of stairs. He starts to head down, carrying me, but I stop him.

"I don't want to go back in there," I say. "I wanted to go outside. I wanted to be free, for one last time. To make my own choices."

"You can still change your mind," Zephyr says. "You don't have to do this."

I swallow and taste blood. "You know I do. I'll fight for my family, even if it kills me. And I can't ask you to go with me. I've taken advantage of your help, expected you to always be at my side. But you're free, Zephyr. Why won't you just *go*?"

He sighs. He sets me down.

"I can't go, Meadow."

"Yes, you can. And you should," I say.

He stares at his boots. "It's like you're hardwired into me, Meadow. I think about you when I'm awake. I dream about you when I'm asleep. My brain was obsessed about you for years because of Sparrow, and the system, and the need, deep down, to murder you." He laughs, but the sound is hollow. "And then I met you in real life, and I realized it wasn't an obsession. It was just . . . you."

"What do you mean?" I ask.

"You're stubborn, and you're always angry, and you *like* killing, I can see it in your eyes. I have a theory that you're one of the worst people in the world," he says. I turn my face away, but he reaches up and gently touches my chin. "But that's what I love about you. It sounds crazy. You make me stronger. You make me laugh, and most of the time, you make me so mad I want to scream. But that's just it. You make me *feel* things, Meadow. Real things, not just fabrications programmed into me in your mother's lab. You're real. *We* are real. There's something here. And I refuse to let that go."

I told myself I wouldn't let him get closer to me. There is no room for anyone else, not now, not ever.

But his words shatter my walls. My body takes over, and it's full of *want, need, now.*

I reach out, grab Zephyr by the shirt collar, and yank him toward me with all the strength I have left.

Our lips touch, and there's fire inside of me.

I feel him groan, feel his mouth press harder against mine. He pulls me down on top of him, and I become a burning flame that wants to devour more, more, all of him, always. But when I slide my fingers beneath his shirt and run my hands across his chest, he pulls away.

"I can't do this," he says.

"Do what?" I ask. "Don't you want this? I can feel your heart beating as fast as mine."

I press my forehead against his; kiss him again, and for a few seconds, he kisses back even harder than before. I'm breathless. Wanting him, even though I don't know why. The kiss breaks as Zephyr pulls away.

"What's wrong?" I ask.

"I did it," he whispers, and then he gasps, like he's shocked by his words.

"Did what?" I ask.

He won't look at me. His lips are out of reach.

When he speaks, his words ignite a flame in me again.

But it isn't a good fire.

"I killed your mother," Zephyr says. "I'm the one who shot that arrow."

The fire is hot and heavy.

It's so angry it could burn down the entire world.

CHAPTER 56

ZEPHYR

She doesn't speak to me.

She stumbles the whole way back to the Outpost, tripping over her own feet as she goes.

Blood drips from her nose, and stars, I want to help her.

But Meadow is beyond help.

"You hated her," I say to her back. "Why does it matter that she's dead?"

No answer. Just the stomping of her boots as she struggles to get back to the others.

"I did it because it was the only way, Meadow. If she didn't die, then the Patients wouldn't have gone after the Leeches. We escaped. We're here, and we're going to find your family."

Finally, she whirls around. Her eyes are wild, and for a second, she looks so much like Lark that I freeze. "She *was* my family," she says. "Regardless of what she did, what she became. She was my *mother.*"

"You're confusing mother with monster," I say to her back.

She whirls around, flings her dagger so fast I don't have time to be shocked.

It grazes my face, then clatters to the ground behind me.

I feel hot blood as the fresh cut opens.

"You missed!" I yell at Meadow's back.

She stops before the door to the Outpost, turns again to look at me. Stars, she's beautiful. And terrifying. "I meant to," she says.

I throw my hands up. "So why don't you kill me, then?"

There's sadness in her eyes. "If I wanted to kill you, Zephyr, you'd already be dead." The guards raise the gate for her. "Keep him out," she says.

They lower it before I can get there.

"Really, guys?" I ask.

Sasha is one of them. "Trouble in paradise?" she asks. I nod, motion to the gates. "The General's orders. What the girl says, goes. Sorry."

"Fine," I say. "I'll just stay out here, then, and bother you until you let me in."

She shrugs, from the other side of the gate. "Try me."

I slide to the ground with my back up against the wall.

I don't get a wink of sleep all night.

CHAPTER 57
MEADOW

Morning comes, and I am staring at my mother.

She stares back at me.

When I move, she moves. When I stumble sideways, she stumbles, too. When my nose drips blood, she lifts her hand to wipe it away.

Her eyes are heavy, dark half-moons beneath them weighing them down. She smiles, and her teeth are blackened. *My* teeth are blackened, from something Ray's wife used.

The New Militia has dressed me in Initiative clothes, all black. They have made me look older, somehow. Martha, Ray's wife, has altered my Catalogue Number to match hers. I held my screams to myself, while she tattooed a new number 8 over my number zero, and the Cure has already healed it. The Catalogue Number looks fresh and new.

My mother and I were only one number different.

It wasn't that hard to do, with the right tools.

"Flux," Sketch breathes. She steps beside me into the small bathroom, stares into the cracked mirror. "Woodson, I swear, you look just like her. I kind of want to kill you now."

"Zephyr already did that for the both of us," I whisper. Anger flares in my heart, threatens to burst from the inside out.

Sketch sighs. "Get it over it. He did what he had to do. You would have done the same thing, right?"

"Before capture, I wanted to kill her," I say. "What she did to the world is unforgivable. But after all the torture . . . She went through what we went through, Sketch. But we endured it for weeks. She endured it for years. It changed her. It would change anyone." I lean against the wall, stare at myself as my mother, and sigh. "Can we come back from the things we've done in this world?"

"I don't know." Sketch shrugs. She runs her hands down the scars that line her arms, tallies of all the victims she's killed, under the influence of the system. "But even if we can, I think there's some of us that wouldn't make the choice to." She looks at me in the mirror. "You might hate your mother for what she did to the world, Meadow. But deep down, you're a killer just like her. We're all killers. And we like being that way."

She's right.

Because of the system, I sway the way my mother used to sway. Because of the torture, I can harness the cold, hard hatred that blackened her heart.

I can become her.

I have become her.

And no one will stand in my way.

CHAPTER 58

ZEPHYR

I'm sitting on the edge of the roof, letting my legs dangle over the world, when Sketch finds me.

"Thinking of jumping?" she asks.

She sits down beside me, hangs her scarred legs over the edge. The wind is strong. It tugs at the laces on our boots, almost like it's whispering for us to just lean a little farther out.

Fall into the abyss.

"Why are we doing this, Sketch?" I ask.

Birds fly overhead, just a few black splotches that disappear into the dark clouds.

Sketch doesn't answer, so I go on.

"Why are we staying with her? She doesn't want us. She's going to die in there. I can feel it. If we follow her, we'll die, too. This whole mission is suicide."

Sketch spits over the edge. We watch it fall until it's out of sight. "Love makes us do stupid things," she says.

I turn to her. "I thought you said you couldn't love."

"I lied." She laughs, a hollow sound. "Did you know I had a sister, once? She was just like Meadow. Reckless. Angry. Strong."

"Meadow reminds you of her," I say. It's not a question. I should have known the entire time, the way Sketch makes excuses for Meadow. The way she stays by her side without questioning it. She's replacing her sister with Meadow.

Sketch nods. "We can't bring back the people we've lost, but we can find pieces of them in others."

It starts to rain, little drops of water dancing down from the sky. I tilt my head back and let the drops burst onto my tongue.

Sketch sighs. "Woodson doesn't care about anyone besides her family. But then there's you. There's always been you. I said she whispered Peri's name, in that dirty cell. But she also whispered yours, Zephyr. Every night, I heard your name, over and over."

"I killed Lark," I say. "She hates me now. Whatever was between us is gone."

Sketch's laughter is nearly lost in the rain. It pounds down now, soaks my clothes, my hair. "Meadow loves you. She's just too scared to admit it."

"And you?" I ask. "What about you?"

She shrugs. "No one loves me. No one ever will. It's better that way."

"You can't really believe that," I say, but Sketch waves a hand, and my voice trails off.

I don't know why I do it. But as thunder rumbles the sky, and lightning strikes overhead, I reach out and put my arm over her shoulders. At first she tenses up. But then, when I refuse to let go, she leans against me. She's warm and solid. If I close my eyes, I can almost imagine the rain is the sound of the ocean.

We're somewhere safe and free. We're not Patients. We're just people.

"We're the same," I say. "You and me. We broke free of the system, and now we're trailing after the girl who holds the key to its life in her brain. Are we stupid, Sketch? Are we cursed to always follow the Murder Complex in some way?"

"We're not cursed," Sketch says. "We're bound by love.

Love makes it harder to see the darker side of things. When I look at her, all I see is the sun."

The rain drowns out the sound of the world.

"We're going with her, aren't we?" I ask.

Sketch nods.

"You and me," she says.

We sit together on the edge of the world until the storm passes.

We don't talk anymore, and we don't have to, because the decision radiates between us. The fear, the questions, but there is no longer any doubt.

We're going back inside the walls.

Only this time, we don't know what waits for us on the other side.

Meadow has brought her mother back from the dead.

She looks at me, and I see nothing but emptiness in her eyes.

"I'm sorry," I say, as we follow the General and his soldiers through the parking garage, up the ramp. I grab Meadow's arm, but she shakes it off. "Meadow. Can we talk about this, please?"

She stares straight ahead. "There is nothing to talk about. You killed my mother. You did it because you had to. And now, I can't look at you without seeing her blood on your hands."

"*She* put blood on *my* hands, from tons of innocent people," I hiss.

Sketch marches beside her, wearing Leech black. "She put blood on my hands too, Woodson. Let it go. Zero did us all a favor."

"You two are idiots," Meadow hisses. She looks at Sketch. "You are only slightly less of an idiot than he is."

Sketch explodes with laughter. She wraps her arm around Meadow's shoulders, and suddenly I'm the ChumHead in the back, alone, marching along in a Leech uniform. Following Meadow like some homeless dog. Sasha, the New Militia member who runs the telescope, is going with us. She falls back beside me, her red hair tied in a bun. It shows off the new Leech tattoo on her neck. The open eye. I've got to hand it to her; she's committed to the disguise.

Talan would have done the same thing, and if she were here, she'd tell me to man up and forget about Meadow for a while. Let her come to me.

"You hanging in there?" Sasha asks. She nods in Meadow's direction.

I blow out a mouthful of air. "You don't even want to

know. I screwed this up, bad."

She laughs. "She seems like a tough one."

"Tough doesn't begin to cover it."

"Well, I've seen the way she looks at you, when you're not looking at her." Sasha winks and nudges me with her hip. "There's hope in there somewhere. There's always hope. Sometimes it just takes a little patience before it shows itself."

The General stops up ahead, motions for the two guards at the gate to open it. Sunlight pours in from the outside, and the sounds of so many people on the packed streets. Sweat beads on my forehead.

It's like we never left the Shallows.

The gate screeches and groans as it rises into the ceiling, just enough for us to pass through. The guards stand at the ready with their rifles.

"Remember the plan." The General turns to me, Meadow, Sketch, and Sasha. "As soon as you get there, you have seventy-two hours to find your family and make contact, as Miss Woodson decided upon. If you don't, we'll assume the worst. You'll be on your own." He looks us all over, then lands his gaze on Meadow. "Remember what I said. I'm counting on you, Soldier."

There's a secret between them. Something that's

hidden, and I don't like it.

Meadow lifts her hand, does what I've learned is called a salute.

I know what it means.

It means her freedom is gone. She's already a part of the General's army.

I lift my hand, salute him, too. Meadow throws me a glare.

"I go where you go," I say, and shrug.

"Oh, for the love of fluxing . . . Can we just get on with it already?" Sketch groans.

The General sends us into the streets.

I hope the plan works. Because it if doesn't, we're all going to die.

CHAPTER 59
MEADOW

The weakness fades inside of me. I feel strength come back in a surge.

I know what is happening to me. But I hold that secret to myself.

At least for now, I'm strong enough to run with everyone else. At this rate, we will make it to the train tracks in a few hours' time. The storm has finally passed.

We pass back through the city, through the packs of people. This time, when they see us dressed as Initiative soldiers, they shy away. They avoid our eyes, like they're afraid of us. We have rifles on our shoulders, the same way the soldiers in the Shallows always did.

But it's not the guns.

It's the look of us.

Even on the Outside, the people fear the Initiative.

"Sometimes the Initiative combs the streets," Sasha says. "They take people at random, load them on to their trains."

"Why?" Sketch asks, as we leave the city behind and follow chunks of an old road, bits and pieces blown away.

Sasha shakes her head. "We think they take them to the Ridge, and to the Drop. Never the Shallows, though. That one is full, from what we've gathered." She smiles for a second. "But you three made it out, didn't you?"

I sidestep a pipe that sticks out of the concrete like it is stretching for the sky. "We didn't make it out without casualties."

Behind me, Zephyr says nothing.

We walk until the large road ends, and a smaller one begins. There are old homes, scattered about. Remnants of a neighborhood that might have been beautiful once. Some of the homes look almost intact, and for a moment as I stare at the boarded-up windows, I think about the families that have taken up residence inside.

I wonder if they are like mine.

An older brother who sees the beauty in art, even when

the world around him is shattered like glass. A little sister who loves to laugh, whose voice is like music. A father who shows love through teaching the art of survival, and a mother who is dead. Then not dead. Then dead all over again.

I trip over my feet, as my body suddenly switches back. Weakness grabs ahold of me.

I go down to the concrete, and I can't catch myself.

"Meadow," Sketch says. She never uses my name unless she's worried. "You all right?" She kneels beside me, sweeps my hair back from my face. I'm dripping sweat, but I feel cold.

I shiver, and she puts an arm over my shoulders, helps me sit up.

"It's okay," I say. "I can keep going. We have to make it to the train on time."

Suddenly I feel a lurching in my stomach. I lean over, spew vomit onto the concrete. My throat burns, as if someone has scalded it with fire. I close my eyes, beg my body to work with me.

I have to make it to the train.

"We have to stop," Sketch hisses.

"It's fine, Sketch, I can keep going," I say. I open my eyes.

Zephyr and Sasha lean over us from above. "It's not fine," Zephyr says. "Look at it, Meadow."

He points at the vomit.

It is full of blood.

CHAPTER 60

ZEPHYR

She's dying.

Meadow is *dying.* That has to be the only explanation for what's going on. Every step is like agony for her. She falls, and her nose keeps dripping, and she's puking blood now on top of it all.

Her whole body shakes. She goes from hot to cold and back again.

Sketch and Sasha and I take turns helping her move along, one of us on each side of her, one behind in case she falls backward. At first she's able to get enough strength to keep up with us. But an hour passes, and she's soaked in sweat. Trembling like it's the middle of winter.

She throws up again.

More blood.

Her nose trickles it and I don't know what to do, how to help her.

"We just have to get to the tracks," she says.

Her voice is so weak.

Sketch and I share a look, and there's a silent message in it.

Fear.

When we stop to rest in the shadow of something called a gas station, I pull Sasha aside. "Have you seen anything like this before?" I ask.

She shakes her head. "No. We don't die, Zephyr. You know that. We don't even get sick."

I look at Meadow and Sketch, huddled together against the back of an old gas pump. Sketch pulls Meadow's curls back from her face. She rubs sweat from her brow and whispers something to her. Meadow nods weakly.

I have to look away. "She's sick. It's plain as day. The Surgeon back in your camp . . . He knew something, and he wasn't saying it. What did he know?"

Sasha puts her hands on my shoulders. "I don't know anything, I promise. If we can make this work, the Initiative has doctors that will save her. We'll take some captive. Force them to fix her. But first we have to get to the Ridge." She raises her voice so we can all hear. "All right, team. Time to move."

We leave one neighborhood, enter another, and then leave that one behind. We go through a wooded area, packed with kids. It's like the Reserve back in the Shallows. I want to stop here, stay in a place that feels familiar.

But *Meadow is dying.*

Stars, I can't stop thinking the words. They aren't true. There's no way they could be, but when I look at her, doubt sinks its teeth into my soul.

"Just get to the train," I say, and I don't know if it's to myself or Meadow or everyone else, but I don't care.

An hour passes. An hour and a half. An hour and forty-five minutes.

We finally see the tracks up ahead.

"We're almost there," I say to Meadow, and by now, she crumples. I put her on my back, and Sketch stays behind me, to help hold her on.

"I'll run ahead," Sasha says. "I'll flag them down." She looks at Meadow, shakes her head. "She has to be ready when the soldiers stop. She has to become Lark."

"I will," Meadow gasps.

Sasha sprints away, red hair dancing like fire. Sketch

and I move along, slow, so fluxing slow.

The train comes, rumbling like a great metal beast. It's a small train, a few cars, but it's got the Leech eye. Luck is on our side, because this train isn't from the Shallows. It's coming from the north, from the Ridge.

This *has* to work.

I see Sasha wave her arms, jump up and down. The train doesn't slow. She swings her rifle around, fires off a few rounds into the air.

By now the driver's face is clear. Other Leeches poke their heads out of a door.

They point at Sasha, and she fires off another round in the air.

Finally, the train squeals, as the driver slams the breaks.

"Yes," Sketch says. "Come on."

We run as best as we can.

We reach Sasha's side just as the train comes to a stop.

The door swings open, and suddenly Leeches pour out, rifles aimed and ready.

"Finally!" Sasha yells, and it's like she turns into another person. She puts one hand on her hip, lets her rifle drop. "What the hell took you so long? My wrist mic breaks, and it's like a ghost town out here. Well? Where have you been?"

The Leech in charge steps forward. He's tall, slim. He

points his rifle at Sasha's face. "Who are you?"

Sasha stares back at him. "I work in the SPC department, back in the Shallows."

The Leech raises a brow. "Shallows? That's eighty miles south of here, Soldier. Care to tell me what you're doing so far from your post? You an Abandoner?" He takes another step forward. The Leeches behind him grunt and shuffle to come closer.

Sasha laughs. "I am the angel of opportunity," she says. "Bring her forward!"

I realize she's talking to Sketch and me. We bring Meadow forward, help her to her feet.

"Lark Woodson, boys," Sasha says. "The *Creator*."

It takes all Meadow's strength to put her feet down, stand on her own, and look them in the eyes.

But what I see in her erases everything from our past, morphs her into someone she's never wanted to be.

"Get me to the Ridge," she says. Her voice is so perfect, so spot on with that twinge of a song, the same voice I hear in my head when the Murder Complex calls to me, that I forget she's Meadow at all.

She is Lark Woodson, through and through.

"You're dead," the Leech gasps.

Meadow laughs, sways on her feet, and I know it's because

she's fighting to stand, but it's perfect. "I'm only dead if I say I'm dead, Soldier. Now get me on that train, turn it back around, and take me and my team to the Ridge."

"Those aren't my orders," the Leech says.

Meadow throws her head back and laughs. Blood drips from her nose, and she doesn't move to wipe it away.

"The Resistance bastards came. They tore apart my lab, and set my own doctors against me at gunpoint. Now unless you're deaf, I suggest you put me on that train and take me to the Ridge, and straight to the team there, so I can finally speak to someone who is not completely incompetent." She looks over her shoulder, at us. "The people we call our employees, I swear."

She sways again.

The soldier lifts his wrist mic. He opens his mouth, is about to speak.

Meadow drops.

Everyone gasps, and because they're soldiers, they instinctively go to help the one in charge. Whether they really believe it's her or not.

It's the chance we need.

We open fire, one round right after the next, until our rifles are smoking.

The Leeches lay dead in a pile.

CHAPTER 61

MEADOW

I drift in and out of consciousness. I hear Zephyr's soft, gentle voice. Sketch's harsh laugh. The train rumbles beneath me, and I know we've made it on.

Sasha's voice comes over a loudspeaker, from the driver's seat. "Settle in, Soldiers," she says. "It's going to be a long ride."

The light of day fades, and the next time I wake, it is dark with night.

I shiver.

Where is the heat of summer? I think of Peri, alone and shivering in the Ridge, on the video that the Commander showed me.

I tell myself she is safe and warm, back on the houseboat in the Shallows. I tell myself none of this ever happened.

Zephyr approaches beside me. A blanket is draped over my legs.

"Try to drink," he says. Water is forced into my mouth. I throw it back up.

I smell blood.

A hand finds mine beneath the blanket. It's strong and warm, and even though I know it's Zephyr's, and I should be mad at him, I hang on. I'm afraid that if I let go, death will come and steal me away.

I hope the General was right to believe in me.

I hope my plan works.

The rumbling of the train beneath my body lulls me back to sleep.

I'm in the ocean.

I'm suspended underwater, and I don't need to breathe.

There's movement, somewhere in the black. And I see my mother.

She swims toward me, her hair splayed out to the sides in the water, and she looks so beautiful. She smiles, just for a moment.

"My Meadow," she whispers.

I reach out to her. I want to take her hand, but there is something solid between us. A wall of glass.

"I need to hear you say it," I whisper to her. "Your apology."

She tilts her head. Opens her mouth, and finally, I'm about to get what I have needed, so desperately, for years.

But blood seeps from her nose. She wipes it away, then gasps, as more pours from it; a stream. It spreads far and wide, until the ocean is crimson. I bang against the glass. I try to get to her, but I can't. She disappears behind a wall of red.

"Mom!" I scream. The glass turns to a mirror.

I stare at myself.

"You'll never make it to the Ridge," my reflection whispers.

"No," I say.

"You won't make it," the reflection says. "Because you left the Shallows. And that means you're already dead."

The glass shatters and pierces my heart.

I wake up screaming.

Hands hold me down, force me to lie still.

"Meadow, calm down!" a voice hisses. The person is wearing Initiative black, and for a moment I forget who he is. I scream, try to rip away from him, because I don't know where I am, and my only rational thought is to get *free*.

"Woodson, get ahold of yourself!" Sketch's voice. *Safe*.

I gasp as memories come rushing back. The rumbling beneath my body, the voices of Sketch and Zephyr, as Sasha drives the stolen train toward the Ridge.

I relax, calm myself.

The weakness has become energy again. The switch, I'll call it. I sit up, look around.

"I'm sorry," I gasp, holding my head. Sketch hands me water. I take soft, slow sips of it, and I'm able to keep it down. No one touches me, and for a time, I sit alone in the train car, watching the world pass me by. I try to hear my father's voice, but I can't reach it. I feel helplessly, horribly alone.

It goes from green to brown, from patches of flat, vast, empty space, grasses swaying in the wind, to suddenly, hills. The hoards of people are ever constant. We shut the doors and lock them, as we pass through the thickest parts of civilization. The train rumbles on, but with it, I hear the cries for help. The voices of the non-dying, wishing that they could.

The world gets colder and colder as we go. Rain pounds the metal, seeps inside through cracks.

The switch happens again, around the time darkness hits. Strength back to weakness, and my head is in Sketch's lap.

She braids my hair, whistles an old Ward song from the Shallows. It is the song Peri used to sing, onboard our houseboat. Hearing the tune brings the memories flooding forth. I sing the words softly:

"Someone save me, I'm falling to darkness.
I met a man in the night who gave me a new start.
Someone save me, I'm losing my sanity.
The man's name was Death and he blackened my heart."

I understand the lyrics now, more than I ever have. Death calls to me from my mother's grave, whispering for me to come close. Threatening me that soon, he will take Peri and Koi and my father, Zephyr and Sketch, too, and I will be the only one left to suffer through this life alone.

My voice trails away, and soon it is just Zephyr and Sketch humming the tune. I close my eyes and let it mix with the sound of thunder in the background. A rumble that sounds like the beating of Death's drums as he comes for me.

"How do you control it?" I ask suddenly.

Sketch stops whistling. She looks down at me. "Control what?"

"The changes," Zephyr says, across from us. He is leaning up against the metal wall of the train, watching me. "She means the changes, from whatever is happening to her."

I nod. "All my life, I've been in control. My father trained me that way." I shiver, and Sketch pulls the blanket tighter up to my chin. "How do you stay sane, when you feel like you can't?"

Sketch shifts her legs beneath me. I can feel her sigh. "You don't control it, Woodson. You just cope."

"There has to be a way," I whisper. "I can't live like this, not knowing when I'm going to switch. Not knowing when I won't even be able to stand on my own two feet."

"I remember when I first met you," Zephyr says suddenly, across from me. I lift my head enough to see the small smile on his face. "You were such a ChumHead, Meadow, you know that? Lying right to my face, saying you didn't know me. But you saved my life. You gave me your blood, and that's the only reason why I'm here."

I listen quietly, lost in the memories of that day. The tube in my arm, going to his, giving him another chance at life.

"I thought I was alone," he says. "I thought I could die, and no one would try to stop me. But *you* did." He leans his head back against the metal again. "And when I lost control, after that, you were always there to help me. And that's what you're missing."

His eyes flick toward mine.

I want to look away, but I force myself not to.

His voice is like music, softening the hardness of my soul.

"You are Meadow Woodson," Zephyr says. "And your entire life, you've been taught that surviving means keeping your distance. It means finding a way to solve things yourself, because you don't trust others. But that's where you're wrong. You're not alone anymore, and you don't have to be. You have me."

"And me," Sketch says.

Zephyr nods. "When you're weak, we'll be there, Meadow. You're not alone in this world, and you never will be again, as long as we're here. And we will be, because you can't get rid of us. We're going to prove to you that love makes us stronger, whether you like it or not."

"Amen, Zero," Sketch says. "A-fluxing-men."

I know I should hate him for killing my mother.

I know I should never want to look into his eyes again.

But Zephyr made a choice. He did what my father would have done, what *I* wasn't strong enough to do. I've killed countless people, sliced a dagger across their throats without stopping to wonder who they were, or what they'd done. But when it came to my own, murderous mother, one of the few people in this world who truly deserved a horrible death . . . I wasn't strong enough.

"I still hate you," I whisper to Zephyr. He goes rigid, but softens when I smile at him. "But you did the right thing. You freed us, Zephyr." I don't thank him, because I'm not ready yet.

But because I don't know what's happening tomorrow, or if we'll survive the Ridge, I set aside my feelings for now. The three of us spend the rest of the night sharing stories, whispering words about the world.

Their voices guide me into sleep, and this time, the nightmares stay far away.

CHAPTER 62

ZEPHYR

In the morning, we see the mountains.

Great pieces of land, stretching high into the sky, so far that their tops disappear into the clouds. The mountains are bigger than anything I've ever seen. It's like nothing can break them.

Not even the Plague, or the Eternity Cure, or the Murder Complex, or anything else from here to hell and back again.

They're amazing. But it's the sunrise over them that really gets me.

It's like liquid fire, spilling into the valleys beneath the peaks, lighting them up with pinks and reds and yellows that come alive.

I know it's the same sun that rises over the Perimeter, back in the Shallows.

But somehow it looks different.

Here it's electric, like the sun is jealous of the intensity of the mountains, so it shines a little brighter to rise above.

Meadow and Sketch sit beside me.

Somewhere up front, Sasha guides the train along. We're nearing the end of the tracks.

Soon we'll be at the Ridge, and we'll have to find a way in. Soon it's going to be hell all over again, and I don't know if Meadow will be alive to go through it with me.

What I do know is this moment is a little piece of heaven. And I'm going to hold on to it until the tracks end, until the train stops.

Until we enter the Ridge.

CHAPTER 63

MEADOW

The closer we get to the Ridge, the fewer people we see. It is as if they can sense the horrors that go on inside there, so they stay far away.

The tracks bend into the woods.

And suddenly the world is full of green. More green than the everglades. That color pales in comparison to these trees.

They tower into the sky, stretching with their needle-like arms, taller than any I have ever seen. They sway as the wind blows, and the deep, natural scent of the woods envelops me, and beyond it, something wet and cold. Red birds flit back and forth from the canopies.

Squirrels leap, rush into hiding as we pass.

For one moment, I feel as if I am inside of a dream. A beautiful fairy tale, from the stories my mother used to tell me, when I was only a girl. I imagine Peri with her hair in braids, her laughter like music as Koi and I chase her through the trees. I imagine my father waiting for us somewhere on the other side, strong and safe and *alive*.

Then in a flash, the trees fade away. The fairy tale disappears like smoke on the wind. The train lurches, then slows down.

We see the Ridge for the very first time.

CHAPTER 64

ZEPHYR

It's a dome.

Bigger than the Catalogue Dome, back in the Shallows.

It's ten times the size, like it holds an entire world inside.
It's just there, right in the middle of the trees, a big circle
of shining metallic gray. So out of place.

"Holy flux," Sketch gasps. "The General didn't think
about telling us this?"

I shrug, look at Meadow. I know she and the General
have a secret. I know she will never tell me what it is. "He
probably didn't tell us a lot of things."

"But we're the idiots going in there!" Sketch hisses.

Meadow is sitting on the floor in between us, with

our shoulders pressed to her sides to prop her up. She's switched back and forth twice. I thought killing the Regulator's computer would stop hurting her, but that can't be the solution. Otherwise she'd be fine by now.

"It's just like going into the Headquarters Building," Meadow says. "We're starting to make a pattern of this, aren't we?"

We watch as the Ridge comes closer, and closer. It looks like it's made of titanium, the same stuff as the Perimeter around the Shallows.

If we even get in . . .

I don't know how we'll ever get *out*.

CHAPTER 65

MEADOW

The tracks come to an end at a building just off to the left of the Ridge.

It's several stories high, perfectly intact.

I run through the plan in my head, forcing myself to remember.

Be your mother. Get inside. Get a look at your surroundings.

They are the General's words, but they come to me in my father's voice, strong and solid, and hearing them makes me feel like a little girl again, wild and windblown from the sea, wanting nothing more than to impress her father by staying alive.. How badly I want to show him that I am the daughter he raised me to be, despite everything I've been through since losing him.

But how can I do this right, when my strength has left me?

I beg it to come back. I beg my body not to betray me, not when I am so, so close.

"You ready for this, Woodson?" Sketch asks me.

We watch the world go from flashes of solid images, to a straight blur.

"I don't know," I hear myself say.

"You have to be," she says. She grabs my hand and squeezes it, so hard that there's a pinch of pain. I gasp, and then smile. She knows what I need, what makes me come back to life when I'm feeling so dead.

We are one hundred yards away.

I can see the door of the Initiative building now.

Sketch and Zephyr help drag me to the piles of blankets and rations. We sit close together, wedge ourselves inside, cover our bodies with as much as we can.

By now, we must be fifty yards away.

Sasha's voice comes over the speaker. "It's been a fun ride, boys and girls," she says. Her voice cracks. "They're filing out of the building. I wish you could see it." She laughs, like she's talking to an old friend. "This is gonna taste so sweet."

Zephyr grabs my hand. I let him hold it. This could be the last moment we ever touch.

Ten yards.

"I imagine I won't be seeing you on the other side," Sasha says. I can hear her breathing quicken, hear the smile that lingers on the edge of her voice.

The train speeds up—a final lurch—as the tracks come to an end.

Sasha doesn't stop. She guns the engine. "Do me a favor?" she asks. "Give 'em hell."

We fly off the end of the tracks, a giant silver bullet aimed at the Initiative building.

CHAPTER 66
ZEPHYR

The world explodes around us.

The train is a roaring beast that's come to life. It screeches and screams, and I can literally *feel* the building tearing apart around us as we crash inside.

Beside me, I feel Sketch and Meadow, jostling around.

I feel a bang against my head, a splash of pain behind my eyes.

The train keeps rolling. Destroying, taking out everything in its path.

And then, as fast as it started, it all stops.

CHAPTER 67
MEADOW

The train stops.

I can't breathe.

I can't think.

Get ahold of yourself. Invite fear into your heart, and then crush it.

My father's voice. I cling to him.

There is commotion, all around. The sound of rubble, falling onto the top of the train. I don't know if Sketch and Zephyr are okay.

I reach out, grab for them.

A hand finds mine, squeezes it.

We're silent.

Voices outside.

Shouts and screams.

I am weak, weaker than I've ever been, and I know that soon the Initiative will come, open the door, and find us.

You'll die soon, my mother's voice calls to me. *You won't even make it halfway, Meadow.*

I shut her out. I refuse to believe her.

The switch happens. My strength comes back to me as a rogue wave.

A split second of weakness, and then, I feel it in the deepest parts of me. Surging forth, until my muscles explode with power.

Right as the door is wrenched open, and Initiative soldiers are staring, wide-eyed, inside the train.

CHAPTER 68

ZEPHYR

Meadow is a blur.

She moves like the wind, a rush of silver and black.

A rifle barrel, aimed at every Leech soldier in her way. She takes four out before I realize I'm supposed to help.

Sketch is alive, and safe, and she's up on her feet, screaming as she shoots.

I can't find my gun.

The supplies are everywhere, spilled like blood. I scramble around, shoving stuff aside, trying to find it. But it's nowhere, and all I can hear is a ringing in my ears as everything explodes around me.

"Clear!" Meadow shouts. I whirl around, see her and

Sketch leap from the destroyed train car, into the building.

"Wait!" I follow after them. Everything is a blur, dust and rubble, bodies broken and ripped open on the floor.

I slip in blood.

Fall onto a body, lying faceup. I get to my feet, run forward, following Meadow's shouts.

There are too many halls. Too many doors.

Too many Leeches.

They take out as many as they can.

Find the exit, find the exit, is all I can think. But there's no chance to find it.

I crash into Meadow's back.

She stands frozen, facing forward, and I realize why when I look up.

Leeches.

Reinforcements, from other parts of the building, aiming their weapons at us. I turn in circles, looking for a way out.

But there's no hope.

We're surrounded on all sides.

CHAPTER 69

MEADOW

I am in a cage that looks like it is meant for an animal.

Zephyr and Sketch are beside me. We are bound, wrists and ankles, with MagnaCuffs. These are impossible to break. Impossible to escape from, without the key. We're in a small white room. Cameras on the ceiling are pointed at us, watching, like eyes.

I wonder if by now, they have contacted the Shallows.

I wonder if they will send us back.

I wonder why I still care.

At some point, my strength disappears again, and I am as weak as ever.

I feel as if I could topple over, with the slightest burst of wind.

"You think they're gonna kill us?" Sketch asks. She slams her boots against the cage.

Again and again, until I want to scream.

It's too loud, too much.

"Would you stop it?" Zephyr snaps at her. "You're acting like a fluxing idiot! Of course they're going to kill us. We just took out half their army with a train!"

"Shut your mouth, Zero, before I shove my boot up your ass!"

They start fighting like children, and our triangle begins to break. We are losing our calm, losing our sanity.

Hours pass.

We're cramped, not able to stand.

I switch again, back to strength, and I want to move, to run, to put my hands around someone's neck and feel it snap like a fresh-fallen twig. I stay quiet and still.

I wait, and I think of the ways I will kill the people who have captured us. I think of the way their hot blood will feel on my hands. I dream of their tortured screams.

I long for revenge.

Finally, the door to the room opens.

A woman dressed in Initiative black marches in.

CHAPTER 70

ZEPHYR

The woman looks strong and courageous, which isn't a good sign.

She's got an angular face, her dark hair pulled back so tight I'm surprised it doesn't rip from her scalp. She looks at us with so much disgust that I know instantly we're all fluxed.

She marches in with two armed Leeches at her sides. One of them pulls up a chair for her, swings it around so it's facing the cage.

The woman sits.

"I am Doctor Jameson," the woman says. "The head scientist in charge here, at the Ridge."

Meadow is still weak beside me. She slumps her head against the bars so she can see the doctor.

Sketch just rolls her eyes, like she's sick of hearing the woman after only a few words.

"Normally, I would kill anyone on sight, for brutally murdering twenty-three of my soldiers, injuring seven others, and destroying years of work in some of my labs. *Years*," Jameson hisses. She crosses her legs, sits straight up in the chair. "But you three don't deserve death. It's too quick. Too final." She looks at us with so much hatred I swear she's going to burst. "I know where you came from, and I know exactly who you are."

"So ship us back to the Shallows already," Sketch says. "We all know that's what you're going to do."

Jameson narrows her eyes. "Did you think you could simply come in here, destroy us all, and walk out with your lives? What are you really here for?"

I don't say a word. Sketch just groans and looks away.

It's Meadow who speaks. "We came to ruin you," she whispers. "Just like we ruined the Shallows."

Jameson's dark eyes meet Meadow's light ones. Together they're two hot flames, out for someone or something to burn.

"The Shallows still stands, despite the death of Lark

Woodson and the Commander." She nods at Meadow. "You are the precious daughter she spoke so highly of when we were in training together. If I didn't support her cause, I'd already have carved you from ear to ear."

Meadow laughs. "You and I both know you can't hurt me."

"No," Jameson says. "But I can hurt your friends."

"I've already been through this, back in the Shallows. Hurt them, hurt me. It's a waste of time. Send us back home and move on with your life."

Jameson stands, paces back and forth. "I would love to send you home," she says. "Especially because you escaped." She stoops to one knee in front of our cage. She's so close I can see the muted brown flecks in her green eyes. "*No one* escapes the Initiative."

Sketch spits at her, then laughs. "We did."

Jameson wipes her face. Then she pulls out her pistol and levels it at Sketch's head.

Suddenly the soldiers rush forward, but Jameson screams an order. They freeze.

"The new Commander has ordered that I send you into the Ridge," Jameson says.

The new Commander?

I hope it's Rhone. I hope he took control, like he said he

would. I hope Dex is there beside him, singing her crazy songs, giggling like the beautiful maniac she is.

"The new Commander is a *fool*." Jameson's eyes go to Meadow. "If you die in there, imagine the waste. I should take out your brain now. I should start my own testing site and use you as my prototype." She growls, runs a hand across her face. "You have put holes in our system. You have *ruined* the order we worked so hard to gain. Don't you understand? We're trying to fix the world. And you're working against us, to break it all over again!"

She throws back her head and screams.

"Doctor." One of the soldiers steps forward, reaches a hand out to her, but she turns and shoots him. I hear his head smack the concrete with a wet squelch of blood and brains.

She turns back to us and kneels, close enough to look Meadow eye to eye. "You were *never* meant to escape the Shallows."

Blood drips from Meadow's nose. She's too weak to move to wipe it away.

"You're dying," Jameson says. "Aren't you?"

Meadow glares at her.

Blood drops. Splatters on the cold floor.

The doctor's lip curls in disgust. "What a waste."

She stands, moves for the door.

"I do hope you enjoy the Ridge. This time, there is no escape. And what you'll find inside, I can assure you, is worse than death. I'd put the new Commander in there myself, if I could."

She marches from the room, slamming the door behind her.

CHAPTER 71

MEADOW

I'm young.

Lying on the bow of the boat beside my mother, the first few weeks we had it.

It's nighttime. The stars are out, and we're staring at the sky, counting the constellations. It amazes me how vast the sky is, even when the world feels so impossibly small.

I close my eyes. Begin to drift away.

I hear my mother's voice whispering, whispering.

"I'm sorry," she says, "for what I've done."

It's a dream, only a dream, and I am too young to understand.

"I will always give you a way out," she says. "Maybe

someday, you'll make the choice to die."

I am nearly gone.

"If you leave here," she whispers, "it will happen. My gift to you, Meadow."

I feel her lips touch my forehead.

Then my dreams whisk me away, beneath the sky and the stars.

PART THREE

THE RIDGE

CHAPTER 72

ZEPHYR

Morning comes like a strike of lightning.

Too fast, and impossible to avoid.

We march down the valley behind the Leech building, skidding on loose gravel and stones, patches of grass.

Every step gets us closer to the Ridge.

Every second gets Meadow nearer to finding her family.

We're almost to the edge of the Ridge when the Night Siren goes off, even though it's morning. But the sound is still the same. It's like the wailing has come right out of my memories, piercing my ears, stabbing my heart.

Meadow stumbles and drops to her knees.

The Leech guards laugh and kick her.

"Get up," they say. "Move."

She's too weak.

Seeing her there, broken on the ground, almost breaks *me*. But then she looks up, and instead of fear or sadness in her eyes, there's the promise of death.

"You're all bastards," Sketch says. "You know that, right? Come on, Woodson."

She helps Meadow up. We put her in between us and practically carry her the rest of the way down the hill.

"I don't need help," Meadow says, but it comes out like a gasp. "If I had my weapons . . ."

Her eyes flick toward me just for a second. "You'll switch again soon," I whisper. "Then you won't need your weapons."

"How long before the switch kills me for good?" she asks. "How long before I'm dead?"

"Don't think like that," I say. "We'll figure it out."

She nods, grits her teeth, and fights like hell to stay on her feet.

From here, I can finally see the Ridge in detail. A giant dome, towering over the world, at least twelve stories high. Probably impossible to break. From here it looks like the top is a thick web of titanium, with just enough spaces to let the sun and rain break through.

There's an outer gate surrounding the dome.

A Perimeter, almost identical to the one in the Shallows. Only this one has coils and loops of barbed wire across the top.

Beyond it all, the mountains look like monsters. They stretch as high as I can see, and somewhere, I can hear roaring water. Almost like the mountains have a voice, and they're warning us.

Stay away.

There are others, making their way from the trees at the base of the valley, heading toward the Ridge, escorted by Leeches. They're chained, like us. Looking scared as hell as the Leeches shove them along, force them to march toward the Perimeter.

"It's going to be okay," I whisper to Meadow and Sketch.

They don't answer. I look up at the Perimeter. Another world full of walls and lies, and whatever else waits for us inside.

I wonder why I ever thought to say it would be okay at all.

CHAPTER 73
MEADOW

We are separated once we get close. Boys left, girls right.

It is like a flashback to the day I got my job as a rations worker.

Two lines. One place to go.

Last time, I was in line to save my family from starvation. This time, I am in line to save them from death.

"Meadow, look at this place," Sketch hisses. I hang on to her, and she holds me up, gasping. She's exhausted, and I am sapping her strength just to stay upright. I grit my teeth, try to force the switch to come, but I can't reach it, don't think it is possible. My body is beyond my control. "There are Leeches, everywhere."

I look up at the top of the black gates that surround the opening. On either side, stationed with guns, are Initiative guards, watching our every move. They march back and forth, probably on a platform behind the barbed wire.

There are also Cams that rise from behind the wall, buzzing about.

Why do they need an extra wall *outside* of the dome? The New Militia will never be able to get us out of here. Even if I send the signal, they could still fail.

One of the Cams dives low, swoops toward us. My instincts tell me to turn my face. Look away. But I force myself to stare.

The line moves slowly forward, and I get a closer look at the entrance.

There are two doorways. One with a male symbol, the other with female, embedded on the front.

There are guards manning the doorways, and a HoloScreen that hangs in between. A woman appears on-screen. She flickers, pale cheeks and white hair. I notice that, like the Initiative guards holding us, she does not have a Catalogue Number. *"Males to the left, females to the right."* She smiles, waves her hands out to both directions. Like we should be pleased to be here.

A boy in shredded clothing stumbles toward the left door. It slides open for him, and he disappears into darkness. The door slides shut. I think I hear him scream, from inside. But maybe it is only my imagination, my fear coming forth in the shadow of this new place. Zephyr is close to the front of the line. He looks at me.

For a moment, I remember the boy he once was, the very first time that I saw him. He was lying broken in a puddle of tears on the floor of the Catalogue Dome.

It would have been easier if we'd never met, if I hadn't placed those crushed white flowers by his side.

But then he nods at me, and his emerald eyes are strong and steady. And I know that without him, I would never have made it here.

Without Zephyr, and Sketch, I would still be on my own.

I'm angry at him. A part of me craves his touch, while the other hates him with a fire that cannot easily be extinguished.

He murdered me, my mother's voice says, in my head. I flinch, shove her ghost away. Focus on what is more important.

Sketch is the first to enter. "You'd better bring that strength back soon, Woodson, because something tells me once we get in there, we're going to need you," she says with a wink. But she looks sad, and I know she's thinking about what we all know to be true. That I'm dying. I'm actually dying. "See you on the other side."

Males to the left, females to the right.

She steps in. The door slides closed. When it opens, only seventy-two seconds later, there is an empty space, a tiny room large enough for one person to stand inside.

The HoloWoman speaks, waves her hands wide.

I step inside, and I am alone.

CHAPTER 74

ZEPHYR

I step into the box.

The door slides shut behind me, and my heart hammers like crazy in my chest.

There's a voice that comes from the walls, the same one as that pale lady whose Holo was out front. *"Please place your left wrist into the designated slot."*

A hole in the wall glows red. I stick my hand inside and wait.

"It is highly advisable not to move."

There are three quick beeps. I feel something solid and heavy snap over my wrist.

"Commence Cataloguing," the voice says.

There's a whirr, and a pinch of pain, like someone's sliced me with a knife.

"Citizen Red. Number P375320. Blood Level—Clean. Please repeat your designated number."

I repeat the number, get it wrong, and have to do it again.

Then, finally, there's a hiss, as the door in front of me starts to open. I pull out my wrist, see the bloodred metal cuff locked around it, the numbers *P375320* inscribed into the metal. There's a small screen on the center of it. A letter *C* appears on it, in bright red.

"Citizen Red, P375320. Operation: The Death Code. Trial Stage: 17." Her voice is happy. Sugary sweet, like Lark's. My cuff blinks bright red, then goes dark again. *"The Initiative thanks you for your service. Welcome to the Ridge."*

A rush of cold air. I take a step out, blinking, as the cold and daylight settle back over me. The door slides shut behind me, locking me in.

And then I get a look at the Ridge, for the very first time.

CHAPTER 75

MEADOW

My strength comes back to me in one solid burst.

I gasp, feel my limbs tingling as energy spills into them.
My head stops spinning. My vision gets clearer, and I
feel as if I could run a hundred miles, fight a thousand
enemies.

The door to the Ridge slides open.

Trees, all around me, as far as I can see.

A forest.

Something about this forest feels different from the
palms that lined the beach in the Shallows. There, death
was around each corner, its whisper calling to me as I
made my way into the city.

But here, everything feels like it is alive. I get the shivery feeling that I am being *watched*. I wheel around, looking overhead and behind me. There is no one here, just me and the trees, Sketch and Zephyr standing in front of me, staring at this new world. I force myself to relax. To *think*.

I expected a city. Destruction. Initiative guards, ushering us inside, rifles in our faces.

This is different.

This gives me the illusion of freedom, and that unsettles me the most.

I turn in circles. Behind us, the wall towers like a dark demon, its arms spreading far and wide. I look up, and instead of sky, I see only metal. Solid and impenetrable.

We've come in.

There is no going back out.

I look down at the red cuff locked on my wrist, the letter *C* a bright, blood red on its screen. Sketch's and Zephyr's are the same.

"I'm guessing you both heard the message?" I ask.

Zephyr nods. "The Death Code. What the hell does that mean?"

"It means what the General told us it means," Sketch says, with a hiss. "It means they're going to try to find a way to kill us, without putting their hands on us at all." She nods at me. "You look better. Back to the old Meadow again?"

"No," I say. "The new Meadow. The old one died a long time ago."

The door in the wall behind us opens. A girl with a yellow cuff steps into the woods. I see the same letter *C* on her screen.

"Hey!" Sketch says.

The girl spins. Her eyes widen when she sees us, and she turns and runs, fading into the trees.

"Fine, run away!" Sketch yells after the girl. She turns to me. "We didn't want her anyways. Idiot."

A shrill cry sounds from above. I duck down to the ground on instinct and reach for the dagger at my thigh that is no longer there.

Zephyr sighs. "Meadow. It's okay. Look."

He points up at the trees over our heads. Perched atop a branch is a large brown bird, staring down at us with one beady green eye.

The bird opens its mouth once and makes a strange clipped sound, then pushes off the tree branch. Its long wings make huge strokes as it disappears into the forest. I watch in awe for a while, desperately wishing I had wings like that bird.

I could soar high.

See my family from above. Find a way to give the New Militia the signal that much faster and get us all away from here.

"We should move," I say. "Find out where everyone is."

"And water," Zephyr says. "I'm dried up like a corpse."

"Really?" Sketch groans, clutching her stomach. "You're disgusting, Zero."

I forge ahead, leaving them to follow.

They argue like children.

We walk for a while, weaving through the forest. Every so often, I stop, listen for noises in the woods. There are voices, far off. I think I hear the trickle of running water, but I can't see it.

The world is one shade, and my eyes hurt from all of the green. "We have to find weapons."

Zephyr and Sketch are shoving each other like kids. She pushes him against a tree, and he tackles her to the ground, cursing while she laughs. It reminds me of Koi and me, fighting on the houseboat, tackling each other overboard into the waves. It reminds me of Peri, how I used to tickle her above her hips, and her bright laughter shattered the darkness of night.

The memories bring on the pain, and suddenly I have

to get away, *do* something productive, before I lose myself to the madness of missing them.

I pick the tallest tree and climb. Branch over branch, hands and feet on solid bark, until I'm at the highest point before the tree threatens to bend.

The forest around me is endless. Trees stretch on for as far as I can see, a line of green and brown like sturdy Initiative guards placed throughout the forest. A thin ribbon of silver snakes its way through them.

"Water!" I yell. "North."

I stay there only for a moment, reveling in the feel of the wind lightly kissing my cheeks. The domed ceiling is far, far overhead. There is no way we could ever reach the top to escape.

The New Militia, and me sending the signal, are the only options. I touch my fingertip to the small protrusion on my inner wrist, given to me by the Commander when we spoke in private.

I pray that no one notices it.

I climb back down, turn to Zephyr and Sketch. They are both bleeding, him with a puffy lip, her with a slit eyebrow. "If you two are done wasting time, we should keep moving."

"Relax, Meadow." Zephyr reaches for my hand. "We're

just having some fun."

"There is never any time for fun," I hiss, and back away. "Especially not now. My family is here somewhere. We have seventy-two hours to find them and give the signal."

"And we will," Zephyr says, his eyes flashing an angry emerald.

Something clicks beneath his boot.

"Stop," I whisper, holding up my hands, as I realize what's about to happen. "Zephyr. Don't move."

CHAPTER 76

ZEPHYR

There's one click, like the sound of a bullet sliding into a chamber. I take a step right as Meadow tells me not to.

And then the world's gone all wrong. Lopsided.

Something tugs at my left ankle. My head slams the ground, and before I realize what's happened, I'm dangling in the air, blood dripping from my mouth and into my hair.

"What the hell was that?" Sketch screams.

Her face is even with mine.

Meadow moves fast, searching for something to get me down with.

But there's nothing. She doesn't have her dagger, and

Sketch and I are just as empty.

There's a crack in the trees behind us. Meadow whirls, fists clenched. I'm spinning slowly, the cord on my ankle waving me in the wind.

One spin. I see movement in the trees. "There's someone out there," I say.

Another spin.

"Get him!" Meadow screams. She dives, but I can't see who she's after, because I'm spinning again.

"What's happening?" I yell. No one answers. I hear grunts. A person cries out in pain, and I don't know who it is. "MEADOW! SKETCH!"

A third spin, and I'm praying to the stars that they're okay.

The rope turns me back around.

And I'm facing Meadow and Sketch again. Only this time there's another person. A dirt-faced boy, and they've got him tackled to the ground, his cheek pressed up against the snow.

"I wasn't gonna do nothing'!" he screams. "Swear it!"

"You'll shut your damn mouth if you know what's good for you," Sketch says.

"Take his knife," Meadow cuts in. "Get Zephyr down."

I spin again, missing the scene, but just before I spin

back, I see Sketch's face.

"No, Sketch, wait!" I yell.

She slices the rope. I drop and land on my face.

"Ugh," I groan, sitting up, spitting out dirt. "Thanks, I guess."

"Don't say I didn't warn you." Sketch laughs.

"You *didn't* warn me!"

My head throbs and I feel dizzy, as blood rushes back where it belongs. But I finally get a clear look at the kid whose trap I triggered. He looks like a Ward, a younger version of me. He's got dark hair, matted to his head in thick, crusty knots. He looks like he hasn't bathed a day in his life.

But that's not the worst part.

It's his body.

He's covered, from his neck down to his bare arms and legs, in boils. They ooze green. One of them pops on his neck, and Sketch backs away, disgusted.

"What the hell's wrong with you?" she asks.

The boy struggles under Meadow's grasp, but she's too strong for him. "Let me up. Do it, 'fore Scout comes for ya."

"He's just a kid, Meadow," I say. A kid covered in some nasty stuff that I don't want her touching. "Let him up."

He wears a green cuff on his wrist, scuffed and scratched. The screen has a number 37 on it. There is no Catalogue Number on his head. He stares at us like *we* are the aliens, but he's the one who looks like he came from another world.

"If you run, I'll catch you," Meadow says to him. He nods, whimpering. "Now just tell me where everyone else is, and I won't hurt you."

"Okay." The kid nods. "Just let me go, please."

Meadow sets him free.

He leaps to his feet. He tries to take the knife back from Sketch, but she lifts it too high.

"You'll pay for this," the kid says.

Then he does the one thing he shouldn't have.

He turns and sprints into the trees.

Meadow laughs under her breath. "That's exactly what I hoped he would do. Come on."

She takes the knife from Sketch, then sprints after him, silent as a predator as she follows his trail.

CHAPTER 77

MEADOW

The boy runs fast, dodging in and out of trees with an animal-like swiftness.

He is well practiced at this, and he knows this land.

But I was trained by my father. Trained to run faster, harder, than anyone in the Shallows. With my strength back, I can make my father proud and be the fighter he always pushed me to be. I don't know how much time I have left. I want to make every single second count.

I stay far enough away that the boy has the illusion of safety. Because I want him to lead me to his home. As I run, I can see things that don't seem right. A splash of blood on a tree trunk. A crumpled bundle lying in a pile of sticks and leaves. A broken shell of an Initiative Cam. I scoop up a curved, sharp piece, tuck it into my belt loop to use as another weapon.

Behind me, I can hear Zephyr and Sketch calling my name, begging me to stop. They'll catch up soon enough.

The boy leaps, cutting across a river that runs through the forest, the same one I saw from my vantage point in the tree. My throat is dry, and everything in me begs for me to stop and drink from it. But I have to keep going. Keep following.

Soon a massive rock formation comes into view, like a small version of the giant mountains outside the Ridge. It is circular, almost like a Perimeter of its own.

I duck behind a fat tree, slide close to the trunk so the boy can't see me.

When I peer back out, I see him smile. He thinks he's lost me. A boil on his face pops, dripping a horrible, purplish-black liquid, and my stomach lurches. He drops to hands and knees and sweeps aside a curtain of tangled vines, then disappears into a small opening in the rock wall.

Zephyr comes up behind me. "Meadow!" he yells, but I whirl, put my hand over his mouth to silence him, slam him up against the tree.

"Just like old times," he whispers, grinning.

"Would you just shut up?" I sigh, then point at the top of the rock formation. Smoke trails into the air. It isn't black, a sign that at least, hopefully, they aren't cannibals like on the Outside.

With smoke comes the promise of people.

Food.

Answers. So far, we have been the only ones with Catalogue Numbers. Which means that the only others in here with them will be my family. The citizens of the Ridge will remember if they've seen them.

"Ladies first," Sketch whispers, as she comes up behind us. She nudges Zephyr in the back. "That would be you, Zero."

"I swear to the stars, Sketch . . ." he says, but I hold up a hand to cut him off.

"Go."

He sighs, then steps into the clearing, drops to hands and knees, and disappears through the vines and into the rocks.

CHAPTER 78

ZEPHYR

I duck into the opening.

The space is way too small for me, so I have to turn sideways to slide through.

And then I get stuck.

I can't see what's happening on the inside of the rock fortress, but Sketch is coming up behind me.

"Go, Zero," she whispers. She nudges me.

"Hang on," I hiss. "I'm stuck!"

And I don't want to go any farther. Because there are voices coming from inside the rocks. Lots of them.

"Stop being such a whiny ChumHead," Sketch says. And then she shoves me, hard.

I fall forward, my face scraping against the rocks. And land right on the edge of a crowd of people. They turn to look at me, at least twenty of them.

Their eyes go first to my wrist. See the red of my cuff, the *C* on the screen.

Theirs are all green, with numbers.

And something tells me that's not good.

CHAPTER 79

MEADOW

Zephyr has fallen right into the entrance of a camp.

It's a large circular clearing, surrounded entirely by tall boulders. A fire blazes in the center, people surrounding it, and all of their eyes are on us.

Zephyr stands up, scurries to my side.

"Way to go, skitzface," Sketch mutters.

Overhead, at the tops of the boulders, the forest starts back up again and the trees are linked together by sharp hooked wires that make a tall fence.

It is a good home, a solid place to stay.

But the people who own it look like savages, like an army of the living dead.

My eyes fall on a young boy by the fire. He has what almost looks like an extra arm sticking out of his side. The others are just as bad.

I see a woman across the bonfire, her face strangely swollen and covered in a mask of angry red boils. An older man lying on the ground close to the fire, one of his arms with thick, rippling muscles, the other arm limp and atrophied.

The General was right about the Ridge.

The people here are mutated. Destroyed.

Horrific, like they have stepped out of a nightmare, come to life. As soon as we can, I will send the signal to him, the one we talked about in whispers, when everyone was asleep, the night before we left to come here.

I take a few steps backward into Sketch.

The people here all wear green cuffs. They look at ours. Red.

Out of place here.

"That's them!" the boy shouts, the one I followed. "Caught 'em right by the entrance. Told you they'd follow me."

When they see us, our faces fresh and clean, our Catalogue Numbers on our foreheads, our clothing unworn, they stare hungrily.

Hatred is a tangible thing, and when I face a predator, I can sense it.

But these people don't look like predators, or fighters. They look weak, and broken.

And starving.

"Who are you?" I ask.

"Reds, huh?" A man rises from the crowd. "Welcome to the Rock."

He has long, muscular arms. And scars littering his entire face. They look like burns, twisting his skin, bubbling up in places, the same way Sparrow's face was. His dark hair hangs in mats down to his shoulders, and as he stands, the crowd watches his every move.

He is definitely their leader.

"What happened to you?" I ask. "All of you?"

"What? There somethin' wrong with the way we look, Cleanie?" The man rounds the side of the bonfire. He looks like a character out of my nightmares. As he gets closer, I see the tears in his clothing. The skin beneath is scarred, too. His entire body is covered, as if he was thrown to a fire, or burned with acid.

He steps up to me and looks me over. Zephyr slides in front of me, arms crossed. I roll my eyes. I can take care of myself. For now.

"What do we have here?" The leader holds out a filthy scarred hand, like he's going to touch Zephyr's Catalogue Number.

But I dive, grab the man's wrist, and twist it backward. I hold it until it's about to snap.

"No one touches us," I say. "We came for answers. Nothing more."

The man smiles, but there is darkness in his eyes. "Easy, now," he says. "You came to us, Cleanie."

"What does that mean?" I ask.

He laughs, but it comes out like a wheeze. "It means you just got here, that's what it means. Letter *C*s, on your cuffs? Clean blood. They ain't got to you. Yet."

I let his wrist go.

He staggers backward, still staring at my Catalogue Number. "We've seen others like you. Things are changing here." He looks back, at his people. They watch with wide eyes, as if they are afraid. "Tell us, Reds. Where did you come from? Why did they send you here?"

"Tell us where the others like us are staying," I say instead. "A trade of information."

His voice crackles like the fire. "Look around you. This place ain't much, but it's home. And when a guest enters a home, it's customary to bring a gift." He looks over his shoulder again. Some of his people stand.

I take another step back.

"Now, Cleanies. What do you have to offer us? Give us a gift, and you can stay the night. There are bad colors out there. Blues and yellows and purples, and more. But we're Greens. We're the good guys, and we can be friends, if you give us a reason to be."

"We have nothing for you," Sketch says.

But the man has other ideas. "Your coats," he says. "Your boots." He nods at the knife in my hand. "And the boy's knife you stole. He'll be needing that back."

"No," I say, wrapping my coat tighter around myself, pulling the knife flat against my chest. I have a flash of a memory, standing on the beach with Peri, when the Pirates made us give up her shoelaces. "These are ours."

He whistles. Two men stand, the one with the muscular arm, and one with bloodred eyes. They cross behind us, and others join, making a circle. Blocking out the exit tunnel. I start to move, ready to fight my way out.

But suddenly sweat beads on my brow. I sway on my feet.

The switch is coming again. Soon I will be useless.

"You understand, I have people to look after," the leader says, and spits blood on the ground. "We won't hurt you.

We just want what you have. The nights are cold. You find your Reds, and they'll take care of you, same as Greens look after Greens. That's the way it works here, Cleanie. But for now . . ."

He motions for his men to move for us.

I clench my fists, beg myself to just *hang on* until we're out of here. My nose drips. Fresh blood.

And then there's a noise in the distance.

A whirring sound, coming from afar.

The men freeze. They glance at their leader. All around, everyone starts murmuring. Children start to cry. Women shush them and pull them close.

"Scout, they're coming," the woman says. "Help us."

"Stay calm," the leader says. "Remember. *Don't. Move.*" The people huddle together, leaving the entrance open and free. Their leader looks at us, and winks. "You got off easy. I'd say you're lucky, Cleanies, but . . ." hHe glances at the sky, and for the first time, I see fear in his eyes. "The Biters are here."

The buzzing grows louder and louder.

"Meadow," Zephyr says, and he tugs at my shirt, tries to pull me back. "Meadow, let's go."

But I'm frozen. I can't move.

Curiosity tugs at me, and I have to *know.* Have to see

for myself what we are up against.

The buzzing intensifies, and I can almost feel it in my bones.

A wave of giant, black winged insects soars over the top of the fortress, blocking out the sky. It's like the world freezes, as I look up at hundreds, thousands of them, buzzing as loud as the Night Siren wails. They look like mosquitos, nearly as large as my hand. *Biters.*

"Well, flux me," Sketch says.

The world snaps back into the present. Biters dive downward, an army poised for the attack, and the Greens erupt into a chorus of screams.

CHAPTER 80
ZEPHYR

My instincts take over.

I dive for the tunnel, pulling Meadow and Sketch with me. I shove Meadow through first, and she scurries inside. Sketch goes next, and I'm about to race after them when something stabs me in the neck.

I scream.

Pain, worse than anything I've ever felt before, like I've just been struck with a white-hot fire poker. I slap the Biter, and it squelches against my palm. An explosion of blood and black goo on my skin.

"Zero!" Sketch yells.

She yanks me in after them.

I fall to hands and knees, and then Sketch is ripping off her jacket, shoving it into the gap behind us. Meadow and I follow suit, and in seconds we've covered the entrance to the Ridge as best we can. Behind the barrier, I can hear the Greens screaming, the constant buzzing of the Biters.

"What the hell were those things?" Sketch asks.

In the darkness, we're crammed together, breathing hard, listening as the screams and the buzzing fade.

"I don't know," I whisper, as silence comes. The throbbing on my neck fades, but now I swear I can feel something running through me. Like there's poison in my veins. "But I think one bit me."

I barely have the words out before there's a strange, speckling in my vision.

Then it goes dark.

"What just happened?" I whisper. "Where'd the light go?"

I feel someone shift beside me.

"Zephyr . . ." It's Meadow's voice. "It's not dark."

"Yes it is," I say. I wave my hands in front of my face, but I can't see anything at all. Only pure oil black, darker than a starless sky.

"No, Zero," Sketch says. "It's not."

"I can't see," I whisper.

It's then that it hits me.

I think I've just gone blind.

CHAPTER 81

MEADOW

This is impossible.

Zephyr was fine, seconds ago, and now he is blind. His cuff changes. The letter *C* becomes a number 47.

I tell myself to stay calm, to stay in control. It is what my father would do, and probably has done, since coming to the Ridge. There is always an explanation for everything, and once I find my father, he will explain this to us.

But this is my fault. This wouldn't have happened to Zephyr if he had just *stayed away from me*.

We crawl from the tunnel, and once we're out, I get a good look at Zephyr's neck for the first time.

The bite is large, a red welt, already leaking white pus. Black streaks spread out from the center of the bite, as if something has seeped into his veins. Poison.

"I can't see," he keeps saying, over and over. His cuff moves to a 53.

"Stop freaking out!" Sketch says.

"I can't SEE!" Zephyr screams. He is tearing at his eyes with his fingers, drawing streaks of blood on his face. "What the hell is happening to me?"

"Zero, calm down!" Sketch yells, but he is beyond consoling, and we are losing him.

So I slap him, as hard as I can, across the face.

He freezes. His cheek is red, with an imprint of the back of my hand.

"Did you just *backhand* me, Meadow?" he gasps.

"Someone had to!" I nod, but then I remember he can't see it. "If I didn't do it, Sketch would have. Now take a deep breath and get ahold of yourself. We need to find shelter, in case those things come back."

I take his hand. Sketch takes his other, and we walk in a chain, telling him when to step over fallen logs and tree roots that could make him stumble.

The switch is coming fast. I can feel it as sure as I can see the poison in Zephyr's veins.

"Where do we go?" Sketch asks. For some reason, she is whispering.

"I don't know," I say. I look at Zephyr, see the fear in his blind eyes. "I don't know anything."

We walk until we reach the stream again.

"We should follow this," I say. "Someone will have made camp near the water."

Zephyr keeps his mouth shut and does not say a word, but I can practically feel the panic seeping off of him in waves. He is drowning in fear.

He clutches my hand like a vise. We move slow, steady. Then I hear a snap.

We freeze.

"It came from above," Zephyr whispers.

"Keep moving," I say. We walk slowly, carrying on, and as we go, I use my free hand to reach for the knife at my waistband. Another snap.

I look up, slowly, as if I am simply searching the world.

And that is when I see the flash of yellow overhead, almost concealed in camouflage. Almost, but not all the way. It is on the wrist of a person who holds a wooden bow.

The arrow is aimed right at Sketch.

"Duck!" I scream. Sketch and Zephyr drop, and I

launch the knife without thinking.

It hits true, rocketing through the branches overhead, and hits the person in the arm. The body falls, crashes to the forest floor in a heap.

The person screams, rips out the knife, and throws it to the side. Their face is covered in a mask of green, so I can't tell if it is a boy or a girl. All I know is that they are the enemy.

I dive.

We both go down together. I land a punch to the face, then another to the neck, before I'm flipped over, and the enemy is on top. We spar, and Sketch is screaming, and Zephyr is shouting, asking what is going on, but I don't care about any of it.

Because I realize the motions of this fight feel as natural as breathing. It is neck and neck, as if we have been competing for the win our entire lives.

I gasp. I freeze, when I see the strong, scarred forearms of the person that is holding me. The silvery hair, hanging to his shoulders, tangled and knotted, but so, so familiar. The strong hands, both for fighting and carving and bringing images to life.

"Koi," I gasp again. "Koi, it's me. It's me."

"M-Meadow?" He reaches up, moves his camouflaged

mask away, and I finally see his face.

The sob that comes from my lips is instantaneous.

It is my brother.

He is just as I remember him. Strength and softness, all tangled into one. The only difference is that he now has oozing scabs mixed in with his sparring scars, gentle drips of blood that coat his skin. But I don't care. He is *here*.

We stand up to face each other.

I launch myself into his arms.

"Meadow," he whispers, and we are both crying, holding each other so tight that I dare the world to try and rip us apart. I tell him about our mother, and he holds me tighter. Whispers that it's okay, that it wasn't my fault, that she was already dead to us both.

"I found you," I breathe. "I found you."

"You came for us," he says. He pulls back to look at me, holds my face in his hands. His fingertips tug at the short, light strands of my chin-length curls. "You cut your hair?"

It is such a normal, stupid question, that I laugh, and then I can't stop laughing, because he is here. My brother is with me, after so, so long. "The Initiative did it," I whisper. I turn, so that he can see the Regulator.

He gasps.

"They . . . they did lots of things," I say, but I can't finish the sentence, because suddenly an image of two other faces appears in my mind. "Dad?" I whisper. Terrified of the answer he might give me. "Peri?"

Koi sniffs, shakes his head. "Dad's with me, back at camp. But Peri . . ."

"She's not dead," I say. "She can't be."

"No," he says. "God, no, but . . . we haven't found her yet, Meadow. The Ridge is a massive place. But we will. I promise, we're looking every day. I'm so sorry."

Pain streaks through me.

And then the switch hits. In one instant I lose all my strength. My knees buckle, but Koi holds me up, wraps me tighter in his arms before I can fall.

"What's happening?" he asks. "What's wrong with her? Was it the fog? The Biters? The needles?" He checks my cuff.

There is an 89 on the screen.

"That's one of the highest number's I've ever seen," he gasps. "I'm going to ask you again. What. Happened. To. Her?"

"Nothing!" Sketch says as she steps forward. Zephyr clutches onto her like a child. "I swear it, nothing happened. We ran from Biters, and Zero got bit. Not Meadow. And we haven't run into anything else."

"Did you drink the water?" Koi asks.

"No," Sketch says. She's frowning at me like I am on my deathbed, and I hate it. I want her to stop. I want to be strong again. "It's a long story," she says. "She just needs to rest."

"We'll go back to camp," Koi says. He holds me tighter, and he smells different, but he *feels* the same. "For now, let's be happy," he says. "My sister is here, alive and well. And that's reason enough for me."

My tears mix with his. Our cuffs clink together, red and yellow. He smiles again, but I can see through it.

I see the fear in his eyes, clear as glass, as he carries me across the Ridge.

It would be worse if he knew the truth.

CHAPTER 82

ZEPHYR

My vision comes back after we've walked for an hour.

"I can see," I gasp. Patches of light trickle in. Then shadows and light together, and then it all comes bursting back in one sudden sweep. "I can see!" I scream.

I reach back and touch the welt on my neck.

But it's not there anymore. My cuff changes, from the new number 53, to a 27.

Then, gradually, it drops in numbers until it's back at the letter C.

Meadow's brother looks back over his shoulder. "Biters got you, right?"

I nod, more confused than I've ever been.

"You won't heal so fast after a while," Koi says. "They carry something in their blood. A disease, or poison, whatever it is. Causes blindness. There's a guy back at camp, Abram. He's lost his sight for good. But he's still alive." He looks at the sky. "No one has died yet, no matter what they've thrown at us. Death is impossible. Our mother made sure of that."

I don't tell him that I'm the one who killed Lark.

That when my arrow nailed her in the chest, I smiled and felt a million times lighter inside.

Meadow nestles against her brother. She groans, and Koi looks down at her and moves her hair back from her face, wipes a drop of blood from under her nose.

She smiles, and damn, it lights up the world.

I haven't seen Meadow smile like this . . .

Ever.

Not even the night I found her. After so long, we were together again. Our kisses, our hearts. Then I told her about killing Lark and . . . I feel worse than a Leech for thinking it. But I'm actually jealous right now.

I'm happy for her. I am. But the happiness doesn't feel good.

I flinch when Sketch puts her arm around my shoulders. "Don't look so grim, Zero," she whispers. "She's not gonna kick you out now that she's found her brother.

There's still room for you in that black heart of hers. Deep, deep down."

I hadn't planned for this, hadn't realized we'd actually find them. Most of the time I've known Meadow, it's been the two of us. I've been her family. I've been her friend.

And now that we've found Koi . . .

"I just need a second," I say.

"Right, okay. Now shut up and let me hold you."

Normally I'd shove Sketch away.

But she looks the same way I do. A little hurt, a little broken, watching Meadow with her brother. "You're thinking about your sister," I whisper.

"We already talked about this. Do we have to bring it up again?"

Sketch and Meadow held on to each other in that jail cell in the Leech building. They kept each other alive. And now Sketch is just as connected to Meadow as I am, in her own way.

"No," I say. "You're right. I'm sorry."

"You're annoying me," Sketch says.

But then she laughs and punches me in the arm.

"You hit like a man," I say.

"And you cry like a girl, but I'm not judging," she says back.

We follow Koi and Meadow deeper into the woods.

CHAPTER 83

MEADOW

Koi carries me until he can't anymore. The number on my cuff rises to a 90.

He walks faster, breathes harder.

I keep my eyes on him the entire time. Afraid that if I blink, he'll fade away. Afraid that this is all a dream, something my consciousness has made up to fool me. A parting gift from my mother's ghost. Maybe she is snickering from the grave.

Maybe I will wake up in my cell, with the Interrogator standing over me, ready to draw blood all over again.

Maybe none of this is real. Laughter escapes my lips.

The wind blows, and I shiver, teeth chattering, fingers

trembling, and it reminds me that this is *real*. That I've found my brother, and now, Koi is leading me back to my father. I swallow the craziness back, hold it deep down inside of me.

We're halfway to whatever camp Koi has, when a dark-skinned boy appears from the trees. He moves like the wind, swift and steady and silent as death. I shout a warning, but Koi greets him.

"Saxon," Koi says, turning to look at the boy. "He's with me. It's okay."

"Well, son of a Scumbag." Saxon whistles. "Your sister?" He rubs his hands over his face. I see his fingernails are missing. "'Course she's your sister. She looks just like you. How'd you find her?"

Saxon is taller than most, his body lean and muscular. He walks by our side, with a hand-carved bow slung over his shoulder. His feet are bare, and they are missing the nails, too.

"I guess she came for me," Koi says. "Just like I knew she would." He hoists me up higher, shows Saxon the 90 on my cuff.

Saxon's eyebrows rise to his hairline. He whistles and shakes his head. "What got her so bad? On day one? There's no good luck here, is there?"

"Nothing did," Koi says. "Nothing that they know, at least."

He changes the subject and explains what happened to him when he arrived in the Ridge. "I don't remember much at all. I was in a train, cuffed, blindfolded. When I started to wake, they stuck me with something, and I went out cold again. I remember waking up, freezing. Feeling like I was in another world. Then I woke up here, with this damn cuff on my wrist," Koi says, stepping over a fallen log. "Spent a few days stumbling around. I nearly had my heart cut out by some Oranges in the West End."

A rat skitters past, and Saxon moves, lightning quick, knocking an arrow onto his bow.

He shoots the animal in the eye. A perfect shot.

My father would be proud.

"Dad found me," Koi says, "and then Saxon found us."

"Crazy bastards, those two," Saxon says, scooping up the rat. "Good additions to our group. And if you're anything like them," he says to me, smiling with several missing teeth, "then I imagine the rest of the Yellows'll let you stay. Normally we don't take in other colors. It's not the way of the Ridge. But your family's changing things. Lots of things."

I focus back on Koi. It's hard to talk. My strength is waning, and all I want to do is sleep.

"What's with the Cuffs?" Zephyr asks. "The colors?"

"Tribes," Koi explains. "You get a color, and that's your tribe. The number on your cuff, there, that's your . . . health level, is all we can describe it as. Dad thinks the whole operation is another sort of experiment, like the Shallows. Every day, there's different trials. Sometimes it's poison gas. Sometimes, the Biters come, and they're full of nasty poison and diseases, all sorts of stuff." He nods at Zephyr. "Blindness is a common side effect of being bitten. Then there are the needles. Those come from the sky. And the water's laced with something. The animals, too. You can taste it."

"The cuffs," Saxon says. "They've got some kind of blood reader in them. When someone gets sick, their numbers go up. They heal, the number goes back down." He lifts his cuff. There is a 29 on the screen. "No one's ever made it to 100. That's the final number."

I look down at the 91 on my cuff. The bleeding scabs on my brother, the missing nails and teeth on Saxon. I think of all the Greens, how afraid they looked. How *sick*.

"We have to find Peri," I say.

"We will," Koi says.

I'm so disgusted, thinking of her all alone in this world, that I hardly notice it when the switch comes again.

My cuff goes back to a letter *C*.

CHAPTER 84

ZEPHYR

We reach the waterfall by the time the sun starts to set.

It's a monstrous being, a huge force of water that pounds down on a deep pool beneath it. The sound is like a roaring giant.

"I've never seen one of these," Meadow says beside me, staring up at the top. She's standing again, back to her normal, stronger self. "Peri would have wanted to see this."

"She will," I say. I want to take her hand and squeeze it. Instead, I just stare and hope she can sense the sadness in me.

She gives me a smile that doesn't seem real. "I know."

"All right, let's move," Saxon calls out from the front of the group. He leads us to the waterfall, down a slope of massive slippery rocks. We climb down, one at a time, and when we hit the bottom, we're so close to the falls that I can feel the freezing water spraying on my face.

It's hell.

"I miss the beach," I hear Sketch groan over the roar of the water.

I never thought I'd say it. But I do, too.

"Dad won't believe his eyes when he sees you, Meadow," Koi says, looking at the sky. It's light pink, the color of raw fish. "No telling what he'll say when he sees Patient Zero with you."

He gives me that same ridiculous glare he always has. He hates me, still thinks of me as the guy who tried to kill his sister. His mother's creation. But I don't give a damn. I'm learning it's easier not to care what people think of me.

The waterfall is built into the side of a cliff. "Swim down, under the falls, up the other side. There's a cave back there. Hidden. Good place for the Yellows to hide."

"You mean we're going *in* that godforsaken pool?" Sketch squawks like a gull.

Saxon laughs. "Unless you'd rather stay out here and

face whatever Colors come this way alone . . . not to mention the Needles. They'll be dropping soon."

Sketch glares.

"I'll go first," Meadow says.

I want to tell her to be careful. That if something happens to her, if she switches while she's under the water and isn't strong enough to fight to the surface, I don't know what I'll do with myself.

But it's like having Koi again has replaced a tiny fragment of her old self. She's fearless as she stomps forward, takes a deep breath, and dives into the water.

CHAPTER 85

MEADOW

My father taught me how to swim almost as soon as I could walk.

The water is like home to me.

A peaceful, safe place, away from the world, away from the threat of murder.

But this water is not the same. I dive, and it feels like knives are stabbing me. Every inch of my skin, seeping into my pores. Strangling me. With my eyes open, I can see my skin reacting. Reddening, to whatever the Initiative has laced this water with.

But I think of my father.

He is on the other side of the falls.

And I would go through hell and back to get to him.

I swim down, my head feeling like it might explode from the pressure.

My father tied weights to my legs. He made me swim with my arms.

My father blindfolded me. He made me find my way to shore, and had faith that I wouldn't drown.

My body is ice. It is almost impossible to haul myself up and out, and the pain is enough to make me gasp when my cheek hits dry land.

Sketch comes up behind me, pulls her body into the cave.

"Son of a Leech-loving ChumHead!" she screams, and I laugh through the pain, as the others emerge behind her.

We are inside of a small cave, surrounded on all sides by grimy, rocky walls that make a dome over our heads. It smells like earth. The falls barrel down behind me, covering the entrance, glittering blue with the light of day.

It is strange, how the beauty of this world begs to be seen. Even in the darkest, most dangerous places, it shines through.

Saxon points at a pile of blankets, folded neatly in the

corner of the cave. "Frostbite is nasty business," he says. "Get warm, and let's move."

Zephyr wraps a blanket around me before he wraps himself. He is selfless and loving.

And yet when he looks at me, I see a darkness in his eyes that reminds me too much of my own.

"Zephyr," I say. "Look, if you want to talk about everything some more—"

"I'm fine," he cuts me off. Then he sighs, runs a hand over the back of his neck. "I just need some time, Meadow."

He turns and heads away, following the others down an earthen tunnel.

I follow his shadow into the darkness.

My father is on the other side of it.

And that thought, the image of his face, and the pride in his eyes when he sees me, warms me more than the blanket ever could.

CHAPTER 86

ZEPHYR

The tunnel leads us upward for too long.

There's no way this could have been made by the earth. The walls are perfectly round and polished.

"The Ridge used to be a big mining place before the Fall," Koi says. I can't see him, but his voice echoes back, bounding through the darkness. "Abram, one of the oldest guys we've got, used to live here. He refused to move when they built the Ridge, so they built it up right around him. He knows everything there is to know about this place."

I feel my way along, moving forward.

"My thighs are burning," Sketch groans.

She never shuts up. She's Talan, but she's a whole hell of a lot worse. And it hurts, thinking of Talan.

Would Talan have come with me, to the Ridge?

I know the answer already. To everyone else, Talan seemed selfish, and broken, but I knew the truth. She was loyal as hell. She would've followed me to the ends of the earth. She *did* follow me, all the way into the Headquarters building.

Right into death. I wonder if the tables were turned, would Meadow follow me?

Would she risk everything, even her freedom?

Stop whining. I can hear Talan's gravelly voice in my memories, coming back. *Just shut up, Zeph, be a man, and get over it. You chose this. You went after her.*

I shake Talan's voice away.

Finally, just when my back muscles are screaming, the tunnel widens.

There's a door, handmade, standing right there in the wall. Two torches hang beside it, throwing light around the small space. Koi knocks three times, followed by two quick staccato beats. I hear a loud bang, then a muffled curse. The door swings open. A pool of orange light shines out.

A dark face stares at us, a tall wavy-haired man with

what looks like a permanent question in his eyes. They're a strange, milky white.

"Who's knocking this early? Not even light yet, is it?" He's looking a little to the right of us. "I can hear your breathing, there's three of you there!"

Saxon chuckles and snaps his fingers, and the man whips his head toward the sound.

"Who goes there? I'll take you down, I will! Got hands big as an elephant, they tell me!" He lifts his hands and swings them toward us. They're way bigger than they should be. Swollen like they're full of air.

"Keep those filthy hands away from my face, Abram," Koi says.

The man's face lights up with a toothless grin. "Oy! It's Koi! He's got stragglers!" His voice squeaks like a mouse. He yells back into the doorway behind him. "Koi and Sax are back, with more Yellows!"

Meadow shoves past me, almost knocking the old man over.

"Where is he? Where's my father?"

"Meadow, hold on," Koi says. He rushes in after her, and then we're all moving forward, spilling through the doorway past Abram.

I finally get a look inside.

It's a massive, towering room, strangely lit by several flickering fires scattered throughout. Tall fingerlike rocks protrude from the floor, reaching almost to the ceiling. I look up and see black winged shapes flitting swiftly from place to place overhead. The air feels cool and moist, and I shiver a little. It's so much like the Resistance Cave that it shocks me.

"Brought some Newbs!" Saxon shouts.

Meadow stops and looks around.

I watch her take in the place, look left to right.

Then she freezes, and her eyes fall on a man lying by the fireside.

"Dad," she whispers.

She runs for him. Koi chases after her.

"Come on, Zero." Sketch grabs me by the shirt and yanks me toward the crowd. Everyone's sitting by a big fire, sparks shooting into the ceiling of the cave, way overhead. We sit down with the group.

"Reds?" a girl asks. Her skin is a weird, yellowy color, peeling away in places.

"They're joining us. Koi's sister came, just like he said. And these two were with her." Saxon motions at Sketch and me. "Koi found them. Seems like he can't stop bringing strays home. They're from the other testing site, same place as Koi and his pops. They got the barcodes, see?"

I hear a couple of gasps, as the group crowds around the fire to get a good look at me and Sketch.

None of them have barcodes on their foreheads. Just big, empty space that shouldn't be there. It's like they're missing limbs.

A dark-skinned boy with long dreadlocks takes a seat next to me, crossing his legs together. There's a big hole in his cheek, and I can see his teeth where they sprout right out of his gums, like a skeleton. "Hey. I'm Onyx." His voice comes out with a hiss. "Any weapon you can think of, real or not, you come to me and I'll whip something up for you."

He leans past me, winks at Sketch. "And if you need anything else . . . I'm here."

"Talk to me like that again, and I'll stick a knife in your junk."

The boys erupt into laughter.

Saxon ignores Sketch's threat. "The tall one in the back is Aiken." A wide-shouldered boy with a buzzed head and a number 80 on his cuff. His eyes drip constant tears of blood. He nods, looks at me and Sketch, and leans back on his elbows. "Guy's got ears like a mouse; he does a lot of recon for us. Knows where most of the other colors keep their hideouts. When we run out of food, it's good to know who to steal it from. Aiken's been here almost as long as I have. Initiative hasn't killed him yet. We've also got Doc." Saxon points out a fat lump of a man with bug eyes and a balding head, no eyebrows or lashes. "He used to work for something called the CDC. He knows all there is to know about what they're pumping us with. And the craziest part? This loony bastard actually volunteered to be in here."

Doc's eyes light up. "Tuberculosis, meningitis, avian flu, Ebola, the SARS virus." He counts out names of things I've never heard of on his fingers. I notice the 77 on his yellow cuff. "Fascinating diseases, all of which should be able to take out the nation, within mere days of exposure. And yet we live on." He smiles, like he's proud of being in here.

I wonder if he's like the Believers, back in the Shallows, in Cortez. The people who supported the cause of the Leeches. Who actually believed in what they were doing, by letting the murders just happen.

I guess there are crazy people everywhere in this world.

Even in the Ridge.

Doc keeps talking. "Six-hundred and seventy-two days in here, and I'm still fat as an Initiative's ego. Healthy as a horse. You got an explanation for that? No," he says, answering for me. "No one does. And that's the most mind-bending science I've ever seen. It's beautiful. Absolutely thrilling."

"So, what's the point?" Sketch asks. "Why keep trying to kill us, if it hasn't worked yet?"

Doc rubs his hands on his chin. "There's always a flaw in every system, always a weakness to every disease, every *anti*-disease, like the Eternity Cure," he says. "The Initiative believes they will find it. Then they'll use that answer, this so-called *Death Code* that they believe can be implanted into our genetic systems, to combat the Cure. Bring death back to the world."

It's not possible.

Meadow's mom made sure of that.

But as Saxon goes down the line, naming off at least twenty other boys, a few girls and women, and finally the introductions end, I realize that maybe the Leeches are on to something.

Maybe, if they keep running through the lines of people, they might eventually find their Death Code.

I'm about to stand up to leave, when I notice there's someone else at the back of the crowd, away from the fire. Someone Saxon didn't name.

It's an old man, all crumbly and gray, with a wrinkled face hidden behind a mess of white hair. His eyes are such a bright watery blue that it reminds me of a summer sea, back in the Shallows. In his creased hands sits a walking stick carved of wood, his fingers scratching intricate patterns down the shaft of it with a rusty old blade. He mumbles silently to himself as he works. His cuff has a number 80 on it.

"That's Tox," Saxon says, waving his hand. "He's old as hell. And bat-crazy to top it all off. He's been here since the beginning, longer than anyone else in the Ridge. It's too bad he's lost his mind. Whatever they gave him, it did something to his brain. He's a mumbling, drooling mess."

I stare at Tox through the flames.

There's something about him. Something different, and interesting.

And I realize it's not *him* that's interesting. It's the images he's carving on the stick. *X*s and jagged lines and circles, and one word over and over again.

Green. I think of the memory I had earlier in the week, while we were walking into the city.

"What's that mean?" I ask. "Green."

Saxon shrugs. "No idea. But don't waste your time talking to him, Cleanie."

I watch Tox for a long time.

He looks crazy, like his mind is fluxed. But his hands are steady, and the word he carves is solid and clear.

Green.

It means something. Has to mean something. And I'm going to figure it out.

CHAPTER 87
MEADOW

Close your eyes.

Relax your mind.

Now survive.

I see my father, sitting beside the fire. Silver hair, like storm clouds.

My father.

Feel your enemies' weaknesses.

I run to him.

You are stronger than you think, Meadow.

You must always be ready to defend yourself, no matter what.

He is alive, and I have found him, and he is in front of

me right now. Close, so close, after weeks of needing him. Missing him. Begging the world to bring us together again.

I reach the fire.

My father looks up, and through the flames, our eyes meet.

His are tinged with red. Not from crying, not from tears.

It is blood.

"Meadow," he says. "My Meadow."

His voice is a raw croak, the sound of sickness. But sickness isn't possible. It isn't *real*, not in the world my mother has cured. There is no way the Initiative has succeeded in breaking the Cure.

I fall at my father's side. He reaches out. My hands close over his, feel his warmth. He is *too* warm, and his forehead is beaded with sweat.

We simply watch each other for a time. The world around us fades away, and for a moment, we are back on the houseboat, father and daughter, lost in our own world.

It is one of training and toughness.

Love is cast aside, and only the art of survival remains.

I can almost taste the salt air. Feel the gentle lull of the waves beneath my feet. Hear the cawing of the gulls overhead, the sloshing of water against the sides of the boat. The sound of Peri's laughter in the background, and the carving of a knife on driftwood, as Koi creates another beautiful image.

"You left the Shallows," my father says, bringing us back to the here and now. The Ridge.

"I did what you trained me to do," I say back, nodding. "I came to keep my family safe."

"You put yourself in the line of danger." He blinks, and more blood drips from his eyes. What is wrong with him? Why does he look this way? So broken. So weak. And yet, when he speaks, his words are still filled with training. Authority. "Why did you come? Why did you leave your home?"

"Because my home is here, with you," I say. "Family is everything. The *only* thing. You taught me that."

He nods. He swallows, hard. And then he does the one thing he hasn't done in years. He reaches out. He pulls me into his arms. And he hugs me.

My father *hugs* me. Holds me.

"I don't know how you made it, and I don't want to know," he says.

I am about to explain anyways, but he keeps going, and I let him speak.

"But I'm *proud*, Meadow." He takes a deep, rattling breath. "I'm so proud of you."

It's all I've ever wanted. My father's pride.

And at his words, I let the tears fall.

For once, he doesn't tell me to stop. He doesn't tell me to be strong, or to wipe them away, or to throw a punch or a kick or wield a sharpened knife.

He lets me break.

And as I break, I whisper that my mother is dead, for good this time. She is no longer a life behind a lie, but a corpse, probably already burned to ashes in the incinerator. I tell him the secret she told me, trembling as the words spill from my lips. His grip tightens. I tell him about Peri, and the Regulator that is on her spine. How she's out there, somewhere, terrified.

As I speak, I see my mother's dead eyes, staring at me from my memories. I hear her whispered words. *I'm sorry.* I hear her begging me to *stay*, to just stay, to *live*.

I tell him that soon, I will die.

I tell him that soon, I will join my mother on the other side, in fire and ash.

I have to set the world right again before that moment comes.

I have to find my sister.

CHAPTER 88

ZEPHYR

I wait for Meadow to join us at the fire.

I fight to stay awake, but eventually, exhaustion takes over. I fall asleep.

I'm only a kid.

Lying in a bed in the Initiative Headquarters, staring up at a screen, as images flicker by, showing me memories. Hopes. Dreams. Desires.

Two Leeches move around the room, checking vitals of everyone in the beds.

They come to me, ready to tape my eyelids open, so I'm forced to watch. I like the videos. They make me feel safe. Alive.

"I'm transferring," one of the Leeches says. A woman. "I'm leaving tomorrow for the Drop or the Ridge, wherever they assign me. And if you love me, you'll come with me."

"You keep saying that," another Leech answers. This one is a man. "But you never actually go. What's so bad about here?"

"It's them," she says. I see her lean over me. She's pretty. Young. She tapes open my first eyelid, her hands gentle and soft. "This is wrong, Peter. We're playing with the natural order."

"And isn't that exactly what they're doing in the other sites? What's wrong is you allowing yourself to think that way. You want to go to the Ridge? Test them, make them wish they were dead? Look at this kid." He points at me. "He's higher than the clouds right now. We're making the Patients happy. They like listening to us. They like killing, doing what needs to be done for the system. We're giving them a reason to live."

They tape my second eyelid open.

The woman sighs. "I just can't get over it. It gives me nightmares. I can't sleep. So maybe we don't go to another site. Maybe we could just go to the Green, and . . ."

"The Green isn't real," he says. He reaches across my body, grabs the woman by the chin. She gasps, but he holds her

strong. "How many times do I have to tell you? You're not leaving here. You'll stay, and do everything the Commander tells you to do, and forget about imaginary places."

"We could have sanctuary," she says. Her voice shakes.

"Sanctuary is here," he tells her. "Face it, babe. The Shallows is as good as this world gets."

He releases her. She holds back tears. They move on, and I'm left to stare at an image of a broken place. Buildings blown to bits, a world that is my job to purge clean.

The Shallows.

I wake up, gasping, drenched in sweat.

Damned flashbacks. I thought they were gone.

I think of Meadow.

She's still alive, which means the system is still alive, too. No matter how far I run from the Shallows, and even with the Creator dead, I'm still a Patient. My mind is still beyond my total control.

I sit up, and a blanket falls from my chest. Sketch is asleep beside me, curled into herself. Shivering. I toss the blanket over her instead, then stand up.

I try to piece together the memory I just had. The Green. It's the second time I've had a memory about it, and now with the old man Tox carving it, I'm sure.

It means something.

The Green.

I have to find Meadow.

CHAPTER 89

MEADOW

Zephyr finds me later, when I am sitting by the dying light of the fire.

His eyes are heavy, with dark circles beneath them.

"Hey," he says. "Why didn't you wake me?"

"I let you sleep. You looked tired."

"Thanks," he says. He sits down beside me, but far enough away that I can't touch him.

My father is asleep a few feet from us, curled up in a blanket. Snoring, which is something he never did before on the houseboat. "He's sick," I whisper. "His breathing is labored. His heart rate is slowing."

"That's not possible," Zephyr says. "I mean, it shouldn't be."

"Everyone here is sick," I tell him. "You've seen them. My brother, Saxon, the people in the Rock. I think the Initiative's diseases are actually doing something. Weakening the Cure in our bodies."

"They're sick, yes. But no one's dying," Zephyr says, running a hand through his dark hair. "The Cure keeps us alive. Even with whatever new diseases the Leeches have made."

"I'm dying," I whisper.

He puts his head in his hands. "Don't believe that. It's just more Leech lies, Meadow."

"It's not," I say. "You've seen it, Zephyr. Every time the switch makes me weak, the number gets higher and higher. It's going to reach a hundred sometime. And then I'll be gone."

He lifts his head, glares at me. "Would you *stop*?"

"I'm only speaking the truth," I say. "Accept it."

He's silent, unmoving. I think back to the conversation my father and I had, hours ago, when my tears dried up, and reality took their place. His eyes dripped a stream of crimson, and he wiped it away, smearing a streak across his face. *If I die, Meadow . . . You have to save Peri for me.*

You won't die, I said. *My mother's Cure will never be broken.*

What if it already is? he asked. *What if this is really the end?*

Our eyes met, and I knew.

"My father is dying, too. But it's from something here, something they did to him."

"Meadow, it's not possible," Zephyr says. "Years of this, and no one's dropped yet."

"It *is* possible," I say. "Somehow, he's the one who's finally going to give them their stupid Death Code, and then they'll use his blood, and his body, to experiment and find a way to kill the rest of us. And if we find Peri soon, and give the signal and get my father out of here, back to the New Militia, maybe the Surgeon can fix him." I sigh, and touch the small lump on my inner wrist. "My mother could have."

"Whoa, whoa, hold on." Zephyr laughs, but it is more of a bark laced with anger. "She wouldn't have saved him. She would have rejoiced with the rest of the Leeches and talked about the *beauty* of the science or something crazy like that. She was a murderer, Meadow. A monster."

"So am I," I say, and I glare up at him with gritted teeth. "And so are you."

"No. You're not the same as her, and neither am I. We've both done things. We've both killed. I did it because I had to, and you did it to survive. But she did it because she believed it was the only answer. Because she *wanted* it to be, without anyone controlling her. Because she wasn't human."

"Don't talk about her like you knew her," I say.

He looks into my eyes, and I see flames of anger.

Pain.

"I knew her better than you ever did," he whispers.

The words hit right to my heart.

He keeps going, fueling off of the hurt on my face, throwing the truth like punches. It's like he has held all of his anger from me, and now it's exploding forth, and he can't quit.

"Stop trying to imagine her as the woman you used to know, the woman who never *was*, and you'll be happy she's dead for real this time." He clenches and unclenches his fists. "I wouldn't change things, you know. If I could go back, I'd shoot her through the heart a million times over, and I'd love it. And if you're still the Meadow I know you are, you'll understand exactly what I'm saying. I think you're mad because deep down, *you* didn't get to be the one to kill her."

I swing out my knife, hold it to his throat. "You might have known my mother, but you *don't* know *me*."

"I do know you, Meadow," Zephyr says. He leans in,

so that the knife breaks his skin. A trickle of blood runs down his neck, bright crimson in the fading firelight. "You disagreed with her, and when we found her in that cell, you saw the truth of who she really was. You're just using her death as an excuse to push me away from you."

He is quiet for a time. When he speaks, his voice cracks.

"You'll never love me, will you, Meadow?"

I am hurting him. I have always hurt him, been the one piece of his world that doesn't quite fit. Pushing him away would shatter him, tear the fullness of his heart to shreds.

"I don't even know why I care," he says. "Each morning I open my heart to you, and you stomp all over it. You're selfish, and you don't *care*."

I put my head in my hands, but I don't cry.

I have no tears left.

"After all of that, I still want you. But not *this* you. I want the Meadow I know is still stuck in there, somewhere. The Meadow who is fearless, even when it comes to love."

"I can't," I whisper. "You need to stop this. You need to pull yourself away, and forget about me, because all I'm capable of is hurting people. I kill and I lose the ones I care about, and it's all because of *me*. You don't think I saw the expression on your face, after we found my brother? I can't have them *and* you. It's too much. I can't keep you all safe."

My voice breaks.

Zephyr takes a deep breath, shakes his head. "You blame yourself for what the Leeches did to your family. The only one you should be blaming is your mother." Zephyr reaches out, takes my hand. He twines our fingers together, and squeezes them tight. "The world can change us," he says. "But it can't tear us apart. Not if we don't let it. And I won't, Meadow. I just need to know that you're in this, too."

"I don't know what will happen tomorrow," I say. "I can only give you today. When I need you, you're there for me. You're always there, Zephyr, and I'm not. I can't take all of you and give you just a part of me in return. It's not right."

"No," he says, letting go of my hand, and I'm afraid this is it.

The end.

I don't want it to be over.

"No, it's not right, Meadow. At all." Zephyr's eyes are so green right now. So full of memories of the past, and I want to go back to the beginning of it all. Before we discovered what he was, what my mother had done, what secrets the Initiative was hiding. Before we kissed, and killed together, and ran for our lives.

But that would mean living in darkness.

Together, we were the sparks that set the world of the Shallows on fire.

Together, we created the light.

Zephyr sighs, his resolve crumbling. "If a part of you is all you can offer, I'll take it." He leans in, kisses my forehead. "I'll take anything you have to give. Because I love you. Every broken piece of you."

Love.

Such a foolish word.

"I can't love anyone but my family," I say. "That's how it has to be."

He nods. "If we get out of this place alive, we'll put each other back together. And slowly, you'll start to see. There's room in your heart for more than just your family. You can add me, too, Meadow. I can fit in."

"I hope you're right," I whisper.

"My moonlit girl," he says. "The first time I saw you in my dreams, I knew I had to have you."

"Now you're just being ridiculous," I say. "No one will ever have me."

"I can try," he says. He leans in, about to kiss me.

That's when the Night Siren goes off.

CHAPTER 90

ZEPHYR

It's the worst sound in the world. The Night Siren.

And yet it sends my nerves roiling. Sends my body into action.

"Time for food, boys and girls!" Saxon shouts from across the cave.

Everyone stands up, straps gear to their bodies.

"What happens now?" I ask.

Meadow shrugs, looks at her father, who lies beside us.

He is hardly awake. "You search for the rations," he says, without opening his eyes. "And if you find them, you do what I taught you to do. You stay alive."

"Let's go," Saxon says.

Meadow squeezes her father's hand.

Then we join a group of Yellows and head from the cave.

CHAPTER 91

MEADOW

Saxon leads the group.

We go back down the tunnel, back through the waterfall and into the pool. As soon as we surface on land, it is like old times. Zephyr and Sketch follow, and Koi and I run side by side.

"We never know where they're going to drop the food," he says. "But we know that when they do, the worst of their attacks come."

We are specters in the darkness, our feet silent and steady on the hard ground. I am not used to the temperature, and it makes it harder to breathe. The wind dances with tiny white flakes, landing cold as ice on the tip of my nose.

But it feels good to move. The action is familiar, running with my brother, like the times he helped my father train me on the beach. Like the times I learned, little by little, to become strong.

At some point Koi stops. Holds up a fist.

I sink to one knee and wait, motionless.

There's a whirring overhead, a sound that makes my hair stand on end.

It is two Cams.

"Damn," Koi hisses.

The Cams swoop down, stop in front of us, and swivel back and forth, taking in the faces of my group.

"It's too late to run," Koi says. "They're fast."

The Cams explode.

We dive for cover, as pieces of metal rain down.

Then the smoke hits. I cough, gag, as something horrid burns in the back of my throat. Everyone else is coughing around me, hacking up green fluid.

I look down at my cuff. It blinks, then skyrockets to a 64.

Zephyr's hits a 50. Sketch's only reaches 36. She was farthest from the blast.

Koi, who stood closest to me, is a 72. The other Yellows' numbers change, too.

As soon as the coughing dies down, there is a giant whirring noise. At first, I think it is the Biters, coming back. But then Saxon points to the sky.

"Pay attention," he commands the group.

A part of the dome opens up, metal spiraling outward to form a tiny hole in the metal sky. Something is lowered through it.

"Rations," Koi says. "Looks like it's about a mile east of here."

"So what now?" I ask.

He smiles. "We run."

CHAPTER 92

ZEPHYR

It's too damn cold to be outside.

And it's snowing, little flakes of white that dance from the sky and land on me, make me shiver like a street rat.

"Stick together. It's about teamwork, but I won't stop to save your ass if you fall," Saxon tells Sketch and me, as we follow Koi and Meadow. The rest of the Yellows run behind us. They're silent, but I'm crashing across the fallen twigs and leaves like I'm a thousand pounds.

I'm not used to these woods.

At least Meadow's strong now, able to run, to help.

Somewhere to our right, I think I see flashes of another color in the woods. Pink. But then it disappears, and I wonder if I ever saw it at all.

Soon Koi slows. The pack follows suit, and we snake through the trees at a brisk walk, keeping as quiet as we can.

We stop before a small clearing.

I can see something dark in the center, a big bundle lying motionless.

"Rations," Saxon whispers in my ear.

I stand up to move for it, but he grabs me, holds me back.

"Wait."

We sit still, and I don't know what we're waiting for. Until I see the figures move into the clearing. They're quick, silent. It's dark in here, without the moon or the stars, but I know they aren't Yellows. Which means, by Ridge rules, they're enemies.

I watch as they reach the bundle, start unwrapping it and pulling things out, putting it into bags they brought with them.

Saxon nods.

"Three," he whispers. "Two"—he rises to a crouch—"one!"

He stands and fires an arrow. Then he's shouting for us to run, and everyone spreads out like a fan, sprinting for the other tribe.

Screaming, weapons raised high. There's got to be twenty, thirty enemies. Some of them turn, stand to fight, while others take the rations and run.

"After them!" Saxon shouts. He tackles a guy, stabs him with his carved spear. I see his pink cuff flash to 100 as he dies instantly.

Meadow goes in for the fight.

Koi joins her, back to back, and they're like death together, slashing knives, taking out enemies.

"Zero, come with me!" Sketch yells. She grabs my arm, and we chase after the people who stole the rations. We reach a girl, tackle her. Sketch kills her quick and pain-less. "After the boy!"

I turn, see someone racing ahead, into the thicker trees. I sprint for him, holding the knife the Yellows gave me.

I leap, and in my head, I tell myself I'm fighting a Leech. It's all a blur, the twist of body against body, punches to the jaw, the throat. The crack of bone and the burst of blood. The slice of my blade against my enemy's desper-ate, sweating skin.

By the time it's all over, we've gotten the rations.

We'll eat tonight.

"Yellows!" Saxon screams. Everyone lifts their weapons to the sky. Sketch screams like a madwoman, but I can't celebrate. Because I see Meadow stumble and fall.

I rush to her side, lift her wrist to my eyes.

93.

She's switched again.

"I'm running out of time," she says. Her silver hair is coated with streaks of crimson. "We have to find Peri. Before it's too late."

"We will," I say.

We head back for the cave.

I have to carry Meadow the whole way home.

CHAPTER 93
MEADOW

Morning comes. I wake with the *C* on my cuff again.

The switch didn't kill me. Not yet.

I eat a handful of rations, just enough to give me energy for a few hours.

Then I find Koi. "We're going after her," I say. "Now."

"Meadow, if you change again while we're out there . . "

"I won't," I say. "We've already wasted an entire day and half. It's now or never, Koi. I won't switch. I'll fight it."

It is a lie, and it comes easily from my lips. But I know he doesn't believe me. We don't know when it will happen again. When it will be the very last time, and I take my final breaths.

"We'll come, too," Sketch says from behind me. Zephyr stands beside her. I sigh, check to make sure my knife is still with me.

"We kill anyone who stands in our way," I tell them.

We leave the cave in search of my sister.

CHAPTER 94

ZEPHYR

Koi has made a map of places he's searched.

It's scratched on a slab of thick bark, and he points it all out, showing the *X*s and marks where Peri hasn't been.

"She could be with others, right?" I ask. "She's obviously got a cuff. Have you checked all the other camps?"

"That's what's strange," he says. "I can't find her in any of them."

Meadow slices a tree with her blade. "Peri is smart. She knows not to trust anyone. She's probably on her own somewhere. Hiding." There's pain in her voice. "If she'd been trained sooner, she would know how to defend herself."

"She was too young," Koi says.

Meadow glares at him. "And we weren't? As soon as we could walk we were learning how to wield knives. The only thing Peri could wield was her teddy bear."

"Dad figured she'd be safe," he says. "We were strong enough together."

"Until you all got caught," Meadow says. "What if she's dead already, Koi? What if someone saw her Regulator, like mine, and thought it was something special, and killed her for it?" She's screaming.

She's shaking all over, and her eyes are crazy. It's like she's staring at an enemy, instead of her brother.

Koi steps forward, until his nose is almost touching hers. "Peri is *alive*. And we're going to find her."

Meadow slaps a thorn branch out of the way and stomps ahead.

We get to what Koi calls the Eye of the Ridge by the end of the hour. It's a big, flat expanse of trees wiped away. An empty clearing, the very center of the whole forest. I freeze when we reach the edge of the clearing.

There're other tribes here. Blues, Blacks, Yellows, Oranges, Pinks, all standing around. No one's killing each other. They're just staring into the clearing with hungry eyes. Waiting hands.

A ring of Leeches is in the center of them, standing beside a few black vehicles that are packed full of what looks like medical supplies.

"I check here, every other day," Koi explains. "The Initiative comes. They give out extra rations to whoever shows up."

"I swear, we're never going to escape these mother-loving bastards," Sketch hisses.

My stomach turns, seeing them. There are at least fifty, dressed in the same black uniforms they wore in the Shallows. They have bigger rifles, too. Ones that look like they could blow a hole right through your gut.

And something else is different about them.

"What's on their bodies?" I ask.

When the Leeches move, something blue flickers across them. Almost like a second skin, glowing pale with electricity.

"Protection," Koi explains, motioning for Sketch and I to follow. "Some kind of electric current. We can't get to them. Bullets, knives, spears. You touch them, you get blown back. It's a hell of an invention. Genius."

"They had that surrounding their Compound, in the Shallows," I say, remembering the night I went crazy with the rifle, trying to take out as many as I could under the influence of the Murder Complex.

"And they had the Cams," Meadow says. One whizzes past, overhead.

"And the Perimeter," Sketch adds.

It's almost funny how similar the Shallows and the Ridge are. Similar, but different. They're both hell, no matter which way you twist it.

We join the other groups, waiting on the sidelines. We get a few glares. Harsh words are exchanged, and Koi tells us to ignore the others. But no one does anything more than that and it's this weird, peaceful moment in time. Like the massacre last night, or the encounter with the Greens on the first day we got here, didn't even happen.

It sets me on edge.

The Leech in charge, a man who's got to be almost seven feet tall, makes his way down the line. Scanning people's cuffs.

He stops in front of a young boy, a kid who could be Peri's age. I look over at Meadow. See the pain in her eyes, and I can't take it anymore. I slip away from Sketch, walk quietly to Meadow's side.

"Cuff," the Leech growls.

The little boy holds out his arm. His whole body shakes

uncontrollably, and he's covered in little specks of yellow, all over his skin.

"A 73," the Leech says. "Interesting." He pulls out some kind of silver tube and presses it to the boy's arm. The kid flinches, and the Leech pulls the tube away. It beeps, and he looks down at it.

"Smallpox," the Leech says, to one of his comrades. "Highest level yet."

"I just wanna eat." The boy starts to cry. "Please." But his tears don't hit the ground.

His body does, instead, when the Leech swings a gun forward.

And shoots him in the leg. The boy screams. The sound echoes across the Ridge. Birds fly from the tops of trees, scatter into the sky.

Meadow grabs my hand. Squeezes it tight, like she's holding herself back from attacking.

I squeeze back, and for this one second she's mine again, willing to open up in the midst of her pain.

Some people flinch. I stand still and steady, because it's just like the Rations Hall. Only this time, I don't have to clean up the boy's body. He's crying, sobbing on the ground, but he's alive.

"Stand up," the Leech yells at him.

The boy can't move.

"I said stand!"

Finally, Meadow releases my hand. "Meadow, don't," I say, but she rushes forward before any of us can stop her, shoving past the other colors standing around. She bends down, grabs the boy's arm, and yanks him to his feet. He's dripping blood. He passes out, but she holds him up.

"Fix him," Meadow says, glaring at the Leeches.

One of them steps up, grabs her cuff. Looks at the *C*, and then at her Regulator on her skull.

"You're the Woodson girl," he says.

"Fix the boy," she says back. "You shot him. Now fix him."

The Cure should be healing him by now, stitching up the bullet wound. But the boy's leg is a blasted mess. From here, I can see the number on his cuff, skyrocketing to a 94.

All I can do is stare.

"He'll survive," the Leech says. "They always do." He takes a glass vial, lets some of the boy's blood drip into it. Corks it shut, and moves on.

Meadow drags the boy over to us. Sketch rips off the bottom of her shirt, wraps up the kid's leg. Gradually, the bleeding stops, and his cuff number sinks lower and lower.

He'll live, just like the Leech said.

"She's not here," Koi says. "We need to move on."

The Leeches go up and down the line, scanning people. Handing over rations bags to some, after they draw their blood. Scolding others, beating the ones that step out of line. I look left, right, searching for Meadow's sister in the crowd. She isn't here.

So where is she?

CHAPTER 95

MEADOW

We search all day.

As we walk, I think of Peri.

How tiny she was, when she was born. The very first time when I held her in my arms. A memory resurfaces like a pang in my gut.

"You will keep her safe, Meadow. Guard her with your life."

My father sits beside me on the floor of our houseboat. Peri is asleep on the yellowed mattress, her cheeks stained from tears.

"I will," I say. "No matter what."

"Good girl," my father says.

He hasn't said my mother's name. It has been a week, and he hasn't even acknowledged the fact that she is gone.

He hasn't asked me if I'm okay.

Maybe he knows that I'm not. The question isn't worth asking, when you already know the ugly truth.

"Is she really dead?" I ask.

My father stares out the window of the boat, watching the sun bleed into the sea.

"She's never coming back," he says. "Trust me." He looks at Peri, the last child he had with my mother. "You are her mother now. Do you understand?"

I nod. A tear slips down my cheek, and my father reaches out, wipes it away.

"Never let her see you cry."

Peri wakes up screaming.

I go to her, hold her close.

My father turns his back on us and puts his head in his hands.

There's no sign of my little sister.

I feel as if I am back in the Shallows, the same day that I went after my mother. Only then, I knew she would appear. Now I can't be sure of anything. We stop, drink from the stream.

Sketch gets a splitting headache.

Zephyr's ears ring so loudly he can't hear us.

I switch back and forth twice, three times.

Koi is carrying me when I notice we're finally on a path, the ground trampled from hundreds of feet. My mind drifts back to the Shallows, the path in the Everglades that led me to discovering my mother's secrets.

The path opens up into a larger, thicker part of the forest. The trees are taller here, fatter around, as if they are ancient. I wonder how tangled their roots must be.

"I haven't come this far yet," Koi says. "I've been taking care of . . ."

He stops.

And I know that he is talking about our father.

"He's dying," I whisper.

Koi takes a deep breath, his silver hair shining in the sunlight.

He scratches his arms, and more of his scabs peel away. "I don't know for sure, Meadow," he says. "The AntiCure comes in many forms. Sometimes, we think we're going to lose a person. But then the nanites fight their way through the system, and they heal." He leans against a tree. "He *will* heal. Just like you keep healing."

"Koi," I say. "It's obvious that every time I switch, I get

worse. Eventually, I'm going to die."

It gets easier, every time I tell someone. They don't believe me.

They won't.

I share with him the secret from my mother, keeping my voice low, so that Zephyr and Sketch cannot hear. Koi is quiet the whole time, and when I am done, he simply nods.

My brother was never one to share many words. When he does speak, though, they are soft and honest.

Understanding, as always.

"We'll find Peri," he says. "Then we'll get help. We'll save you."

The wind blows, pulling strands of my hair into my face. I turn away, my back to the wind, just as I see movement in the clearing.

"I think I see something," I whisper.

"There isn't a tribe here," Koi says. "Shouldn't be, at least."

It happens so fast.

A spear whistles through the air and lands in his shoulder.

Blood spurts, and Koi cries out. He falls, and I tumble from his arms, into the ground. I crawl back to him, rip the spear away, close my hand over Koi's mouth so he doesn't scream.

"We have to run," I say. I try to get to my feet, but I can't. I'm too weak.

"Meadow!" I hear Zephyr's voice in the trees, but I can't see him. He's too far away, and it's getting dark already.

Another spear lands in the ground, close by.

"Get back to the cave!" Koi yells.

I see a flash of motion, twenty paces to the left. It's Sketch yanking Zephyr along, back through the trees, even as he shouts my name and tries to fight her.

Koi helps me to my feet. Puts his good arm around my waist and starts hauling me after them.

A person steps in front of us, their body masked by leaves and sticks, the perfect camouflage. "Hand over your clothes!" she screams. A woman. She holds a bow, and when she shoots, Koi and I separate, and the arrow soars right between us.

The fear brings the switch back to me.

I'm strong in a flash.

I sprint for the woman, shove her against a tree. She yells and tries to fight me off, but I slam her head back. I can hear Koi fighting someone behind me, but I know he can handle himself.

I slam the woman's head against the tree again and again, until there's blood, and she goes slack. I let her slide to the ground.

"Come on!" Koi shouts from behind me.

He's taken out a guy half his size. His shoulder is dripping blood.

"Only two?" I point at the dead woman's cuff. Orange.

"No," Koi says. "Never just two."

Then there's a shout, like the caw of a bird, and others pour from the darkness.

The chase is on. We run.

"Left!" Koi yells. I follow his command, leaping over the river as it comes into view.

Another spear whistles past, barely missing my head.

We duck beneath a cluster of low-hanging branches, roll to our feet, and start running all over again.

I dodge, weave, make myself a harder target to hit. Koi follows suit, and soon I take the lead, blindly running through the woods, trusting my instincts to guide us.

The ground slopes, cutting to a ravine so steep that I don't have time to stop. Right as the switch hits. I stumble, and Koi knocks into my back.

My feet go out from under me.

Together, we fall. Trees rush at me in fast-forward. I

can't stop, can't slow my falling.

My body slams against a tree trunk. My head cracks against something hard, but the Regulator saves me.

Koi isn't so lucky. His shoulder is out of the socket, dangling like a half-broken stick.

Everything fades in and out of focus, but I grit my teeth, force myself to stay alert. I'm able to stumble to my feet, stagger over to Koi.

"No, no, just wait a second," he says, as I reach for him. But I'm too weak to snap it back into place right now.

"It happened again, didn't it?" he asks.

I nod and show him my cuff.

96.

"It's happening more often," I whisper. "I'm not going to make it out of here, even if we find Peri."

"No," he says. "Meadow, just . . . stop. Right now, we need to find shelter."

We both look up. We're in the middle of a deep ravine, a natural dip in the ground, with steep rocky walls all around us. We'll have to climb our way out.

But how can we, with his shoulder? And with me, weakened again from the switch?

"We'll stay the night," Koi says. "Find a place to hide, in case there are Needles or Cams or other tribes. You'll be able to rest. You'll be okay once you switch back, and then we'll keep hunting for Peri."

"Where exactly are we going to hide?" I ask. Blood drips from my nose.

Koi looks away, like he can't bear to see me like this.

"We could go there," he says. He points behind me with his good arm.

There's a tiny cave opening, up against the rock wall.

Together, broken and bruised, we make our way inside.

CHAPTER 96

ZEPHYR

We make it back to the cave wounded, but alive.

Meadow and Koi are nowhere to be found.

I can't believe we ran, left them behind like that. But I figured, with her brother . . .

"Woodson is fine," Sketch tells me. "It's her dad who's not going to be, once he sees us come back without his kids."

"I forgot about him," I growl, as I knock on the door. Abram opens it, and we step inside.

Meadow's dad is watching, waiting.

He sees Sketch and me enter, alone.

His eyes might be bloody, but they're still able to see. And the look he gives me could kill.

I know right here and now that he'd beat me senseless, until I was dead.

We wait for hours.

They don't come back. I keep myself busy by watching Tox carve.

He still has that long walking stick in his hands, and a sharp black rock. He leans over, carving and carving. Never stopping.

There's dried blood on his hands. Like he hasn't quit for days. The number on his cuff still reads high.

"What's he doing?" Sketch asks.

That's when Doc comes up behind us. "He never stops," he says. He hands Tox a leaf full of rations.

Tox doesn't look up. He keeps carving.

"You have to eat, old man." Doc sighs, then reaches out to take the stick from Tox's hands. He reacts, faster than I thought possible, slicing the top of Doc's hand with the rock.

"No rest," Tox says. "Paddle for days and days."

"Damnit! Forget you!" Doc curses, holding his cut hand to his chest. "Sad sack of bones, you are."

Sketch follows Doc back to the fire.

But I stay behind, staring at Tox's symbols. Crude representations of mountains. Strange waves that could be the sea. Twisting, turning patterns that go around the stick, and all sorts of numbers, jagged lines, strange shapes I've never seen before. The wings of an eagle, spreading outward. A sketched letter *X*.

"Is the Green real?" I ask him. "Is there a safe place, in our world?"

He doesn't answer. There's just the scratching of his rock on the smooth, old wood.

"The Green," I say again. "I need to know how to get to the Green."

He looks up, only for a second. "Green?" he asks, and I swear he understands, knows exactly what I'm talking about. "Outside. With the eagle."

The eagle. Is he talking about the New Militia?

I don't think so. If he was, they'd have told us about a place without Initiative control, without fear. Wouldn't they have?

"Yes. The Green," I say. "Is it real?"

Tox stares at me, and I can almost see the pieces sliding together in his mind. Clarity in his eyes. "Green," he says. He holds up his cuff. "Red."

He goes back to carving, and my hope fades away. I settle down across from everyone, alone, and wait for Meadow to come back.

CHAPTER 97
MEADOW

The cave is bigger than I thought it would be.

We crawl inside, slowly at first, our stomachs sliding on sharp rocks. But soon it opens up, and our ragged breaths echo into the darkness.

I lean up against cool, smooth stone, gasping.

Koi slides in next to me, and we sit like that for a while.

At some point, I think I hear something somewhere else in the cave. The pitter-patter of feet. I freeze, listen as best I can, but I think it is only a small animal. Or more bats.

"She tried to apologize," I say, suddenly, when the screams have faded. "Before she died."

I can't see Koi, but I can feel him shift next to me. "Our mother?"

"Yes," I whisper. "Do you think . . . ?" I can't find the right words to say. "Did she really . . . ?"

"Do I think she meant that she was sorry?" Koi asks. He finds my hand in the darkness and grabs a hold. "Dad told me once, that she didn't want to have children. She didn't think she could handle the pressure. But then it happened, and she had all of us, and she loved being a mother. You know she loved it, right? Loved us?"

I think back to the good times. The laughter, the tickle fights in our apartment, the way she'd try in vain to smooth my relentless curls back into a braid, because she knew how much I hated it when the wind blew my hair into my eyes. "She loved us," I say. "A long time ago."

"Love doesn't die, Meadow. It starts out small at first, and then it grows, and it keeps growing, until it takes over our entire heart. I think some people are born to love. Others fall into it, and when it becomes too much, sometimes, they're afraid. Mom was afraid. She knew what she was doing to the world wasn't love. It was . . . something entirely its own. She knew what we'd think of her, how it would break us, once we found out about her work. So she left." He sighs, squeezes my hand. "She probably didn't think she'd ever see any of us again, Meadow. You were with her as she died. And I think, in that moment, she meant every word."

We sit side by side like that for hours, until I switch back again.

When I'm strong enough, I pop Koi's arm back into the socket.

"It's time to move," I say. "I'm ready. We've wasted enough time."

He nods, grins so big it lights up his face. He looks so much like my father. "Time spent with my little sister is never wasted."

I peer out the cave, into the ravine. "Race you to the top?"

"I don't know, Meadow," he says.

But before I can argue, he sprints past me, starts to climb the rock wall. I charge after him, laughing, and in this moment we are children again, climbing higher and higher and higher, desperate to get away from a world that begs to hold us down.

It is only when I reach the top that I turn around and stare out at the world below. We had fallen into a giant hole in the ground, like an open mouth. All around it, there is a ring of land and trees. A hill sinks down, leading to lower ground that seems to stretch on forever. There is a field of yellow flowers. Bright as day, beautiful as the sun. Peri would have loved to see this. I would have taken her there, and we would have danced in the blooms, stretched out on our backs in the middle of a sunshine sea.

Beyond it, the forest picks back up. It looks never-ending from here.

The morning is foggy.

Or maybe it isn't fog. It's smoke.

I skirt around the ravine, to the edge of the hill, and look past the meadow. I see a flickering fire in the distant trees. Another camp.

Koi climbs up next to me, breathing hard. "You beat me," he says. "How did that happen?"

"What tribe lives over there?" I ask, pointing.

He shrugs. "I told you, I haven't come this far yet. It's only been a few weeks. The Ridge is massive, bigger than the Shallows." He smiles. "I'd love to draw this."

I walk along the edge of the ravine, closer to the peak. I look left, far away, and see movement in the trees. Hear that awful, horrible buzzing. A wave of black swarms through the trees, like a giant, moving shadow.

Biters.

"The swarm is heading toward that camp," I say.

Koi bites his lip. "We should move. In case it changes directions. We don't want to get caught up in that."

I turn, take a few steps after him. We are almost out of view of the meadow, at least a mile or two away, when I hear the scream.

It's undeniable. It echoes through the woods, across the field of flowers, up the ravine, finally ringing so loudly in my ears that I swear the voice is calling to my soul.

I know that scream. Its sound used to pull me from a dead sleep, so many countless nights back in the Shallows.

Koi and I whirl around to face each other.

And then in a flash, we are both sprinting as fast as we can, skirting around the edge of the ravine, tearing down the giant hill toward the meadow.

Because we both know who that scream came from.

Peri.

CHAPTER 98

ZEPHYR

Talan lies beside me in her tent back at the Reserve. Holding a pre-Fall book she bagged from the Library. How she got in there, I don't know, but I never ask.

The book is flat. Thin, with faded images of Pirates. Not the kind of Pirates we have in the Shallows.

But they're just as dirty, out for gold.

"It's a treasure map," Talan says. She traces her fingers across one of the pages. Shows me images, little hash marks along the way. "X marks the spot." Her muddy fingers stop on the X.

I smile. "X marks the Ward, Talan."

"You're no fun." She pouts. "For once, imagine you and

me. Free. Following a treasure map to some amazing place. Think of all the food we'd have once we got there . . ."

My eyes open. The memory fades away. I look back at Tox, his carvings, his steady hands.

"Can I borrow that?" I ask. I won't take it from him by force..

He nods, hands it gently over to me.

Sketch comes back, and together, we look down at the walking stick. I twist it in my hands, and suddenly all the images make sense.

It's not the carvings of a crazed man with a lost mind.

They're the carvings of someone who's very, very sane. He's just trapped beneath the surface. He can't bring the words forth because they're stuck.

So instead, he's given us what he can.

"It looks like the map inside the New Militia's place, doesn't it?"

"Holy hell, Sketch. You're right." It's like my eyes open wide, and finally, I can see.

I look past her, right into Tox's eyes. "You've had the answer this whole time," I say. I hold up the stick. "That's what this is, right Tox? It leads to the Green."

"Green," he says, his smile showing through his wrinkles. "Yes."

I look down at the walking stick.

But it's much more than that. Because looking at it, I finally realize the reason why it's stuck out so much to me. The New Militia had something very, very similar, sprawled across one of their walls. The same mountains, the same ocean. The same large piece of land, floating in the middle of it all, where Tox has an X instead.

The stick is a different format, but it means the same thing.

It's a map. The same map the New Militia has.

And it leads to the Green.

CHAPTER 99

MEADOW

My feet cannot carry me fast enough.

My boots hit the meadow, crush the flowers with every step. I am soaring, flying, lost in the rush of being so close to her, after so long.

Koi is at my side the entire time. We're a blur of silver in a world of yellow, and then green, as we hit the tree line and push forward.

There are screams, everywhere.

I can't think.

The fire is just ahead, darkened by the swarm of Biters. Wood huts are scattered about the place, forgotten. There are ten, maybe twenty people, running away. I see a man waving a fiery stick, trying to fight the Biters off.

Hundreds of them swarm him. Women and children rush for the trees. People fall and are left behind, and the Biters dive down on them like predators to wounded prey.

"Where is she?" I scream. I'm whirling in circles, searching for her. "Peri!"

She was here.

I *know* she was here.

A Biter lunges at me, sticks itself into my arm. I cry out, slap it away, but the welt is already there, and the poison is spreading.

Will I go blind, like Zephyr?

I have to find her first. I have to *see* her.

"This way!" Koi grabs my hand, yanks me into the trees, after the group of people still fleeing. I wait for my vision to go spotty and dim, but it doesn't come.

Instead I'm sprinting harder, and finally I see a figure up ahead, running fast.

Peri always ran fast. She loved to run on the sand and chase the gulls.

"There!" I scream. "She's there!"

"Peri!" Koi yells, but she can't hear us.

I sprint and leave him in my wake.

I am close to her, so close, enough that I can see her

bald head, covered in cuts and bruises. Her Regulator is so large on her tiny body that I wonder how she stays standing, has the strength to carry on. Her arms are covered in giant purple bruises and mud, her clothing ripped to near shreds. Her cuff is a teal that reminds me of the ocean in springtime.

"Peri!" I yell, one final time, stretching out.

She doesn't stop.

I leap. I wrap my arms around her, twist as we fall, so that she lands on top of me.

She screams, bites at my arms, claws with her fingernails.

The Biters dive at us. I flip around and push her flat against the ground, cover her body with mine. I can feel the hardness of her Regulator against my face. The Biters make impact. The pain is straight from my nightmares, piercing bite after bite into my skin. I cry out, beg myself not to move, so that they can't get to Peri.

And then, suddenly, it stops. The Biters lift off. Their buzzes carry them away into the woods, after the others who escaped.

"Meadow!" Koi yells. I can hear his footsteps as he catches up.

Peri squirms beneath me, whining, trying to get away.

"Peri," I gasp. "It's okay, it's me, it's Meadow!"

Koi reaches us, hauls me off of her.

Peri scrambles backward, whirls to look at us. She lifts her arm, and she is holding a tiny, hand-carved blade, made from rock. It isn't sharp enough to do any damage at all. Her hands shake, and her eyes are wild, like she is seeing a monster. Like she has seen too many horrors, all of the things we tried to keep her from for so many years, but we failed.

We failed.

"Peri," I gasp. I drop to my knees, hold out my arms. "It's *Meadow*."

I see the pieces click together in her mind. See her look at me, *really* focus, for the first time. She looks past my Regulator, past my newly cut hair, into my eyes.

"M-Meadow?" she says. Her voice is soft, timid.

"It's me," I say, and then I realize I am crying. "It's me and Koi. We found you. It's okay now. We're here."

She lowers the knife. It drops to the ground with a dull thump.

"Meadow," she says again.

She stands up.

And throws herself into my arms.

I wrap her up tight, hold her close, feel the soft fuzz of

new hair growing on her head. Koi drops to his knees, puts his arms around both of us. We hold each other so tightly that for a moment, I almost think that our three beating hearts are the very same one.

CHAPTER 100
ZEPHYR

If there's anyone here who knows anything about this world, it's the person who hates me most.

Meadow's father.

"Zero, do you *want* to die?" Sketch asks me. She chases me across the cave. "He'll gut you like a fish!"

"If there are rumors of the Green, he'll confirm them," I say. "He was on the Outside before it all happened. He was Lark Woodson's husband. He'll know."

"This I gotta see," Sketch says, laughing behind me.

I reach the fire. Sketch stops a few paces away.

Meadow's father is awake, slumped against the rock wall of the cave, sipping water from a woven basket.

437

"I need to talk to you," I say.

He glares at me as I sit. It takes me back to the day he stuck a fishing hook through my cheek, yanked on it until the skin popped and the hook ripped through. I shiver, but I refuse to look away.

"I told you to stay away from my daughter, did I not?" he asks.

I nod. "You did. But I'm the only reason she wasn't captured with the rest of you."

Meadow's father rises to a sitting position. He wipes his eyes with the back of his hand. Blood smears on his skin. "If you came for my gratitude, you're going to be disappointed," he says.

I crack my knuckles. There's a lot I'd like to say to this man. But I have to focus on what matters right now. "What's the Green?" I ask.

He chuckles under his breath. Takes another sip of water. When he swallows, he coughs it back up. I wait patiently.

"The Green," I say, again. "Have you heard of it?"

His eyes flit upward. "Why?"

I decide the truth is better than any lie I can come up with. "Because I think it's real. I think it's out there. And I think we need to find it."

"It's a natural reaction, in the midst of so much death and decay, to hope for a better place. For Patients, like you, I guess it's normal to believe in reaching the impossible. You aren't used to getting no for answer."

"Is it real or not?" I ask.

His bloody eyes turn to slits. "Don't get an attitude with me, boy. Do I need to remind you what you did to my home? My family?"

I lean forward, my hands in my lap. "I killed your wife," I say. His mouth drops open, and I keep going. "After my arrow went through her chest, the entire army of Patients attacked the Initiative. After leading the fight, I then used your sister-in-law to my advantage, and got her to unlock the Perimeter, so that your daughter and I could escape. I was free, for the first time in my life, but instead of running away, I followed Meadow. I fought people. Killed people, so that Meadow could make it here. I gave up my own freedom so that she could come and buy yours." I lean closer, so close I can smell the blood on his breath. "Now, *sir*, I'm going to ask you again. What do you know about the Green?"

He's silent, for a long time.

At first, I think he's going to kill me.

I just told him I murdered his wife and followed his

daughter across the country to get here.

He takes a deep breath.

And then he nods. "I don't like your kind, Patient Zero. I never have, for obvious reasons. But you make a good argument." He takes another sip of water, keeps it down. "I know that there once was a place, *years* ago, that was free of the Initiative. A small community of people that decided to branch off and do things their own way."

I gasp. "Where was it?"

He shakes his head. "I don't know for sure. Somewhere in the Pacific. Somewhere far. An island, off the grid."

Tox's map. The New Militia's map. They both lead to a place in the middle of a giant sea.

"There's a Perimeter around the country," I say. "Is it outside of there?"

Meadow's father shrugs. "Hell if I know. Everyone was spreading rumors. This place was ruined, that place was safe. It's all talk."

"What if it wasn't just talk?" I ask. "What if I heard the Leeches discussing it, too?"

He raises a brow. "That would be interesting," he says. "But not necessarily any more true or false than anything else the world has said before, about sanctuaries."

"But the Leeches know things," I say. "They have more

facts than any of us ever have. And besides. I have a map."

"And where did you get this map?"

I wave my hand. "That doesn't matter. What matters is if it leads to the Green. What would it be like there?"

He sighs, runs a hand through his hair. "If it were real, it would be off the grid completely. It would be a place where there is no testing. No all-seeing Initiative. And best of all, there would be freedom."

There's a lift in his voice as he speaks about it, like he wants it to be true, but he's afraid to have hope.

"Meadow says you're dying," I tell him. "Are you?"

He shrugs. "I don't know. But after all this time, wouldn't it be just my luck, for the man who married the Creator to be the one whose blood has the power to reverse her Cure?"

I hadn't thought of it like that.

"If you die, and we get out of here, I'm going to take Meadow to the Green," I say. "But if you survive . . . I want you to come with us."

"I don't want to burst your bubble," he says, sighing. "But freedom isn't real, Patient Zero. It never was. Not before the Cure, and not after."

"That's where you're wrong," I say. I stand up, look

down at him. "Freedom is a choice. And I'm going to choose to make it."

I turn, about to head back to Sketch, when he calls out to me.

"Patient Zero."

I look over my shoulder.

"Meadow is smart. If she let you follow her here . . ." He sighs, shakes his head, like he can't believe what he's about to say. "Well, you must have something good to offer. If you find the Green, take her with you. Take all of them with you."

I nod. Then I join Sketch across the cave and tell her what I know.

CHAPTER IOI

MEADOW

We trade off holding Peri as we head for home.

First she is in Koi's arms. Then she's in mine. She reaches up and touches my Regulator. Then she touches hers.

She doesn't speak. But there is true fear in her eyes.

"It's okay," I say. "They can't hurt us anymore. I made sure of that."

The world smiles down on us, because I do not switch. For now, I am strong, and that is all I could ever have wanted. To hold my sister, alive and well, and make her feel safe.

We make it to the waterfall.

We swim together, Koi and I kicking beneath the surge of water, Peri in between us. We shove her through the hole in the surface, haul her to safety.

She gasps, and she trembles. But she does not cry. Without the mud and dirt, she almost looks like she used to. But she is broken. She stares ahead, empty as an eggshell.

By the time we make it to the cave, Peri is asleep in Koi's arms. My heart is hammering strong and steady.

We found her.

I knock on the door, three times, and Abram answers, swinging his massive hands in our faces.

Koi pushes through. We carry Peri inside. My father is there, gently snoring in his sleep. I touch his shoulder and he jolts awake, eyes wide like he is ready for a fight.

"You need to see something," I say.

I help him sit up.

His eyes adjust. He blinks, like he does not believe what he sees. But Koi approaches, Peri in his arms.

"Is she . . ." My father's words trail off. Horror in his voice, like he is afraid to ask the question. He glares at her Regulator like he wishes he could tear it from her skin.

"She's only sleeping," I say. "She's alive. She's safe."

"Good." He is in shock, the same way I was, and still am.

He stands up, wobbling on his feet, but he recovers, crosses the fire to stand at Koi's side. "Peri," I hear him say. "My Peri."

Koi sets her into our father's arms. He trembles as he holds her, wraps her up like she is an infant again, and he refuses to let her go.

A single, bloody tear slips down his cheek.

And he smiles.

CHAPTER 102

ZEPHYR

I wake to Meadow's voice, whispering my name.

My eyes fly open, and she's there, alive. Safe.

"I wanted to come after you," I blurt out.

"It's okay," she says.

And then she actually smiles. She sits beside me, a blanket draped across her shoulders, her bare toes warming by the fire.

"We found her, Zephyr," she says. "We found Peri."

"What?" I sit up.

And I see her. Peri, sitting beside Koi and her father. Stars, they actually found her.

Peri is tiny, wrapped up in a blanket that swallows

her whole. She's covered in bruises. Her Regulator looks somehow worse than Meadow's. She's so small, and it's taking over her. And her curls are gone, her head looking even smaller bald. She sits motionless, staring. Like her mind has disappeared.

Her eyes are swollen, ringed with purple. There's a fresh scar on her face, and she looks like she's been in a war.

It's sick. It's so sick my stomach aches, my heart throbs, my hands beg to hurt the Leeches who did this to her, put her in this place.

"She's in shock," Meadow tells me. "After all she's been through . . ."

"She'll come around. Kids bounce back easy. She's safe now, Meadow. You found her."

Meadow nods. Her eyes are red, and sweat beads her brows. Still, there's new light in her as she watches her sister.

"Are you okay?" I ask. I gently take her hand, and lift it. Damn.

Her cuff is at 97. The highest it's ever been.

"I did what I came here to do," she says. Her voice cracks. She swallows, hard, and then she spits blood. "I can die happy now, Zephyr."

"You're not going to die," I whisper. "The New Militia

can help. We're going to make it out of here. We just have to give the signal. Tell me what it is, Meadow. I'll do it for you, and they'll come for us."

"You can't help me with this," she says. She smiles sadly.

Then she gasps. "This could be the last switch," she says. I watch her cuff change, slide slowly back down to zero. Then it goes to the letter *C*.

She's about to say something else when there's a wailing, like the Night Siren. But it is different. Almost like . . . voices.

Shouts.

"War!" Tox shouts, from somewhere in the darkness. "Fight!"

That's when the door of the cave bursts open.

Abram falls in, his meaty hands waving in the air.

A knife sticks out of the middle of his forehead.

"RAID!" Saxon screams.

The cave turns to chaos, as people pour in through the doorway, weapons aimed for the kill.

CHAPTER 103

MEADOW

Oranges fill the Cave.

I don't know how they found our hideout. Did they follow me and my brother?

I see an Orange man, his ponytail swinging as he turns in circles, ordering his army to attack.

I leap to my feet.

I sprint for him, screaming hatred from my lungs. Not now, not when Peri is here and safe. No one will touch her tonight. A woman jumps in the way. I slam her to the ground, ignoring her screams.

She waves a knife in my face. I slam my forehead against hers, then rip the knife from her grasp.

She spits in my face. I use the butt end of the knife to knock her out, then move on. I have to find my father and Peri.

Everyone is screaming, running around the cave.

Two of the fires have gone out, and the world is a mix of shadows, voices bouncing off the walls.

There are more screams, more footsteps. At least fifty Oranges pour through the doorway. With this many, we don't stand a chance.

I hear Peri scream, and it is just like the days of torture. I want to drop, put my hands over my ears, but I force myself to remember. That was then. This was now. I turn, see Koi trying to fight off two men while Peri cowers behind him, her face frozen in horror, mouth hanging open.

I don't think.

I just fling the knife, watch as it sinks into the back of the first man's neck. He drops, and Koi is able to get the other down to the floor. They grapple, and I rush for Peri. I scoop her into my arms, then rip the knife from the man's skull.

"Are you okay?" I ask, looking into her eyes.

"Daddy!" she screams. Her first word since we found her.

She points behind me.

I turn in time to see my father, stumbling toward us in the chaos, a spear through his thigh. His eyes are wild, desperate, like he knows he doesn't have the strength to carry on, and that is far more terrifying than anything I have ever seen. He has a woman on his tail, and she whirls a wicked-looking spiked ball in his direction.

He's not going to make it.

"Duck!" I scream.

My father drops.

The woman lands on top of him, a snarl on her face. She slams his back with the spiked ball.

I see a rush of blood. Still, he fights.

"Stay here!" I shove Peri into Koi's outstretched arms, then run to help my father.

I dive, my body slamming against the woman's. She rolls off my father, and I'm on top of her, throwing punches into her face. She punches me back, and for a second, the world spins.

I slap the sides of her skull, pop her eardrums. Her eyes go wild. Feral. She lunges and sinks her teeth into my neck, draws blood.

"End her!" my father commands from my left. "End her now, Meadow!"

The woman spits my own blood into my eyes. She digs a blade into my thigh. There's pain, white hot and angry.

And suddenly I want revenge. On everyone. The Initiative, for putting my family into this world, for making Peri look like a ghost of herself, for putting her through agony that no child should ever have to face. I'm angry at the other colors, for disturbing the last peaceful night I might ever have.

I'm furious at my mother. The entire world.

I stick my fingers into the woman's eye sockets.

I press hard, until she's fountaining blood, and it's like everything inside of me breaks.

I hear myself laughing, memories of the Commander and his torture and Peri's screams, and my screams, and everything up to this point flooding out from my soul. I pretend this woman is the Initiative, and I'm finally getting my vengeance for what they did to me, my family, Zephyr. Everyone in the Shallows.

"Meadow!" Koi's voice comes up from somewhere beyond, but I don't really hear him. "We have to go! There are too many of them!"

The woman's already dying, probably dead, but I can't pull away.

I scream until my voice runs ragged. Until hands grab

me from behind. I spin, yanking the knife from my thigh, ready to thrust it into my attacker's throat.

But then I see Zephyr.

"Meadow," he says. Only my name, and for a second, I almost thrust the knife at *him*. There's honesty in his eyes. Truth. Desperation to save me not from the woman, but from myself. "That's enough! You've done *enough*!"

I see Peri in the shadows. Tears sliding down her cheeks. Looking at me like . . . like I'm a monster.

I gasp when I see the woman's face. Feel the hot blood on my hands, the roughness in my throat from laughing and yelling. There's fighting all around, and Koi drags me to the side, conceals us in the shadows. "We have to run, Meadow. We can't stay here with Peri. We're outnumbered."

I look past him, as the other Cavers fight. A stray boy runs toward us, trying to escape, but a knife gets him in the skull. He drops.

Sketch appears, helping my father walk. His blood-tinged eyes stare right into mine, and in this moment, he commands my every motion. "We will do what it takes to keep Peri safe, Meadow. We'll run."

"To where?" Koi asks.

I realize that now is the time. We're almost ready to

leave this place. I have my sister back, my entire family. There is no reason to stay here any longer.

I have to give the signal, but first, we have to run to the extraction point.

"The south end," I say. "Hurry."

Tox hobbles forward. "I know South," he says. He lifts his walking stick, holds it high.

"We'll follow him," Zephyr says. "He knows the way. He's been here longer than any of us, and he knows *more* than you realize. You have to trust me on this."

He looks strong. Like a leader, arms rigid at his sides, chin tilted up, so he can stare down at us all, using his height.

"Okay," I say.

Tox disappears into the darkness of the cave, leading the way.

CHAPTER 104

ZEPHYR

Meadow lost it. Right in front of her sister.

She stuck her hands into that woman's face like she was digging through sand and . . .

I shove the memory away, force it deep down, where it won't bug me until later. For now, we have to run.

I don't know where Tox is leading us, but it's somewhere deep in the cave. The darkness folds itself around us like a blanket, only it isn't comforting.

It feels like a cage. I can hear Oranges, tracking us from behind. We move fast, our breathing labored. There were too damn many of them.

"He's just a loonyheaded old bag!" Saxon hisses from ahead.

"Trust him," I say. "What other options do we have? You want to go back there and die at the hands of Orange soldiers?"

"I *am* a soldier!" Saxon snaps. "We just left the other Yellows to die. We left them like bait."

"Then why did you even come?" Sketch yells. "We did what we had to do. And if you're with us, then you'll shut your mouth and enjoy the ride."

I focus on my breathing. Taking short, quick steps, so I don't lose my footing in the darkness and fall into Sketch's back.

My forehead hits the cave ceiling. A snap of pain.

"Oh, right. Duck!" Sketch says, from ahead.

"Could've said something sooner," I grunt, then stoop lower, hauling Meadow with me, our hands glued together from the dead woman's blood.

Soon the talking fades.

The cave gets so short and so small that I'm on hands and knees.

"This is a dead end," Meadow says.

But at the very front, Tox uses his walking stick to beat against a pile of rocks.

They tumble, and I see the light.

CHAPTER 105

MEADOW

The darkness dies when we reach the light.

It is only a small flicker, like shadowed sun. But it is there.

"Dig." The old man's voice echoes from up ahead. *"Dig!"*

Koi is closest to him.

I can hear scrambling from ahead, muffled curses as my brother does what Tox says.

It's a tiny opening in the tunnel ahead.

We have to go one at a time, crawling on our bellies, and by the time it is my turn a tangle of vines is in the way. I slide through them, out onto the forest floor.

"I told you he knew," Zephyr says to everyone. He stoops down to help me up.

His eyes hold mine. "You can't slip away again," he whispers. He grabs my hand and I tell myself I am going to leave my insanity behind in that cave.

But I know, and Zephyr knows, that it is not the truth.

There's no time to talk.

When I look up, I can see the dome ceiling lowering. Like it is getting closer to connecting to the Perimeter. Overhead, the sun is fading.

We are nearing the end of the seventy-two hours.

If I don't send the signal soon, the New Militia will hold off their attack. They won't come for us.

We run.

"We have to stop," Koi says from behind, after an hour of running.

My father is leaning against him, gasping for breath. The wind blows, moving his hair back from his face. And in this moment, I see the paleness of his skin from the loss of blood.

So weak, so unlike himself.

I hear a clicking noise overhead, like the sound of locusts.

It is a sound I have not heard yet in the Ridge. I look up, but I don't see anything different on the dome. Just silver, more silver, the webbed lines of metal or titanium, patched together like spiderwebs.

Suddenly something dark falls from the sky, far off in the distance.

Then another right after, crashing to the forest. They sound like rain, trickling from the sky, soaring down in a rush of wind and whispers. *They're too far away to reach us,* I think. But maybe I thought too soon.

One lands in the ground, beside me.

It is like the stinger of a giant bee, about three inches long, jet black. So sharp at both ends, and serrated along its edges. Perfect for drawing blood, no matter which side of the Needle hits skin.

There is one moment of silence, where my father and I stare back at each other, and everyone else catches their breath.

"Run," Peri says. Her voice is clear and solid. It is the first thing she has said since we found her. "RUN!"

Hundreds, *thousands* of Needles fall from the sky.

CHAPTER 106

ZEPHYR

It's like the sky is crying knives.

We run through the trees, holding our arms over our heads like they can protect us, but it's totally useless.

A Needle lands in my arm. I yank it out and keep going, but the spot turns black in an instant, and I can feel a sick, horrible sensation as whatever the Needle was laced with pours through my veins.

Tox takes the lead again, using his walking stick to brave the path, and we follow behind. Every few seconds, Meadow's dad stumbles. Koi helps him back up, and we keep going.

Meadow is beside me, running in tandem, holding

Peri's hand. The little girl is fast, but what amazes me is that Tox manages to stay ahead of us.

The Needles keep falling all around, whistling as they soar past my head.

One lands on Peri's Regulator, bounces off. Another gets me in my back.

Around me, everyone's getting hit. Everyone shouts as they're jabbed through the skin.

But there's one shout that's louder than all the others. It's Koi's voice.

Meadow stops and turns, pulling Peri with her.

We all look back and see her father crumpled in a heap on the ground.

He's covered in Needles like the rest of us.

"We have to run!" I scream. But Meadow hands Peri to me and turns back. She falls at her dad's side.

I see the flash of his wrist cuff, 98, as Koi hauls him under the canopy of a tree, trying to protect him from the Needles. They're still falling, not as many, but it seems like it won't ever end.

Sketch rounds back, comes up beside me. "Zero, let's go!"

"Meadow's dad!" I yell. I push Peri into her arms.

"Go, get to the Perimeter!"

She shakes her head, dark eyes wide, but she wraps her arms around Peri. The little girl is crying out for her daddy, trying to get away, but Sketch is strong enough to hold her.

"GO!" I yell. "Peri can't see this."

A Needle falls between us.

Sketch nods, takes off after Saxon and Tox. I turn and stay behind with Meadow and Koi, as they lean over their father.

He's coughing up blood.

"You're okay," Meadow says. Her eyes are rimmed with tears, but she swallows them back, refuses to let them fall. "Just get up, keep walking. We don't quit, remember?"

Meadow's dad coughs again, spits crimson. "I'm done," he chokes out. His chest is rising and falling too fast.

"We'll carry him," Koi says. He looks over his shoulder, sees me standing on the edge. "Zero, come help!"

"No!" Meadow's father yells. He tries to lift an arm, but it falls.

Either from the weight of the Needles or weakness or both, but I see the number on his cuff now: 99.

His eyes are wild as he looks back and forth between Meadow and Koi. I'm invading this moment, an outsider who needs to be far away, but I can't go. I won't let

Meadow out of my sight.

"You keep Peri safe," Meadow's dad says. He chokes on his own blood. His eyes start dripping it, like he's drowning from the inside out and it's trying to escape from every place that it can.

"You'll keep her safe with us," Meadow says. She's crying now, real tears that won't stop. Then she starts yelling. "We don't *die*! We're survivors, remember?"

Her father shakes his head. At this point he can't get any words out.

Koi and Meadow stare at him, frozen.

It's a horror scene, the Needles in his arms, in all of our arms, the black spots spreading on everyone's skin.

"Go . . ." their father chokes out again. "Go!"

The word is muffled, like he's shouting from underwater.

Meadow shakes her head. "No," she whispers. Another Needle falls, lands in her dad's outspread leg, but it's like he can't feel it anymore.

He takes a deep, rattling breath. *Go.* He mouths the word, but it doesn't come out.

He gasps, one final time. His cuff changes to 100. Suddenly, as he dies, his eyes flick toward mine. There's a look in them I haven't seen before, like he's pleading with me. Begging.

I nod.

He looks at his children, one last time.

And then the strongest man in the world, the one who would do anything to survive, dies.

CHAPTER 107
MEADOW

My father.

My father.

My father is *dead*.

But he can't be dead, not now, not ever. He has always been strong, always taught me to do whatever it took to survive. Killing, stealing, fighting to the last breath.

I roll him away from me, see his gray eyes open and still.

Not blinking at all.

Koi is moaning, sobbing. "No, no, no."

The world is a blur, as Zephyr comes up behind me, tries to tug me away from my father's body.

"Wake up!" I scream. "Wake up!"

"He's gone, Meadow!" Zephyr shouts. "He's *gone*!"

The Needles have stopped, but the world feels like it is screaming, raging all around me.

He was supposed to escape with us. He was supposed to *survive*.

It might be minutes, or seconds, that pass, when my brother rises to his feet. "We have to leave," he says.

I try to shut my father's eyes with my fingertips, but they won't close. They stay open, staring at nothing. I can't leave him like this.

He is the strong one. He was supposed to be there for my family when I couldn't be anymore. The switch hits, and I'm so weak that I collapse beside him.

"We have to go!" Zephyr yells.

He lifts me, hauls me away from my father. I'm screaming, writhing, and even in my weakness Koi and Zephyr have to hold me together so I cannot get away.

They start moving, pulling me from my father.

We leave him behind, stuck with Needles, lying on the floor of the Ridge.

Soon the Initiative will find him, and that will be his end. Captured by the very people he spent his entire life trying to hide from.

CHAPTER 108

ZEPHYR

We make it to the Perimeter.

Saxon and Sketch and Tox are here, waiting, and everyone seems fine. The Needles hurt us, but they didn't kill anyone else here. I set Meadow down on the forest floor. Koi sits beside her, holding her up as her nose drips and she coughs blood. Just like her father.

I wonder when the Leeches will take his body. I wonder if they'll finally get their Death Code from his blood.

Peri sprints for Meadow and Koi.

"Where's Daddy?" she asks, but Koi shakes his head. Meadow just stares, blankly, into her sister's eyes.

Meadow's cuff is at 98.

Her father's cuff was there, and it took him minutes to die.

But Meadow can't die. She's stronger than death, and she'll switch again soon. She has to. *She has to.*

"Woodson," Sketch says, taking Meadow's face in her hands. "Woodson, what's the signal? We're here. We've made it. We have to alert them now."

Meadow shakes her head.

"Not without him," she whispers.

Peri is sobbing in Koi's arms, and Tox is mumbling something about the Green, and right now it all seems so stupid.

In a world without Meadow, there is no Green.

She can't die. Not like this. Not ever, not in Lark Woodson's world.

CHAPTER 109

MEADOW

"Give the signal, Meadow," Zephyr says. He kneels in front of me, beside Sketch. "We have to give it now. They'll come, and they'll save you. They have to know a way."

But I can't tell him that there is no way.

This is how it was always going to end.

I look around, at all the faces of the people who have come so far with me.

Sketch, with her defiance, with her ability to bring laughter to a world where darkness is more common than light.

Saxon, who welcomed us into his tribe, defied the ways

of the Ridge because he trusted my brother and father.

Peri, who sits a foot away, while Koi whispers soothing words to her. Rubs her back and kisses her on the forehead. They are soft in a place that demands survivors to be hard as steel. But they have survived. They have made it, and that is their way of denying the world.

"Meadow," Zephyr says. "I know it's hard to think, right now. But we have to give the signal."

He touches my cheek, gently.

His green eyes are so bright, so soothing. I could sink into them and find peace, and maybe that's what I will do when it's all over. Maybe death is green, instead of black, full of light summer breezes and soft grass on bare toes.

"I'm sorry," I whisper.

I think of everything we have been through. The pain, the wins and the losses, the journey we've taken to get to this moment in time. Hoping for freedom. That is all I have ever wanted, and now I am going to give it away, to him.

To all of them.

There is a jolt of pain, then the pressure of relief, as the switch happens. The number on my cuff slides down, down, until it reaches a *C* again.

Zephyr is smiling, holding me to his chest, and Sketch

is shouting that I'm okay, that we're going to give the signal now and get the hell out of here.

But I won't be with them. I can't be.

My mother's secret whispers into me. *Once you leave the Shallows, Meadow . . . you will die.*

There is a Needle in the ground, fallen and forgotten, beside me. I slide my fingers toward it. Wrap my hand around it, tight, and Zephyr only notices when it's too late.

"Meadow, what are you . . ."

"I'm sorry," I whisper, and as I say it, I look at him and Peri and Koi and Sketch, and my heart swells with that one horrible thing I always ran from.

Love. But it's enough, the sweetest thing in the world, and for the first time in my life, I welcome it.

Then I plunge the Needle deep into my chest.

"No!" Zephyr screams.

My heart slows.

My vision wanes.

Zephyr falls in front of me, his hands turning me over, hauling me into his lap.

His body is warm. And I am so, so cold.

"No," he says. "No! I love you."

I try to answer.

But my lips won't move. I see everyone rushing over, sprinting for me. Sketch rips the Needle from my chest and tries to stop the blood, but I know it won't stop. Peri screams. Koi screams along with her. They are shouting my name, sobbing.

It's my final offer, the General said to me, the morning we left for the Ridge. *You die, the Murder Complex dies with you, and they'll never be able to replicate it again. Either you go in there and die, or you never come back out. If you die, I'll give them all a good life. I'll set them free. The choice is yours. Death is the signal, Meadow Woodson. The question is whether or not you'll send it our way.*

I didn't have to make the choice. Leaving the Shallows did it for me. Now death calls to me, a song that whispers in the wind.

It sucks me under, the one thing I've tried so hard to escape. But as I die, I realize this is what I was always meant to do.

Live for a while. Then die, for peace. The Murder Complex will die with me, forever fade, impossible to replicate now that my mother is gone. The New Militia will come and break down the walls, and the war will begin. The Initiative will fall.

I can feel it in my head. Almost hear the Murder

Complex system screaming, as together, we turn and face the last Dark Time, the one that I have heard ends with pain and fear and unanswered questions, but that there is hope, and light, and love on the other side.

The sound of my father's voice carries me away, calls me forth into the unknown.

Close your eyes.

Relax your mind.

Die fearlessly, Meadow.

You are so, so brave.

CHAPTER 110

ZEPHYR

I can feel the Murder Complex die with her.

I can feel it like I feel my own heartbeat.

It's a pierce of pain in my skull. A gasp of my breath, a scream that comes from my lungs.

And then it's gone forever. And I'm free.

But she isn't with me. Nothing in the world can make this right, and I want the Murder Complex back, because when it lives, Meadow lives.

I scream.

Everyone screams with me. Koi and Peri hold each other tightly.

Meadow's eyes are still open, staring up at mine. Gray

and soft and gentle, in death.

My tears fall into them.

And seeing them splash against her face, seeing how peaceful she looks . . . "Come back!" I scream. "You aren't done with this life yet, Meadow. Please."

I press my lips against hers, beg them to feel warm.

But they are only cold.

"Come back! Don't leave me, not like this!" I shake her. I sob, screaming her name.

Someone arrives behind me, pulls me back. Sketch, I think. Koi and Peri fall over Meadow, mourn for her, but she is mine to mourn, too.

"Meadow!" I reach for her, as Sketch hauls me backward, and Saxon helps. "No!"

And I want to kill. Kill anyone, if only it would bring Meadow back, trade their life for hers. Why did she do it? Why did she *leave* me?

I see the first memory I have of her when I was just a boy. It was like moonlight, falling on the face of a girl I felt like I knew.

Her laugh, on the swings in Cortez.

Her hands, skimming mine as we swam in the ocean.

Her scream, as she told me to kiss her ass in the Graveyard.

Her lips, pressing against mine as she sacrificed herself in the Leech building.

Her blood, running through my veins.

She saved me, a guy who should mean nothing to her.

Now I am alive, and she is dead.

The world rocks, as an explosion happens. Fire, blazing fire, then cracking and groaning. Behind me, the Perimeter falls. Rocks fly. People dive for cover, but I sit frozen, unable to move.

Something hits my head.

I fall against Meadow's body, lie still beside her. Through the dust and the smoke, I think I see hundreds of pairs of black boots, climbing over the rubble.

Someone touches me, lifts me away from Meadow. Another pair of hands grabs her, presses black paddles to her chest. They haul her onto a board and she's out of sight.,

Gunfire. Leech guards arrive.

Shouts.

"Meadow," I gasp.

I reach for her, but I can't touch her. She is already gone.

I fall into darkness, and my last thought is this:

My moonlit girl is dead.

CHAPTER III

MEADOW

I am standing in a world of white.

Fog drifts back and forth, all around me, dancing across the tops of my toes.

It is silent, except for the lightest kiss of the wind on my curls. My hair is long again, tickling my arms.

I look down.

I have no sparring scars. No blood beneath my nails. No cuff on my wrist or wounds from Needles.

I lift my arm, look for my fearless tattoo, but there is only fresh skin.

"Hello?"

My voice rings out, disappears into forever.

And then, through the fog, my father emerges.

He looks younger, stronger, and the first thing I notice is that his Catalogue Number is gone. His face is alive with the flush of life.

"Meadow," he says.

I try to walk toward him, but I cannot seem to make my feet move. "Dad," I say.

"You were always so brave," he tells me. "You fought hard."

"I'm tired," I whisper. I want to sink to the floor, bury myself beneath the fog, and sleep for an eternity.

"I know you are," my father says. He smiles, and the light explodes into his eyes. "But you're not done yet."

He walks toward me, reaching out. His hands look soft and new, free of any scars from his fishing hooks or his years training me and my brother. "Wake up, Meadow. Live free."

He places his hand over my heart.

And I become one with pain.

I think I wake up, but I can't be sure.

The world feels far away. I can't feel my body, only a strange heaviness all around. Slowly, the sensation of *me* returns. A tingling in my fingers, my toes. A numbness that shakes itself from me, until I know I am a body, instead of just a mind.

There is a rocking beneath me. The steady hum of something.

And the feeling of a hand, wrapped gently over my own.

I try to open my eyes.

They are heavy, so heavy, but I fight. Gently, light pours in, as I look at the world.

And I see whose hand holds mine.

Zephyr.

He is sitting beside me in a chair, asleep. Snoring. We are inside a small room, and there is that strange rocking, rocking.

A familiar feeling, the thing that used to finally lull me to sleep when the nightmares threatened to haunt me into staying forever awake.

The walls and ceiling are silver.

The bed I lie on is a cot. I look up, see the inscription in the metal above my head.

US NAVY is scratched out. *NEW MILITIA* has been roughly carved above it; a new name. A new meaning.

I want to sit up, but there is too much pain in my chest. It's hard to breathe.

A tube is in my arm, dripping blood into my veins. I follow the tube with my eyes, see where it leads.

Zephyr's arm. It is his blood in my veins, that brought me back to life.

I feel myself smile. The smallest tug at my lips, but the effort is so much.

I close my eyes and sleep.

CHAPTER 112

ZEPHYR

Meadow's signal was her death.

She had to die, in order for the New Militia to offer to set us free. Maybe they'd planned it from the second they saw her, when Ray brought us to their bunker. They wanted a war.

They just needed a reason to jump-start it. A reason to take that first step. When Meadow came in, with the key to ending the Murder Complex for good, the General took the chance.

She offered to die to save us all. What she didn't tell anyone, was that her mother's dying words to Meadow were not to leave the Shallows.

If she left, the system would kill her. She left anyways. Sacrificed herself for her family.

We're on a boat, an old Navy tanker, just off the coast of Northern Washington. After the attack on the Ridge, it's where they took us. Where I woke up, screaming Meadow's name, ready to kill the New Militia.

It was the General himself who told me their deal.

And it was on his orders that the moment they found her, they'd try to bring her back to life. It worked. Meadow's a fighter, and she always has been, even in death.

I don't know what she saw on the other side. But she's back with us, she's here now.

She just has to open her eyes.

Sketch forces me to come down to the mess hall and eat. We weave through the metal halls of the ship. Close walls, low-hanging ceilings, metal ladders we have to climb to get from one floor to the next.

Everyone is eating when we join them.

The hall we're in opens up to a wide room. A giant kitchen, and there are metal tables all over the place, filled with New Militia soldiers stuffing their faces.

I look left and right. I don't recognize any of the faces until I see one table, all the way to the left.

Koi and Peri sit side by side. Soldiers stare at Peri's Regulator, but she doesn't seem to notice it anymore. Saxon is across from her, and Tox is nowhere to be found. Probably with the captain as he has been this whole time, holding his stupid walking stick. Trying to compare maps to the Green.

"Let's go," Sketch says. She tugs me along the rows of soldiers, until we take our places at the table.

"Zephyr," Koi greets me with a polite nod.

Peri looks up at me and waves. She's clutching a doll to her chest, one that Ray's wife Martha gave her. She's also cleaner, wearing an oversize green T-shirt that's more like a dress. She looks happy. Almost.

It'll take time for the smiles to come back. For all of us.

"How's she doing?" Koi asks. "Still sleeping?"

He slides me a plate full of rations. The food's the same, and I don't have much of an appetite, but I eat it anyways. Otherwise, Sketch would tear me apart.

"Still sleeping," I say. "But she looks good. Her color is coming back."

Koi nods. "She'll wake up soon. I know she will."

Sketch sighs, chugs down a metal cup of water. "I'm gonna kill her when she wakes up, for what she did."

I glare at her.

"What?" she holds out her hands. "Too soon?"

I'm about to tell her that yes, it's way too soon, when the room falls silent.

The General walks in. Everyone stands, salutes him.

Our table is the only one that doesn't.

"At ease," he says, and then he's marching through the rows, heading for us. He stops just a few feet from me, arms crossed behind his back. "I've got good news," he says.

We all whirl to look at him, questions in our eyes.

"She's awake."

CHAPTER 113

MEADOW

I am too weak to ask questions. Too weak to ask what's going on, where we are, as voices carry, and faces of people I love flood the tiny room.

I let them come to me. Sketch curses at me, and calls me a ChumHead, and then she actually sheds a single tear.

Peri and Koi stay with me for a while, talking. We share stories about old times. We don't talk about our father. I don't tell them that, when I crossed over, I saw him. That he was safe and at peace, and that someday, he will be waiting for us, ready to welcome us with open arms when we reach the other side.

After a while, the Surgeon tells everyone I need to rest.

Peri kisses my forehead and leaves her doll at my side. Koi squeezes my hand and places a carving of our father on the pillow next to my head.

Everyone leaves, and I fall asleep.

Later, I wake up to the sound of snoring that isn't my own. I roll over, see Zephyr lying beside me on the tiny cot. I close my eyes, lean close, and listen to his heartbeat until morning comes.

EPILOGUE
THREE WEEKS LATER

MEADOW

The ocean is endless, at night.

I stand on the deck, on the highest level of the tanker, watching the waves far below. They crash and groan against this great metal beast, whispering, calling to me, speaking in voices that only the sea understands.

Footsteps come up behind me. I tense, but then I remember.

I don't have to be afraid anymore.

"Beautiful night, isn't it?"

I turn to look at the General.

He is dressed in his usual uniform of army greens, pressed neat and clean. Even in this world, where we have almost nothing but what we need to stay alive, he manages to make sure he always looks in control.

"It's like any other night," I say. "Cold. Dark. Somewhere out there, people are still dying."

"But not you," he says. He stands next to me, leans against the railing. His breath comes out in a puff of white that is carried away by the wind.

"No," I say. "Not me, and not my friends or family. Like you promised. I'm grateful to you, for saving us."

I look down at the scar on my wrist, where the tiny tracker used to be. When my heartbeat stopped, it sent a signal to the New Militia.

I have hundreds of scars. But this one is is my favorite.

The General nods. "I'm a man of my word, and it seems that you are a woman of yours, too. Not many would have done what you did, Soldier."

He doesn't know that my mother's secret is the reason why I died. Because she wanted me to stay in the Shallows, so badly, that she rigged the system to kill me if I ever left.

I should hate her.

But lately, all I can do is remember who she used to be. Remember that once, she was the woman who gave me my name, who gave me my brother and my sister. I can love the memory of her, if I leave out the darkest parts.

White flakes dance from the sky. Snow, something I had never heard about until I came here. It's cold, and when it touches my nose, I shiver. I was not made for this place.

But I can't go home.

I have no home.

Not anymore.

"What happens next?" I ask. Somewhere out there, my father's ghost is watching me. I can feel him as surely as I can feel the wind, an ever-lingering presence that makes me feel safe. And there is always his voice, strong enough to carry me into each new day.

The General shifts beside me. "The old man you brought with you."

"Tox," I say. "What about him?"

"He seems to have made advances on finding this . . . *Green.*"

Zephyr and Sketch told me about it. Fantasies of a world where the darkness stays away, where people live in the constant light. I don't know what I believe about it.

I know that the soldiers have hope in their eyes that I didn't see before.

I know that we got new word on the Shallows just last

week. The New Commander is Rhone, and he is the only reason why I was able to continue on into the Ridge, why they didn't ship me back the second they discovered who I was. He told us the Initiative fell at the hands of Patients, and the ones who remain are being held captive. Soon, Commander Rhone will work with the New Militia to safely take down the walls.

The Ridge is a graveyard. The Initiative soldiers that weren't killed in the fight scattered like ants across the country.

My father's body was probably buried beneath the rubble, never to be seen or disturbed again. When the New Militia went back to find him, he was gone.

I know I should fear the reality that the Initiative might have found his body, that they might have gotten the Death Code from him.

But I don't have room for fear anymore.

"The world is broken," I say. "How can we even imagine trying to piece it all back together?"

The General turns to look at me. The moonlight casts a glow on his face, the smoothness of his clean-shaven chin. "One day at a time," he says.

"And you'll expect me at your side."

He nods. "Yes."

I shouldn't have hoped for freedom. Even now, I am still a prisoner to my debts, my promises.

"Unless you wish to go elsewhere," the General says.

I turn.

He is staring out at the sea again. "I can't afford to lose a good soldier," he says. "But I *can* afford to let you choose your way, from here on out. I need to know if this Green exists. I need to hear the truth with my own ears, from someone I trust."

I listen closely, hardly believing his words.

"You can take a small team. Weapons, rations." He takes a deep breath. "Your friends and family. Mind you, it won't be easy to find. But we've gained control of the outer Perimeter. We can cross it now. For once, I can't tell you what's on the other side. But wouldn't you like to know?"

It isn't freedom.

But it's close.

What he's offering me is a chance to forge my own path. See the world on the Outside, truly, for the very first time.

"You'll be monitored, of course. We'll be in touch at all times. And should you find this Green, you'll show us the way."

"Yes," I say, my heart racing. There is still pain in my

chest, even though the wounds have healed. This is the kind that takes time. Years, and maybe not ever, to fully fade away. "Yes, sir."

"You have one week to prepare," the General says. He starts to walk away, but before he's out of earshot, he stops. "You're nothing like her, you know," he says. "Your mother. You might be a killer, Meadow Woodson. But there is light in your heart."

He leaves me on the deck, alone with the wind and the waves.

ZEPHYR

I find her on the highest part of the ship, alone.

She's wrapped in an army coat, and from here, the Regulator is almost hidden. Her curls dance in the wind.

She watches the waves. I sit down beside her, close enough that our knees touch.

"Hey," she whispers.

"Hey," I say. "I heard about the Green."

She nods. "Word travels fast on this ship."

"We're going to try and find it? We're actually going to try?"

She takes a deep breath, releases it. "I'm tired of making

the plans. If my father believed it might have been there, then maybe I should believe, too. It's time we do something you want, for a change."

"I want a lot of things," I say.

I feel her lean in.

"Like what?"

She's looking up at me through her lashes. She's shaking, but I'm not sure it's from the cold. I'm shaking, too.

"Do you want . . . this?" Meadow asks. "Do you want me, Zephyr? After everything that's happened?"

She leans closer. Touches her lips to my cheek. Once, twice, and then suddenly I'm on fire.

"Yes," I say. "Always."

She smiles against me.

Our lips crush together, our breathing becomes one. We fall backward onto the cool metal of the ship, and oh, *stars*, she's on top of me. My moonlit girl is *on top of me*.

She puts her hands in my hair. She's kissing me so hard she's eating me up, devouring me whole.

And I'm alive.

Her fingers are cold as ice when they slip beneath my shirt. I gasp, and she presses harder, almost like she wants to disappear into me. Become a part of my soul, and me a part of hers. I touch her skin, kiss her down the length of her neck, and she's soft, *so* damn soft, even with her scars.

"Meadow," I gasp, but she won't stop.

I don't think I want her to. Not ever.

"You want me to love you," she whispers. I can see her struggling, see her fighting to say it. She looks right into my eyes, green and gray. "And I do. But I'm not good with saying the right thing, and I never have been. So let me show you, the only way I know how."

She falls into me.

And under the sky and the stars, on a ship in the middle of an endless ocean, we become one.

MEADOW

We eat a full meal on the night before we leave for the Green.

There are about thirty New Militia members that will join us.

We don't know what we will find once we cross the Perimeter. We don't know if we are only chasing a dream, or if we will find reality, somewhere out there. A better place.

But tonight, we sit around and share stories about happier times. Better places, where the sea breeze sweeps across our faces, tickles our skin. Where the ocean waves tug at our toes, and gulls cry overhead, singing a sweet summer song.

The Shallows was hell. The Ridge was hell.

But I look at Peri, see her smiling, finally, for the first time in weeks. I hear Sketch's cursing, her obnoxious laugh, her terrible jokes. She kisses Saxon out of the blue, and he's so shocked that he just stares at her, open-mouthed, until she slaps him in the face and he kisses her back. Koi finds a pen and paper and sketches images of trees that look real. Tox grins, and his walking stick is finally cast aside.

I can literally feel the freedom inside of my mind, the emptiness. All of the *space*. Without the Murder Complex, I can just *be*.

Zephyr looks over. Then he reaches out and takes my hand in his. Squeezes it tight, and this time, I squeeze back.

Family is everything, Meadow. It is my father's voice that calls to me from the beyond. I can almost feel his presence right here, beside me. My protector, my guide.

He is gone, like all of the others we've lost.

But I look around at these people, these faces. This broken family come together to make a new one.

And I realize that I will never be alone again.

I think of the places we've come from, the things we've had to do, the monsters we have all had to become.

Maybe, in life, hell is all around, hiding in the shadows, whispering our fears in the middle of sleepless nights. But there is always a little bit of heaven, a little bit of sunlight, to melt the darkness away.

Happiness can always be found.

You just have to be strong enough, fearless enough, to open your eyes and really *look*.

ACKNOWLEDGMENTS

This book was incredibly difficult for me to write. The Murder Complex series has been a part of my life for so many years now, and bringing it to a close also meant having to let go of these characters.

Thank you to Meadow and Zephyr, for being so alive to me. Thank you for being my first characters ever. I will always love you.

Thank you as always, to God, for giving me the gift of writing. Thank you for giving me all of the wonderful people who have helped me get to this point.

To all of the amazing people at team Greenwillow, specifically my editor Virginia Duncan, for helping carry this series to the end. Thanks to team Epic Reads for the support!

A million hugs to Julie Scheina, for helping me save this story.

To my agent, Louise Fury, for rocking and being my voice of reason.

To my parents, Don and Karen, and my sister, Lauren, for praying me through so many drafts and releases and fears. My husband, Josh, for loving me in my moments of crazy.

To Alex Bowles, for being a super fan and friend.

To my in-laws and my three new little brothers. I love you guys!

My friends Rebekah Faubion and Cherie Stewart, for being like sisters to me. Nerdy, beautiful, book-loving sisters. Erin Gross, for helping me with so much!

Sasha Alsberg, who is my book pimp. Ben Alderson, who is adorably awesome. All the #booknerdigans, who love and support me and my work.

Thanks to all the amazing readers I've visited at schools, who have been such lovely audiences, and helped heal me of my public speaking fear.

Thanks to all the members of the YA Valentines, who are always there to hear my crazy fears. You and your books are beautiful. Patrick Carman, for his reassuring phone calls. The YA Binders, for their reassuring Facebook threads.

And because I'm almost 100% sure that I will forget to thank someone, here's to YOU, whoever you are, wherever you are reading this. Thanks for supporting me, and for sticking with me through the Shallows and beyond. Here's to future books, and future #booknerdigans.